TWISTED FATE

BOOK 2 OF THE FRACTURED TIME TRILOGY

MICHAEL D'AMBROSIO

TABLE OF CONTENTS

CHAPTER 1

NEW TECHNOLOGY

Ruger crept down black stone steps into a large cavern, laced with small, fiery pools of lava. He cringed at the eerie shadows rippling across the rough, stone floor around him. Diomedes cursed him for his failures and left his face disfigured and grotesque. Only when Billy is dead and Diomedes is released from her imprisonment in the underground cavern could he ever hope to be healed. The spells of his enemies confined her for eternity with only one way to free her. He needed to kill them to end her curse. The gnarly wizard sweated profusely from the heat as he approached a charred wooden table with seven skulls next to a cauldron. "Diomedes!" he shouted nervously.

"Have you solved the device yet?" boomed a raspy voice from the rear of the cavern.

Ruger's twisted and distorted face reflected his fear. "No, I haven't," he said humbly.

The shadow of a tailed creature shone across the wall. "And what of the outsider?"

"He will be dealt with soon enough." Ruger looked around nervously for Diomedes but saw only her shadow.

"He must not be permitted to ally himself with the Firenghians," warned Diomedes.

"I'll take care of it immediately."

"If not, you'll join me in my hell! You are jeopardizing all my plans, you idiot!"

"I will do my best, Diomedes."

"That's not good enough! You have repeatedly failed me and now we are on the defensive."

"I meant that I will succeed, Diomedes." Ruger bowed to her and fled the cavern.

— ☒ —

Doc Smith peered through the blinds at the sunlit yard and pondered the events of the last few months. After battling for survival against the Neanderthals and the giant spiders, he now found himself at Dr. Miller's research facility, immersed in a civilized atmosphere once again.

The observatory and the surrounding buildings were the last remnants of functional civilization that he knew of on this world. Across the way, he studied the mountains and forests that reminded him of wild animals eying their prey.

Joe Miller entered the conference room. "Good morning! Did you sleep well?" he inquired jovially.

"Good morning, Joe. Quite well. Did you have any luck with the satellite imagery?"

"A little. It appears we can access the satellite but only for brief periods of time."

Doc wore a gray, wool sweater and corduroy pants provided by Dr. Miller's people. His shaved head and big-rimmed glasses belied his true age of fifty-five. Joe was a longtime friend and colleague. The two men jointly investigated changes in the earth, which they believed induced the frequent earthquakes prior to the event that tore them away from their own planet.

Joe was older than Doc at sixty-two. He was only five-feet tall and balding. Many scientists regarded him as the most brilliant eccentric in the world. His theories were quite ahead of their time and he had a rational way of explaining them. He refused to let the disappearance of civilization change his routines. He continued to show up for work every day in a suit and insisted on punctuality among his coworkers.

"We need to figure out who is responsible for this mess," remarked Joe. "Then we have to undo it."

"That may be easier said than done," replied Doc. He examined the icons on the computer screen then shifted his focus to the projection on the wall.

After several keystrokes, Joe made the large projection screen change from a map of the planet to four satellite images. He used a laser pointer to draw Doc's attention to four blue patches on each of the images. "These shades indicate very intense energy fields," he explained. "They're comprised of odd varieties of wavelengths and frequencies of light and sound. In addition, it seems like the fields are made up of energies, blended together unlike anything we've ever seen."

"That's astounding!" exclaimed Doc.

"These are the first images taken about the time your plane landed in Philadelphia. In fact, when you contacted me by radio, I was in the process of analyzing them."

Doc focused on each of the images and tried to make sense of them. He recalled how Maggie repeatedly warned him over the years about his tendency to look too hard into problems and overlook the solutions because of it. "Now, if I didn't know better, what would I see?"

"Think about the big picture," said Joe patiently.

"Each of the large fields was centered on Philadelphia and Washington. The energy fields extracted part of our continent and transported it from the Earth. That's how we got here!"

"It does appear so."

Joe pressed three keys and new images appeared on the screen. He pressed another key and the screen split into two halves. The left half retained the original images, while the right half exhibited the new images. "Look what's happened. The large energy fields are gone except for two small pink ones. I think the large fields operated like magnets that pulled us out of the Earth and replaced us just like swapping out pieces of a jigsaw puzzle," explained Joe.

"Hmm. Like a huge tractor beam," Doc surmised. "But what about the small field up there? It's near my camp."

"That's a smaller quantity of energy. It established a different sort of field, but not a very big one. It could be a portal for transporting someone or something into the region. If I didn't know better, I'd say someone discovered how to use 'wormhole' technology."

"This is fantastic!" exclaimed Doc. "Now, if we could only find out who and how." He stared at the images with his hands on his hips and pondered aloud, "It all makes sense. A trio of energy beams of significant power forms the field. With this quantity of energy, a wormhole could be positioned anywhere using a positioning device."

"Perhaps this is one of the keys to understanding the secrets of the universe, Doc."

"But, the army of creatures that attacked us: what if there are thousands of them? If our theory is true, then they could come through the portal in larger numbers next time."

"I understand your concern but do you realize what this means if we're right?" Joe queried zealously.

"Yes, I do. But think what it means if someone caused this cataclysm. It's too much power for anyone to possess especially if they can't control it."

"I believe that if the energy fields are directed through wormholes, we can predict the length of time it takes before they can complete the transformation of landmasses," suggested Joe.

"I don't care how long it takes!" exclaimed Doc. "How do we reverse it? How do we go home?"

"We have to keep our wits about us and dissect this problem one piece at a time."

"I don't know how you can be so calm about this, Joe. We're stranded on an alien planet."

"We could be on the verge of understanding something miraculous!" Joe responded excitedly.

"The other pink field formed south of here. We could fly over the area and investigate what's happening. Then we'll see firsthand if it's really a portal," recommended Doc.

"That's a good idea, but it won't be us going. Our work here is more important. We'll send scouts to investigate the field. In the meantime, why don't you get some lunch and I'll make the necessary arrangements."

"Alright, but let me know immediately if you find out anything new."

— ⏳ —

Maggie and Penny sat on an old iron bench in front of the observatory. Maggie transcribed several pages of her husband's shorthand notes into a copybook while Penny stared quietly at the eerie mountains looming in the distance. The sky was bright blue and the temperature was about seventy-four degrees. A cool breeze rustled the trees around them. "This would be perfect weather to go shopping in if we were home," Penny commented.

"Yes, it would. I'm going to miss the stores," replied Maggie. Penny stared down at the ground and wondered what Billy was doing back at the camp.

"How are you making out without Billy?" asked Maggie.

"Okay, I guess."

"Have you thought about what you're going to do if you go back?"

"I don't know. If I could be part of his daily activities, I'd be much happier with him."

"Maybe you should take the initiative and make yourself a part of his activities. Don't think about it, just do it."

"That's easy for you to say."

"Not really. I had to make the same decision with Doc and it's not easy. I wanted to be with him so badly that I forced myself to be a part of his everyday activities. If he took issue with it, things would have turned out differently between us."

"Do you ever regret giving up your life to be with Doc?"

"Sometimes, but that's what love is all about. Being with him was more important than being alone. When I made my decision, I promised myself that I would never look back. The only problem I ever had with it is that people came to know me as Doc's assistant instead of Doc's wife."

"I would love to be part of Billy's life but every time we're close to making things work, he gets spooked."

"Maybe it brought back the pain of a bad experience."

"If he's still interested when we get back, I'll have that talk with him. I'm afraid he's already given up on me, though."

"I don't think so. I'm sure if you talk to him, you'll feel much better."

"Hey, Maggie, not to change the subject but it's lunchtime. Are you hungry?"

"I sure am. Let's go to the cafeteria and see what's for lunch."

A young Marine stood in the distance, ogling the two women. He was enamored with Penny. She was very attractive to him, wearing tight blue jeans and a white blouse. He was only nineteen and young men were scarce since the cataclysm. When the women walked away, he decided to make his move. He rushed across the green stretch of grass and caught up with them. "Hello, ladies. I'm Corporal Jarret Kincaid." Maggie and Penny were startled.

"That's nice, Corporal, but we're going to lunch," replied Maggie.

"Great! Mind if I join you?"

The two women looked at each other curiously. Maggie preferred their privacy but wasn't sure how to convey her feelings. Penny didn't want to seem ignorant and buckled first. "I don't see why not. What do you think, Maggie?"

"It's your call."

"Alright, Jarret. You can come." Jarret cheerfully accompanied the girls across the courtyard to the cafeteria.

The front of the observatory was like a small park with a smooth, green carpet of grass. The walkway wound through tall trees and crossed the lawn, giving them a pleasant view of the surrounding area. "So, ladies, do I get an introduction?" asked Jarret.

"I'm Maggie Smith. My husband is Dr. Robert Smith. This is my friend Penny Nichols."

"Penny Nichols. That has a ring to it," kidded Jarret.

"Are you making fun of my name?" asked Penny defensively.

"No, just small talk. My, you're a feisty young lady."

Who's this kid calling 'young'? I'm older than he is by at least five years, Penny thought.

The corporal was captivated with Penny. He walked by her side and admired her. Maggie felt uneasy about his presence and worried that he would cause trouble for Penny. Unfortunately, it wasn't her place to interfere. "So, Miss Nichols, how long are you here for?" inquired Jarret.

"Probably another week. Once Maggie's husband finishes his work with Dr. Miller, we'll fly back."

"What business brings you down here? You're not a scientist, are you?"

"No, I needed to get away for a while. Things were a little hectic at our camp."

"I presume that you'll return to Philadelphia with Dr. Smith."

"Of course. Why wouldn't I?"

"Oh, I thought you might change your mind. We still have some semblance of civilization left around here."

"Like what?"

"Do you have a real bed to sleep in or a building to live in?"

"No, we're literally roughing it. My friends are building huts and we just got running water in the compound last week."

"I'm surprised you'd choose that lifestyle over this. Anyway, I do think it's interesting that part of Washington might be the last remnant of civilization on the continent or the world for that matter. Most importantly, we still have power, even if it's only for a little while."

"I have friends back at the camp, Jarret. We've been through a lot together. Besides, I've grown accustomed to the camp and it's like home now."

"Well, it does sound more exciting than this place. I was hoping that we might get to know each other before you leave." Penny blushed and bit her lip. "Aren't you going to answer, Penny?" he asked anxiously.

"We'll see, Corporal Kincaid. If you behave yourself, we just might get to be friends." Maggie fretted as she realized the game Penny was playing. When they arrived at the cafeteria, they got in line for the grill. It wasn't very long since there were only about sixty people at the observatory and its surrounding buildings.

Doc entered the cafeteria and quietly approached Maggie from behind. She was surprised when she turned and saw him standing there. "How long have you been there?" she asked irritably.

"Not long. Have you had a chance to look around?"

"Uh-huh. Penny and I have done quite a bit of sightseeing since we got here. Were Dr. Miller's people able to tell you anything helpful?"

"They sure did and you won't believe what we've discovered." Doc looked curiously at the young Marine escorting Penny. "Who's the new kid?" he inquired.

"That's Romeo and he's courting his Juliet," Maggie whispered.

"I think Penny should stay away from men. Every time she gets near a guy, she has a meltdown," he joked.

Maggie smacked her husband's elbow. "Robert, that's not nice. She has issues."

"That's exactly what I mean."

Maggie frowned at her husband although she was used to his cynicism when it came to younger people. She enjoyed working with him, but regretted that they never had time to start a family of their own. Doc and Maggie were both eager for a hot meal. When it was their turn, the cook served them cheeseburgers and fries.

"Sorry, we only have a limited selection these days. Tomorrow we're having hotdogs and potato salad," he informed them apologetically.

"No need to apologize. This is a big improvement from what we're used to," said Doc.

The four of them took their trays and sought an open table. Doc and Maggie sat first, while Penny and Jarret took a table further down. Conversation was somewhat strained with all the chatter. Word of the potential discovery of wormhole technology traveled quickly around the group.

Penny was silent and picked at her fries. But Jarret continued his efforts to court her. "You can call me Jarret. Can I call you Penny?"

"I guess so," she said coyly.

"Are you married, Penny?"

"Boy, you don't waste time. Why do you want to know?"

"Is there any reason you wouldn't tell me?"

"No, it's just that I've known you all of twenty minutes and you're already asking personal questions."

"Okay, let me rephrase the question. Is there a significant other in your life?" Penny hesitated, unsure if she wanted to answer the question. Jarret read her reaction immediately. "Let's try this one more time. Do I have a chance with you or not?" he inquired stubbornly.

Maggie couldn't help overhearing the conversation. She noticed that Penny's face was red with embarrassment. "Penny, you may want to hear what Doc and Dr. Miller have discovered. It sounds pretty important."

Penny was relieved that Maggie interrupted when she did. "Sure, Maggie. We're coming right over,"

"Penny, are you avoiding the question or ignoring me?" Jarrett relentlessly asked.

"No. I mean I'm not sure. It's a long story and I'd rather not talk about it right now."

Doc kicked his wife in the shin. She glared at him and tapped her fork on the table in a threatening gesture to her husband. He was quite amused with Penny's current situation and grinned.

"Our situation is no random act of nature. We believe someone has the use of advanced wormhole technology," explained Doc.

"Does that mean we can travel around the universe," kidded Jarret.

Doc frowned and Penny poked Jarrett in the arm. "Behave. Dr. Smith is serious," she chided.

"Sorry, Doc."

As Doc ate a cheeseburger, Maggie urged him, "Don't stop now. Tell us the rest."

Doc reluctantly put the burger down and finished chewing. "We suspect the phenomena that altered our world may be part of a plan orchestrated by someone with technology well beyond anything we have. Huge energy fields were created and directed with a powerful instrument to this region and the Philadelphia region. We believe that these fields were strong enough to transfer large sections of the Earth to this world."

"What kinds of energy fields can exert that much power?" queried Penny.

"We're still not sure. They're quite complex."

Penny was amazed by his revelation. "Why would someone cause such a disaster?" she asked.

"That's what we're trying to solve. Dr. Miller has arranged for a scout to fly our plane over one of the smaller fields. If we are correct in our thinking, we'll find an army of the alien soldiers like the ones Billy encountered."

"How many of these smaller fields exist?" asked Jarrett.

"So far, this is the second such location. If Billy's friends finished off the first army, then they're safe for now. If reinforcements come, they could be in big trouble."

"So, you think the creatures that attacked Billy are responsible for everything that's happened to us?" inquired Penny.

"They're involved somehow. They seem too primitive to execute a scheme of this magnitude on their own. I believe there's a higher intelligence involved."

"Then we need to go back and warn the others, don't we?"

"Yes, we do. There may be more of these things coming. We'll wait and see what the scouts find out first before we make any moves."

"These armies could be the leading edge of a much bigger invasion force," fretted Maggie.

"It's possible. I think the key is to understand how they're using the wormhole technology. Only then can we focus on stopping them." Doc finished his second cheeseburger and his fries.

Maggie and Penny lost their appetites over the news. Jarret wasn't concerned in the least about the situation. He focused on Penny and considered what his next move would be.

"You girls had better eat something. We may be going back today," Doc informed them. He got up and left the cafeteria. Maggie remained at the table and sipped from her cup of soda. She worried that their friends at the compound were in danger.

"Can I go back with you, Penny?" asked Jarrett innocently.

"I don't think that's a good idea. Besides it's not up to me."

"I'll go make the arrangements. This will be fun," he said eagerly and rushed from the cafeteria.

"Jarret, no!" Penny hollered but to no avail. "Well, Maggie, I guess I handled that well."

"Let's go for a walk. I'd like to take in the scenery around here one more time," said Maggie as she stood up.

"Do you think we'll really go back today?"

"I'm sure of it. Dr. Miller is a brilliant man. If he and Doc agree on what they've found, then I'm sure their assumptions are correct. We'll need to warn the others as soon as possible."

Maggie and Penny walked slowly through the park. "What are you going to do about Billy?" asked Maggie.

"What do you mean?"

"Well, you have Jarret in the picture now."

"Oh, don't worry about him. He'll get bored and go away."

"I'd be careful if I were you."

"Why? He's just a kid."

"Have you looked into his eyes? He has lust written all over them."

Penny giggled. "Oh, Maggie, you worry too much."

They returned to the observatory. "Don't lead him on. He's not playing," advised Maggie.

"I understand."

"I need to speak with Doc about some things. I'll see you at the plane in a bit, Penny."

"Alright. See you then." Penny walked out to the small landing strip at the edge of the facility. She sat on a bench and pondered, *Maybe I can make Billy jealous and have a little fun at the same time.* She gazed at the sky with a devious smile.

The small commuter plane landed and taxied down the gravel strip. Penny watched passively, as she considered how to handle Billy and Jarret.

Maggie, Doc and Joe approached the plane and waited anxiously for the pilot to exit. The engines shut down and the propellers gradually slowed to a stop. The pilot stepped off the plane and approached them.

"Well, what did you see?" asked Doc anxiously.

"It was just as you said. We saw an encampment of about two hundred soldiers in black uniforms about twelve miles southwest of here. We flew over several times but didn't see anything that resembled a portal, though."

"How much do you know about these creatures, Doc?" asked Joe urgently.

"The soldiers are primitive and appear to be controlled by a higher intelligence. They wear transmitters on their wrists like a watch. The leaders are tall and I hear they have some special mind-altering ability. One of them attempted to use it on a friend of mine. He is back at the compound and has met them up close and personal."

"How soon are you leaving?"

"I should go right away. I'll contact you by radio if we find out anything new. What's your next move?"

"I'll speak to our resident Marines and see what they can do about dismantling the alien army. I'd prefer if you stayed but I understand your concern."

"Thanks, Joe. I'm worried that the camp may be in danger, otherwise I'd stay longer."

The pilot informed Doc, "I need time to gas the plane. It'll have to be by hand so give me an hour or so."

"That's fine. We'll come back." Doc left them and returned to the projection room.

Maggie sat with Penny, staring at the mountains. "Are you alright, Penny?"

"Yeah, I'm wondering what to expect when I get back."

"Just relax and let nature take its course. You'll be fine."

"I hope so, Maggie. I really hope so."

When Doc returned with the pilot, Penny became excited. There was no sign of Jarrett and she would see Billy again soon. *He'll be so surprised to see me return. Should I play hard to get? No, maybe I'll just go for a romantic kiss. Perhaps he's realized how much we mean to each other.* Penny's mind was filled with so many questions.

Maggie couldn't help noticing the grin on Penny's face and was glad for her. Her sister, Celia, was killed in a car wreck when she was about Penny's age and Maggie couldn't help thinking about how much Penny reminded her of her sister. "I can see you're looking forward to going back, Penny."

"Yeah, I can't wait to talk with Billy." Maggie and Penny arrived at the plane first and waited anxiously. Doc arrived a few minutes later, carrying a large folder, full of maps and notes. He handed them to Maggie.

Maggie quickly stowed it in her carry bag. "I hope this is it, Doc? I'm out of room," she complained.

"That's the last of them."

Jarret raced toward them and called out, "Penny!"

Maggie pretended not to notice him. "Come on, Penny. Let's get on board," she urged.

"I'm right behind you, Maggie."

Jarret caught up to Penny and grabbed her by her hips. "Hey, Penny, did you think you could sneak off without me?"

"Jarret! What are you doing here?"

"I'm going with you. I told you I'd work it out."

"But, Jarret, I don't think that's a good idea."

"It's got to be more exciting in your camp than this stuffy old place. Besides, I'd like to see some of those creatures that Dr. Smith told my friends about."

"Jarret, I don't ..." Jarret cut her off with a quick kiss on the lips. Penny was stunned and speechless. She looked to Maggie and Doc for help.

Doc shrugged his shoulders and smiled. Maggie was appalled by the boy's brashness but left Penny to handle her own affairs. They boarded the small plane without saying another word.

Penny sat in the last row of seats, waiting curiously to see what Jarret would do next. Maggie and Doc sat in the front seats. Doc wanted to be close to the pilot in case he saw anything on the ground that required a closer look. Jarret entered the plane last and sat next to Penny. She immediately realized that she made a mistake with Jarrett. Maggie wasn't sure how to help Penny with her predicament.

Doc sensed her concern. "She's a big girl. She can take care of herself," he reminded her.

"But, Doc. That boy is so bossy."

"Penny will be fine. She's an adult." Maggie sat uneasily in her seat.

The plane took off smoothly into the blue sky. The pilot leveled off at five hundred feet so Doc could survey the ground below. Jarret wasted no time in his relentless pursuit of Penny. He placed his arm around her. "How do you know you wouldn't like me? I may be younger than you, but I would do my best to take care of you."

"You don't understand, Jarret. Things are complicated right now and I don't want ...," she paused and stared into his eyes. Jarret seized his moment of opportunity and kissed her. At first, she wanted to push him away, but then realized how much she missed the warmth of a man. She relaxed and enjoyed Jarret's advances. Then she blurted, "Jarret, I want you to know that there is someone else in my life."

"I can wait," he said coolly and kissed her again.

Penny responded with a long passionate kiss of her own. "But what if I don't want you to wait?" she asked playfully

"I'll wait anyhow."

During the remainder of the flight, Jarret and Penny coddled and kissed. Penny missed being romanced as Billy had done in the past and was anxious to make up for it.

CHAPTER 2

HUNTERS AND PREY

Billy summoned everyone into the main hall of the post office. "I think it's a good time to delegate responsibilities," he announced. "We have a lot going on here and our security is vital."

"How do you propose we do that?" asked John.

"I figure we need four sentries at all times: one each on the northeast and southwest corners of the roof and one at each entrance to the building."

"We could assign some of the men to handle that responsibility."

"Good. Any volunteers?" he asked. Six men raised their hands.

"You six will be responsible for rotating and covering the posts. If you need help for any reason, let us know," instructed Billy. "We need a group to handle the collection of food and supplies from the other buildings."

A few men and women raised their hands. "Good. That will allow us to work on our defenses and make sure we don't have any more surprises."

"Does everyone have sufficient quarters?" inquired John. Everyone nodded.

"How many rooms are left unused?" asked Billy.

"Just two," replied Ronnie.

"So, everybody's happy."

"So far. Don't spoil it," teased Randy.

"Gee, always the comic."

"What's on the agenda for today?" asked Ronnie.

"We'll scope out the areas north of the city and look for any sign of our friends."

"Just a cruise in the mountains for all practical purposes?" inquired Randy.

"Yeah, but maybe we can stop by Sam's station and see what he's up to."

"Well, let's get going," urged Ronnie. "I might have something better to do later."

"In your dreams."

"Oh, bite me, Brock!" snapped Ronnie.

Billy saw Melanie and Tanya standing near the stairs. Melanie dressed in shorts and a blouse tied up at the midriff, accenting her well-developed figure. Tanya, dark-skinned, tall and thin, wore a tank-top and cut-off jeans. "Want to come along, girls?" Billy offered.

"No, but I'll be waiting for you when you come back," Melanie replied coyly. Billy and his friends left the table and exited the hall.

Ronnie drove the Expedition north through the city toward the mountains with Billy in the passenger seat. Randy and Seamus sat in the back seat. Snakeskin seat covers adorned the inside of the vehicle. Billy leaned out the window from the passenger seat. His light brown hair blew freely in the wind.

"So, Billy, what are you doing about your little girlfriend?" asked Ronnie.

Billy was surprised by her interest. "Why are you worried about it?"

"She and I were talking about you yesterday."

"That's pretty sad if all you can talk about is Billy," kidded Randy.

"Don't be jealous," retorted Billy. Ronnie laughed at the two of them.

"What did you talk about that's so special?" asked Randy.

"It's not for me to say."

"Oh, tell us already. What did you talk about?" asked Billy curiously.

"Well, if things don't work out between you and Penny, Mel wants to start a family."

"What did you just say?" he asked nervously.

"She's almost out of birth control pills and obviously can't get any more. Plus, today is her birthday. She's officially eighteen."

"So, what does that have to do with me?" blurted Billy uneasily.

"She wants a family with you."

Billy had the deer in the headlights look in his eyes. "That's not happening."

"Billy, she's a young girl. Don't hurt her."

"Ronnie, we're good friends. I like her a lot, but she knows that Penny is my priority until I find out otherwise."

"Does she really?" asked Randy cynically.

"Don't complicate things."

Randy looked to Seamus for support. "I know nothing," replied Seamus innocently.

Ronnie parked the Expedition outside the police station. Billy got out just as Sam exited the station. "Billy! How the heck are you?" he greeted him.

Billy shook hands with Sam. "Not bad. I haven't seen you in a while."

Sam noticed the bruises on Billy's arm and cheek. "Whom have you been fighting with now?"

"You wouldn't believe it. Any word on your boys?"

"Not yet."

"We're going into the mountains to scout for any sign of the soldiers."

"Good. Help me put a few boxes in the back of your truck first."

"There had better be some for me, Sam," kidded Ronnie.

"Billy says that you only like 'bad' stuff," Sam teased.

"I've got something bad for Billy, Ronnie stated. "Just wait 'til I put my foot …"

Billy interrupted, "I thought you were in a hurry."

"I am," replied Ronnie.

Billy and Sam loaded three cases of ammunition in the back of the truck and climbed into the front seat. Ronnie drove them along a worn path into the mountains.

"You sure you want to poke around the mountains for those soldiers? I mean we could wait to see if they come to us," suggested Ronnie.

"Have you seen any evidence of them since the battle?" asked Billy.

"No, but I have a feeling they're still out there," replied Sam.

Ronnie drove faster along the side of the mountain. Billy yelled, "Whoa, girl! Where's the fire?"

"I'd like to be out of the mountains by lunchtime. Is that all right with you?"

"Keep driving like this and we won't make it at all!"

"Do the two of you always get along so well? If I didn't know better, I'd swear you were married," joked Sam.

"That's a bad topic for Billy," Ronnie remarked.

"That's low, Ronnie."

"So, what's the deal with you and your woman, Billy?" asked Sam.

"Which one?" interrupted Randy.

Billy ignored her and explained, "Penny's a little ticked at me. She wasn't thrilled when I declined to make a commitment with her. I guess I'm not the smoothest talker in the world."

"Are you so sure of that?" asked Randy.

"I don't know. Sometimes it just doesn't matter."

"Ah, but it does," replied Sam.

A group of triceratops loitered along the trail. Ronnie slowed the vehicle to a crawl and teased, "Looks like cattle crossing up ahead. Is this slow enough for you, Billy?"

"That's right, Ronnie, keep it up."

Ronnie chuckled as she parked the vehicle and waited. They watched patiently as the herd of triceratops plodded down the trail.

"I've got an idea," said Billy.

"I can hardly wait," remarked Ronnie cynically.

Billy jumped out of the vehicle and approached the herd from behind. When he came within ten feet of the creatures, he drew his pistol and fired three shots into the air.

"Yee-hah!" he howled. The creatures bellowed in unison. Their roar shook the jungle, sending thousands of birds fleeing from the treetops. The herd quickened its pace, sending up a cloud of dust. Suddenly, the mother emerged from the front of the pack.

"Hey, Billy, I hope you know what you're doing. She looks peeved," taunted Ronnie.

Ronnie and Sam laughed as Billy's misfortunes unfolded. "I don't think this is a laughing matter," said Seamus.

"Don't worry. Billy knows what he's doing," replied Randy. Ronnie laughed harder at her statement.

The triceratops charged after Billy. He dashed toward the trees on the side of the trail. When he cleared the bushes and leaped behind the trees, he lost his footing and slid down the side of the mountain. He desperately grabbed at the bushes but they ripped out of the soil easily and whipped at him as he tumbled down the steep slope. He landed abruptly in wet sand beside a wide stream and lay stunned.

The mother triceratops turned and charged at the Expedition. "Oh shit!" screamed Ronnie. She quickly guided the vehicle backwards up the trail. After a short distance, the triceratops stopped chasing them and returned to her young.

Sam wiped sweat from his forehead and complained, "Remind me to smack the living daylights out of Billy."

"No, you'll have to wait in line behind me. I'll thank him all right!" Randy and Seamus said nothing as they watched from the back seat.

Ronnie inched the vehicle forward, keeping a safe distance from the herd. When the Expedition reached the trees where Billy disappeared, she parked and honked the horn.

"Come on, hero! It's getting late," she shouted impatiently. Ronnie honked a few more times. "You know, Sam, he's really getting me ticked off."

"Maybe, he's stuck or something. I'll go check it out." Sam searched beyond the trees and looked down the steep slope. "Ronnie! Come, quickly! I think we have a problem."

Ronnie reluctantly approached him. "What is it, Sam?"

Sam pointed to the gap between two bushy branches. Ronnie looked down the mountainside and panicked. "Can you see him down there?"

"No, there are too many trees. That's a long ride down, though."

"Billy! Can you hear me?" yelled Ronnie.

Randy and Seamus peeked over the side. Randy grew teary-eyed as Seamus comforted her. "We gotta' get some rope. We can't go after him without it," suggested Sam. Ronnie urgently drove the vehicle back to the post office.

— X —

Billy's head spun and his body ached. He rolled over and felt a ripping pain in his left shoulder. "Wow! That was a hell of a fall," he groaned. An odd slurping sound caught his attention from beyond the trees. He saw a moose drinking from the stream. He was amazed at its splendor and thought, *What a beautiful scene! This would make a cool Currier and Ives card.*

Billy grimaced and massaged his shoulder. He was covered with cuts and bruises. When he touched his left eyebrow, he felt a bump swelling up. Billy surveyed the steep slope and estimated that he tumbled about four hundred feet through bushes and trees. "I guess I won't be going back the same way I came down," he muttered dejectedly.

The moose froze, as it sensed danger nearby. The head of a giant carnivorous dinosaur with a crocodile shaped head craned from the trees and clamped its powerful jaws on the helpless beast.

"Oh shit! The Crocosaurus!" exclaimed Billy.

The dinosaur shook the moose like a rag doll, ripping it to shreds. Pieces of bloody flesh splattered across the sand near Billy. He was terrified as he scurried into the dense forest and hid. Billy peered out of the trees fretfully and watched the dinosaur gulp down the last chunk of flesh. It left the area as quickly as it appeared. Its pulsing footsteps slowly faded away.

Immediately, the scavengers arrived and fed off the remains. Vultures descended in flocks and numerous small predators emerged from the forest. They eagerly picked at the flesh and bone that littered the area. Billy felt nauseous and trembled. He stumbled to his feet and scanned the area for any more dangerous creatures.

When he staggered upstream to higher ground, the sand grew wet and slushy. Billy stopped for a moment and studied the path ahead. When he looked down, he sank into the wet sand. Lunging at a nearby tree limb, he grabbed onto it. As much as he tried to pull himself out, the muck kept pulling at his legs. "Somebody help me!" he shouted frantically.

His frantic cries were interrupted by noises in the bushes ahead of him. A furry creature, resembling a black bear with a lion's head and mane, emerged from the trees. Billy gawked at the creature in amazement. The creature stared back at him briefly and disappeared into the forest.

Billy listened but heard only the shrill whistle of the wind through the trees. His knuckles ached from gripping the branch tightly and his hold was weakening. The mysterious creature appeared again. It perched upright on top of a large boulder and stared down at him. "Help!" shouted Billy desperately. The creature disappeared into the trees once again. His strength weakened and he slid deeper into the cool muck. He accepted the fact that he was going to drown in the quicksand. His eyes filled with tears as he ranted once more, "Somebody help me, please!"

The sound of rustling bushes filled the air. Billy sensed someone nearby. "Who's there? Help me, please!" He felt a glimmer of hope as the sounds drew closer. The quicksand reached his chin and his hands slipped down the branch.

A man and a woman emerged from the trees. The man promptly reached out and grabbed Billy's arm. The woman retrieved a broken tree limb and extended it to Billy for support. After several attempts, they were able to pull Billy from the quicksand.

Billy breathed heavily and leaned against a tree. "Thank you! Thank you so much!" he said, exhausted. His first impression of his rescuers was that they weren't quite human. Their eyes had pupils shaped like those of a cat. Both wore fur tunics made from animal hides. The man stood about six-and-a-half-feet tall with long, brown hair and huge muscles toned to perfection. His facial features reminded Billy of a lion.

Billy turned his attention to the female. She was also over six-feet tall with long, dark hair and reminded him of an Amazon queen. She, too, was muscular and well-toned. Her face was plain but she had a certain quality about her that caught Billy's attention. "Those eyes!" he uttered to himself. "The creature on the rock had those same eyes!"

Billy's body was covered with the slimy, brown muck and smelled foul. He wiped some of the mud off and threw it against the ground. The two strangers observed him and looked at each other as if they were communicating. Billy noticed their expressions and wondered about them. He went to the stream and rinsed himself off.

When he returned, he removed his wet shirt and draped it over his shoulder. He stared at the woman and fixated on her eyes. They were so strange, but so beautiful. The female gracefully approached him and said, "I am Seneca, Queen of the Firenghi tribe. This is my brother, Cassius, King of the Sarcasson tribe."

Billy was stunned that they spoke to him in his native tongue. "I'm pleased to meet you, your Highnesses. I'm surprised that you can speak my language." The two were amused by Billy's politeness.

"Who are you?" asked Seneca.

"I'm Billy Brock."

"We should really get moving. It's dangerous here," warned Cassius, who then led them into the bog.

"So, Billy Brock, where exactly are you from?" asked Seneca.

"I know this sounds kind of bizarre but I'm from another world. I had a little accident and fell down the side of the mountain."

"You say you're from another world?"

"That's right. My friends and I have been fighting Neanderthals, dinosaurs and alien soldiers ever since we got here." Seneca turned her attention to her brother. She didn't speak, but, again, she appeared to communicate with Cassius.

Billy wondered again about their strange silence. *Perhaps they are telepathic or use some other means of understanding each other*, he thought.

"You are very perceptive, Billy Brock," remarked Cassius.

"About what?" questioned Billy, baffled by his comment.

"About our telepathy."

"Please tell me of your encounter with the soldiers," Seneca requested. "How close did you get to these creatures?"

"I've been in battle with the soldiers and the wizards. One of them seems to have a vendetta against me."

"Did anything peculiar happen in your encounters?"

"They tried to put a spell on me. I was able to deflect the spell and injured the wizard who cast it."

Seneca was impressed with his success. She turned to her brother, and they silently acknowledged each other. "I believe we can use your help," said Cassius.

"We share a common enemy," added Seneca. "We are quite different from you but if we put that aside, I believe we can work together."

"I don't see why not. After all, you did save my life."

"I'm sorry that we took so long to rescue you. I wasn't sure if you were friend or foe, so I waited for Cassius to arrive."

"You could have asked me."

"We had to be sure you weren't one of them," reiterated Cassius firmly.

"And now?"

"Now, we trust you."

The trio proceeded up the mountainside. Billy was curious and wanted to know more about his new friends. "Right before you rescued me, there was an unusual creature with eyes just like yours. It appeared a few times, then disappeared. Do you know anything about it?" Cassius and Seneca chuckled.

"I'll let you explain, dear sister," said Cassius.

"Do you know what a shape-shifter is, Billy?" asked Seneca.

"Well, kind of. I don't know if there really is such a thing, but if there was, I think I'd know."

Seneca stared at him with seductive eyes. "I was the creature that you saw at the sand pit. I was in my alter-shape."

"You're serious?"

"Yes, I am. All of our race can change into an alter form. Unfortunately, there aren't many of us left, thanks to the Mideonites."

"So, you're a real shape-shifter?"

"Yes, I am."

"And the Mideonites. Who are they?"

"The Mideonites are the wizards who lead the minion army."

"And who are these minions?"

"They are the soldiers who fight for them. Evil spirits who have been summoned by a conjuror are given the bodies of sacrificed victims. The bodies tend to become horribly disfigured when the spirits enter them."

"You've got to be kidding me!"

"No, I'm not. This world is probably quite different than what you're used to. It's full of magic, both good and evil."

"I suspected that the wizards attempted to use magic on me. I still find it hard to believe, though."

"You will surely die if you underestimate their powers of magic," warned Cassius.

"How did you first encounter the Mideonites?" inquired Seneca.

"It's a long and complicated story. It has to do with Ruger, the chief councilor and wizard."

Cassius stopped abruptly in his tracks and scanned the area ahead of them. A moment later, he sniffed in all directions as if he was searching for something. A concerned look flashed across Seneca's face as she did the same.

"What's wrong? What are you two doing?" asked Billy nervously.

"Stay put. We have company," ordered Cassius.

Seven black gorillas emerged from the trees and closed on them from three sides. The gorillas were nearly thirteen-feet tall and very hairy. Their eyes were wide and bulbous and their snouts were shaped like a pug's nose. They had long arms and big hands. One gorilla had shades of white on its back and stood out among the others. "That's the leader," indicated Cassius.

"I never saw gorillas that big in my world," uttered Billy.

"I'm sure the creatures here don't behave the same way as in your world either," warned Seneca.

"I've already found that out."

Cassius grunted and growled at the gorillas. Seneca pulled Billy back toward the stream. "If they attack, dive into the water and swim upstream," she instructed.

"What about Cassius?"

"Don't worry about him. Just do as I tell you."

Cassius followed the gorillas into the trees. A loud roar broke the silence and rocked the jungle. A second roar immediately sounded in response, followed by several growls.

"Cassius will be back shortly," said Seneca confidently.

"How do you know?"

"We have telepathic abilities."

"But what was he sniffing like that for?"

"We both have a very sharp sense of smell. This territory belongs to a large family of primates. They're afraid of something. That's why they're behaving aggressively toward us."

Billy grew concerned and complained, "Well, that's just great!"

"Don't worry. Cassius is taking care of it," Seneca assured him.

Cassius returned and complained, "The foul-smelling simians had the nerve to think that we would pay them a tribute for crossing their territory!"

"What brought that on?" asked Seneca.

"They've seen Ruger's minions in the area and they're a little nervous. I'm sure they won't bother us, though."

Billy became annoyed, hoping that he had seen the last of the minions. "What is it, Billy?" Seneca asked curiously.

"The minions need to be dealt with."

"And what do you propose?"

"I've got to track them down and finish them off, once and for all."

"There's a lot more of them than you think. Besides, you aren't ready to confront the Mideonites again on your own. You were lucky last time."

"So how do I get ready?"

"I'll prepare you for your next battle," Seneca informed him.

"There is a lot more to this than you realize. You'll see what we mean soon enough," cautioned Cassius.

"But my friends will be looking for me, too. I need to let them know I'm okay."

"You can't go back, Billy. You would put them at risk," Seneca said somberly.

"If you want my cooperation then I want to know everything that's going on. No secrets."

Seneca and Cassius glanced at each other. "We're the best trackers and hunters from among our people, gifted with certain skills that the others don't have," explained Cassius. We're here to stop Ruger and his followers. They invaded our lands and if we don't stop them, they'll overrun yours as well."

"So, the two of you are like assassins."

"More like hunters," replied Seneca. "The Mideonites know why we're here. Our people have fought many furious battles with them and lost. That's why we're interested in why they pursued you and how you survived."

"So where are we going now?" asked Billy.

"Around the mountains. We need to avoid the minion stronghold."

They were suddenly pelted by a barrage of stones and retreated behind a large tree. "I thought you said they wouldn't bother us!" Seneca shouted at Cassius.

"I was wrong!"

"Billy, swim upstream as fast as you can. We'll meet on the other side."

The three of them dove into the stream headfirst and swam underwater. The stream was wide and slow moving. The warm water was only five-feet deep and clear. The rocks left trails of bubbles as they struck the water around Billy. When he came up for air, only two of the apes remained on shore. They persisted in firing stones randomly at them.

Billy ducked underwater again. He saw Seneca and Cassius ahead of him, moving swiftly underwater. He followed as quickly as his bruised body would allow him. When he approached the bank, he saw a school of fish. Each was a foot-long and wore a series of multicolored stripes on its sides. One of the fish drifted close to Billy's face. He reached out to touch the fish, but a large set of teeth flashed from his right. A snake-like fish darted from a hole and clamped its mouth onto the striped fish. Its sharp teeth cut cleanly through the body, leaving only the head and a piece of the tail. Billy trembled as he watched the pieces spiral slowly to the stream's bottom. He shot to the surface and swam as fast as he could.

Seneca and Cassius had already emerged from the water and waited on the bank for Billy. "What's all the splashing about? You'll attract every creature in the land," chided Cassius.

Billy gasped desperately for air. He crawled from the water and lay on the ground. "What happened, Billy?" asked Seneca worriedly. He tried to speak but couldn't. He coughed repeatedly as he tried to get to his knees. Seneca rolled him over and pressed down on his back several times. Billy coughed again and water spilled from his mouth.

"Did you Did you …?" he stammered. He pointed to the water and made a frantic motion with his hands.

Seneca felt sorry for him and pressed his head against her bosom. Cassius waited impatiently with his hands on his hips and frowned at her. Seneca glared back at him. "He's pretty shaken up."

"He'll be alright. We passed through the feeding ground of the tiger eels. He probably got too close to one of them."

Seneca helped Billy to his feet. "Can you walk?" she asked.

"I'm alright. Let's go," he said weakly. When he was over the embarrassment, he said humbly, "I'm sorry. I never saw anything like that before."

"Be careful about touching things you aren't familiar with. If you don't know what it is, consider it dangerous and leave it alone," advised Cassius. Billy appreciated the advice and decided he would heed Cassius' warning.

Cassius always stayed ahead of them by twenty feet allowing Billy and Seneca the opportunity to talk alone. They hurried through the valley where the forest grew thick and the terrain was difficult to cross. The three of them grew fatigued and slowed when they reached the base of the second mountain.

Billy's legs were heavy and his body ached. "Can we break for a rest soon? I'm in bad shape and the hike isn't helping me any," he pleaded.

"We'll be at a safe location very soon," answered Cassius.

When nightfall came, the trio stopped on the slope of the third mountain. Billy was exhausted, as was Seneca. "I'll scout ahead while the two of you rest. I'll return in the morning," Cassius informed them.

"Be careful," warned Seneca.

Cassius gazed briefly at his sister, and then dashed away. Seneca had a bad feeling about her brother's safety but it was too late to stop him. Billy sat with her and they talked at length.

CHAPTER 3

STALKED

Ruger sat at the oak table in the center of the chamber in the upper tier of his castle. He stood at six-feet tall and looked anything but human. His eyes were black and bulbous like those of a fly, leaving his vision somewhat impaired. At the end of his arms were gnarled hands with three stubs in place of the five fingers he once had. His mouth resembled that of a scorpion. Somehow, he still had his vocal cords. Talking wasn't easy but he adapted with time.

Two of the four walls were covered by burgundy drapes. The other walls were ebony blocks of stone, each with a doorway. A glowing, blue sphere was positioned in the middle of the table. It resembled a snow ornament at Christmas time but slightly bigger.

Ruger tapped his fingers impatiently and eyed a complex device that was strapped on his right arm. The device was the size of a large calculator and consisted of two keypads and a viewing screen. The first keypad had five rows with six buttons, each row with a different color. The second keypad consisted of ten white buttons, each with a different arrangement of dots etched on it.

As soon as he pressed one of the keys, the screen came to life. It displayed a soft blue color with seven cryptic icons. After depressing three more buttons, seven portals appeared around the room, each like mist but of a different color. Ruger aimed the device at a vacant spot on the wall and pressed a red button followed by a blue one. The sphere dimmed and the portals shrank somewhat. Ruger reached for a small valve on top of the sphere and rotated it slowly until he heard a sucking sound. The sphere grew brighter as it absorbed oxygen and the portals returned to their original size. He pressed three of the white buttons and waited patiently for the screen to change. The device emitted a series of beeps and the image of a starry sky appeared on the wall.

Ruger became frustrated and pushed several of the colored buttons randomly. The image changed to a variety of unusual landscapes before going blank. The sphere grew dim again. He reluctantly opened the valve further to increase the sphere's power. A blip of light flashed from the device and painted a green portal on the wall.

Ruger raised his arms in frustration. "This is a waste of time!" he complained and stormed from the chamber. He reached a landing with stairs on either side and descended the left stairs to a larger chamber on the main level of the castle. He crossed the floor and opened a thick wooden door with black iron hinges. It squeaked loudly when he moved it.

Reluctantly, he descended the stairs into a fiery cavern. His furry face became matted from sweat. He considered turning around but was interrupted by a loud, raspy woman's voice. "Ruger, you wretched creature! Do you have them yet?"

"No, Diomedes, but they will come soon. Their thirst for vengeance will make them come." Ruger saw her shadow across the fiery wall. He cowered when he couldn't see her. Even worse, he feared when he did. "We're running out of time and I'm running out of patience!" she shouted at him.

Ruger held out his arm, revealing the device. "But Diomedes, I still can't operate this device. What good is it if I can't use it?"

"That's your problem, Ruger. Did you slay the stranger?"

"My army is hunting him as we speak."

"I want Cassius and Seneca soon, or else!" Diomedes' voice roared. "Their imprisonment is necessary to defend the castle and end the siege."

Ruger shook his head in futility and departed from the chamber. At the top of the stairs, he paused and swore that one day he would have his revenge against Diomedes. He trod back to the upper chamber and hesitated in front of an orange portal. He stared at the new green portal he created earlier on the far wall. There was something about the portal that bothered him. He pointed the device on his arm at the portal and haphazardly pushed several buttons. The portal continued to emit a green glow from its swirling mists.

"I can't even get rid of the portals I made. This is hopeless," uttered Ruger disgustedly. He remembered Diomedes' impatience and feared what her wrath upon him could be. *What if Seneca and Cassius have already allied with the human?* Ruger considered. *He's done more to impede my plans already than anyone else.* He stopped abruptly and grumbled aloud, "I need more minions and I can't do that without bodies." He returned to the orange portal and followed a sandy path encased in mist. His vision, impaired by the curse that Diomedes placed on him, made the trip even more difficult.

Ruger felt the edge of the path with his foot and realized that he could fall, possibly into oblivion if he strayed from the path. When he reached the end of the portal, he stepped down from a platform in front of a massive, silver gate. He surveyed his army of minions and considered his next plan. The minions immediately acknowledged his presence and knelt before him.

"Search the city and find more prisoners," ordered Ruger. He held his left arm out and waited patiently. A small gargoyle descended from the sky and perched on his arm. Ruger admired its ability to disappear into the sky at will without detection. He would surely flee far away from Diomedes' reach if he could. The little gargoyle stared back at him with scorn. It was aware of the curse that Diomedes bestowed upon him and felt not one bit of sympathy for him.

Ruger whispered something to the winged creature and it disappeared into the evening sky. He barked orders to a group of minions until he saw Pirocles, one of his disciples, standing nearby. Pirocles' face was badly scarred and his right hand and forearm was a black stub. He wore a cloaked robe with the hood over his head and was quite humble after barely surviving his injuries from the explosion that Billy caused.

"Pirocles, you'll come with us to trap Seneca and Cassius," instructed Ruger.

"I'm at your service, Ruger."

— X —

Ronnie parked the Expedition in front of the post office. She called frantically for her friends as she raced toward the entrance. Jerry came out and asked, "What's happened?"

"Billy's had an accident!" she replied, nearly in tears. "He fell down the side of the mountain and we have to rescue him."

"I'll get some rope and a first aid kit."

Ronnie spotted John at the edge of the field and rushed to him. John sharpened a sword against a flat stone as Ronnie approached. "What happened now?" asked John.

"Billy's had an accident and he needs help."

"Not again!" John went inside the post office. He returned a few minutes later with Jerry and a large brown canvas sack. Jerry carried a coil of rope over his shoulder. "Let's pack everything into the truck and get moving," said John irritably.

— ⊠ —

Ruger led his army of minions through the dark forest. He saw something flitter through the night sky above him. "Ah, my pet. What news have you for me?" he whispered. When he stretched his arm out, the tiny gargoyle landed upon it and emitted a series of noises.

Ruger was satisfied with the gargoyle's information. "Pirocles, lead the minions to the west into the mountains."

"Yes, Ruger. Right away." Pirocles summoned the minions to follow him and departed.

Ruger took a different route back through the valley. "Tonight, I'll have all three of them," he uttered confidently.

— ⊠ —

Billy sat on a log and contemplated what he should do about his predicament. He rubbed the bump on his eyebrow and cringed from the pain in his shoulder. Seneca watched sympathetically. "Why don't you start a fire? I'll be back shortly," she suggested and then went to the stream to fill a flask with water.

Billy said nothing as he stared sadly at the trees. He missed his friends and feared he'd never see them again. Reluctantly, he gathered dried branches for firewood and prepared a small fire. He stared at the forest and wondered what other frightful surprises awaited them. When he sat by the fire, he tried to position his arm to minimize the pain in his shoulder. In his misery, he noticed two shiny objects in the trees. *Now, what in the hell is that?* he thought.

Billy's curiosity led him to act carelessly. He approached the bushes and realized he was staring at a pair of eyes, but it was too late. Ruger lunged from the bushes and tackled him. He tried to get up but was pulled down again. "You'll pay for everything you've done to me!" Ruger warned.

"Why can't you leave me alone?" Billy pleaded.

"How much has Seneca told you? Never mind, I'll know soon enough when I take the very essence of your life from you." Ruger's eyes bulged, big and black, like those of an insect. He laughed at Billy as he gazed coldly into his eyes. "You thought you were rid of us. Well, you are going to pay for what you did to my disciples. I have something special for you."

Ruger opened his mouth wide and a pair of tentacles extended toward Billy's face. Billy grabbed at the tentacles and wrestled desperately with them as they strained to reach his nasal cavity. Suddenly, a black furry creature shot from the forest and lunged at Ruger, knocking him away from Billy. He was stunned by the creature's lightning speed. Before Ruger could react, the furry creature leaped on him and ripped the tentacles from his mouth. After a brief scuffle, he scurried to his feet with blood seeping from his mouth. "You'll pay for this, Seneca. You and your friend!" he shouted as he fled into the woods.

Billy lay on the ground with both hands covering his face. He wore a pained expression. Seneca knelt by him and extended a hand to help him up. "What the hell just happened, Seneca?"

Seneca placed her hand gently on his cheek and asked, "Are you okay?"

"That was Ruger!"

"It doesn't matter. He's gone. Are you hurt?"

Billy felt weak and distraught. "What in the hell is he doing here? Were you that creature?"

"Yes, I was."

"But how did you change so fast?"

"It doesn't matter. Try to relax while I'll get you some water."

Billy was visibly shaken by the attack. He never expected Ruger to track him down in the forest alone like this. "Why does he want to kill me, Seneca? What are you hiding?"

Seneca was uncomfortable with Billy's distrust. "It seems that Ruger is determined to hunt us both down since he rarely leaves his castle," she remarked.

"Oh, he leaves it alright! He's come after me several times already."

Why did Ruger attack Billy if it's me he wants? Why does he fear him so much? she pondered.

Billy nestled down on a pile of leaves and closed his eyes. Seneca perched on top of a nearby rock and watched over him. Billy knew she had her eyes on him and wondered what was going through her mind. Seneca hopped down from the rock and sat in front of him. A chill swept over him as he considered that maybe she could read his thoughts. Seneca broke the silence and said, "Yes, Billy, shape-shifters are telepathic. What else do you want to know?"

"Can you read my thoughts?" he asked.

"It doesn't work that way," she revealed. "I can read a Firenghian's thoughts at any time but not yours."

"Skills like that would make you a pretty powerful leader," he suggested. "You'd always know what your enemies were thinking."

"But they would know what I'm thinking as well," she countered.

"Then no one would have an advantage," he relented.

"You make a pretty interesting leader," said Seneca coyly.

Billy was flattered and cracked a smile. "I don't see myself as a leader. I just have a habit of doing things that have to be done," he explained humbly.

"A true leader is determined by traits that are sometimes genetic and sometimes learned," Seneca explained. "Whether you like it or not, you are a leader." *Where have I heard a sermon like this before? Ah, yes, Jerry K,* thought Billy.

"Billy, you will become a very important weapon for us against Ruger and the minions. There are things that will happen to you that require your trust in me."

Billy felt a surge of bitterness as he thought of Charlene and Penny. Trust never quite worked for him when it came to women. "You'll have to earn that trust, Seneca. My days of giving it away are over."

Seneca gazed into his eyes and he relaxed. Something about her was innocent. He wondered if she could ever care for him or if he was just another passing whim to be forgotten at the first opportunity. As if on cue, Seneca placed her arms around Billy and kissed him passionately. Billy felt an animal magnetism grow within him. Soon he felt immersed in a magical world. He was oblivious to his pains and discomfort.

Seneca made no effort to disguise her intentions. She laid Billy on his back and undressed him. Billy anxiously removed Seneca's fur tunic and slid on top of her. The two lay comfortably on the ground in each other's arms and made love. Billy felt helpless in an erotic way as he succumbed to her passions. Seneca rolled on top of him, nibbling and kissing him in ways that made him tingle all over.

Billy felt himself change, as if he was transformed into someone or something else. The heat of passion grew and engulfed him, taking him to heights he never imagined. When their experience ended, he opened his eyes and breathed deeply.

"Wow! That was awesome," he said giddily.

Seneca smiled seductively at him. "I've waited a long time to have this experience with someone."

"What? You've never made love before?"

"Of course not. The consequences are complicated with my race."

"Tell me more about your people," he requested.

Seneca placed a finger over his lips and then kissed him. The two nestled together and stared at the approaching sunrise.

A dull brightness appeared over the mountain and became the first of two sunrises, one for each of the two suns. He was amazed at how quickly the night passed them by. Seneca ran her fingers across his chest and asked, "How do you feel?"

"Fantastic! My body doesn't hurt at all." Billy sat up and admired Seneca's perfectly sculptured body. She appreciated his adoration.

"You'll feel many more changes. I hope you like them," she said eagerly. Billy pondered what she meant but quickly dismissed his concern. Seneca extended her hand to him and said, "We must go. Cassius will return soon and there's much to do."

"I'm still not sure what happened between us during the night. Was I dreaming, Seneca?"

"No, but remember what I told you. You must trust me."

"Why wouldn't I?"

"Because you won't understand things at this time." Seneca kissed him and giggled. As anxious as he was to know what else was behind Seneca's motives, she convinced him to be patient.

— X —

Cassius perched behind several rocks and watched the minions march toward their camp.

Pirocles should be with them. That's odd, he thought. A voice from behind startled him. "Looking for me, Cassius?"

Pirocles held out his hand and blew a small amount of white dust at Cassius. The dust quickly expanded and covered Cassius before he could react. Within seconds, he was immersed in a white cloud that became a solid, transparent bubble. Cassius was frozen inside and could do nothing. Pirocles laughed and guided the floating bubble back to the castle. "How much easier could this get? The great hunter captured without even a whimper," taunted Pirocles.

— X —

Seneca took Billy's hand and led him to the stream. They bathed together in the water and frolicked. Billy kissed her over and over. He felt consumed by her and couldn't get enough of her.

Seneca climbed onto a flat slab of rock. She took Billy's hands in hers and pulled him out of the water. "Come on, Billy. It's time to go."

"Just a little while longer," he pleaded. Billy was overwhelmed with joy. *I think I'm falling in love with her*, he thought. *That wasn't supposed to happen?*

Seneca knew what he felt for her and was elated. She never knew true love before, because of the traits she and her people possessed. *I hope Billy doesn't change when his powers are equal to mine. He's a very special man,* she thought to herself as her heart raced. Together, they set out across the valley to meet Cassius. As they walked, Billy felt as though he could read Seneca's thoughts. At first, they were only partial thoughts, but became more complete as time passed.

Billy saw Seneca as a young girl in a white tunic, wearing a wreath of flowers in her hair. "Seneca, am I reading your thoughts?" Billy asked curiously.

"Yes, you are."

"How is this possible?"

"We did a lot more than you think last night. I've given you some of my traits which will help you in our fight against Ruger and the minions."

"How can your traits help me against Ruger if they weren't enough to help you? I've already held my own against him."

"In time, you'll understand."

"I don't get it. What's the big deal?" asked Billy impatiently.

"You'll understand later. Now, please don't ask me again."

Billy was ready to argue the point but Seneca suddenly appeared ill and fell to one knee. Tears welled in her eyes.

"What's wrong?" he asked urgently. Seneca buried her head in her hands and cried. "Seneca, what's happened?" Billy asked again.

"Something horrible happened to Cassius," she replied tearfully.

"How do you know?"

"His last brief thoughts to me were of fright and helplessness."

"Was he nearby?"

"No, he was on the mountainside."

"You can communicate to each other from that far?"

"Telepathy is often fueled by emotions. That's how he could project his thoughts from such a distance. Cassius wasn't afraid of Ruger but something must have happened to frighten him so."

"Was he chased?" asked Billy.

"No, I don't think so. Why do you ask?"

"Cassius may have stumbled across something important. If he was as frightened as you say, then maybe he found out something that threatened Ruger." Seneca broke into tears again and sobbed.

"Is it possible that Cassius was captured and Ruger prevented him from communicating with you? Perhaps that would explain his fear," he suggested hopefully.

"No, Cassius would have found a way to get through to me."

Billy considered their circumstances and inquired, "How well do you know this area?"

"Not well. We believed that only primitive creatures inhabited the area. The minion army never came this far east before."

Billy nestled Seneca against him and consoled her. He pondered what might have happened to Cassius and if they were in the same danger. Billy released her and stood up. "I'm going up the north side of the mountain to spy on the minion camp," he informed her.

"Maybe we should go back. It's too dangerous for the two of us," she suggested.

"No, we need to find out what Ruger and his cronies did with Cassius and what they're up to. It seems they're going through a lot of trouble to get to us."

"I won't leave you. If you go, then I'll go with you."

Billy placed his hands on her hips and pulled her close to him. He hugged her and whispered in her ear, "Trust me, Seneca. We'll get through this."

"I give you my trust. Will you give me yours?" she asked, gazing into his eyes with tear-streaked cheeks.

Billy couldn't resist her request. They had the same fears of being hurt emotionally. "How could I not trust you?"

Seneca felt better knowing that she could lean on Billy for strength when she was frightened. She embraced him tightly. The two of them hiked eastward until they were safely away from the southern face of the mountain. By nightfall, they circled to the rear of the mountain and began their ascent. They stumbled upon a small cave and stopped to investigate. Billy searched inside the cave while Seneca guarded the entrance.

When he returned, he put his arms around her waist and kissed her neck. "I see you're in a good mood," she commented.

"You've changed me and I love you for that," he replied. "I think I'm a better person for it."

"I hope you feel that way later," said Seneca with a note of concern in her voice. "You get a fire going and I'll find us something to eat."

"I like having a huntress for my woman," he remarked,

"Am I your woman?" she asked coyly.

"I certainly wouldn't mind."

"How do you know I'm hunting?"

"I sense it."

"We'll see," she teased and then disappeared into the forest.

Billy pulled together some pine branches for a crude bed. He sat down and flexed his shoulder, surprisingly with little pain. *How did it heal so fast?* he wondered. Then he thought about the traits and Seneca's many references to 'later'.

Seneca returned with a handful of berries and three fish tied together with a thin, wiry vine, much to Billy's surprise. "What? No dino burgers?" he joked.

"These are healthier for you."

"You don't mess around when it comes to food, do you?" he mentioned.

"It's the art of survival." Seneca handed Billy some berries. She hung the fish over the fire and waited patiently as it cooked. Billy admired her immensely. She was independent, strong, beautiful, and in his eyes, caring.

"When we defeated the minions, there could only be two of the wizards left at most," he pondered aloud.

Seneca pulled the fish off the fire and slit them lengthwise. "It would seem so," she replied sadly and placed the fish back over the fire.

Billy continued to mull over the situation. "Imagine this, Seneca: what if Cassius was captured in a beam of energy and taken to another time or place?"

"What difference would that make?" she asked, confused by his example.

"It could prevent him from communicating with us."

"You have a way of making me believe in the best of things," she admitted and took his hand in hers.

"Without hope, we have nothing. That's what keeps me going," said Billy humbly.

"Maybe you've given me something, too, Billy."

"Yeah, but it didn't come with the thrill that you gave me."

Seneca giggled as she laid the three fish on a rock. She separated the meat from the bones, minced the berries and sprinkled them across the fish. "Eat up, Billy."

Billy eyed the meal. "It's not what I'm used to but it looks interesting," he remarked. The two of them ate quietly.

"Ruger is smart. If he knows you're the last threat, he may be using Cassius as bait to lure you into a trap. Is there anyone else from your clan who can help us?" asked Billy.

"No, they are engaged in a battle with Ruger's army. They fight at the walls of his castle as we speak."

"How about Pirocles? Do you know of him?" inquired Billy.

"He's a coward of a wizard who does whatever Ruger says."

Billy lay on his back and stared up at the sky. "You know, Seneca, you and I are the only ones left who pose a threat to him. Perhaps that's why he wants us both dead more than ever."

"Can you help me find a way to defeat him?" requested Seneca.

"We'll deal with it tomorrow. Right now, I'd like nothing more than to rest."

Seneca lay next to him and kissed him tenderly. Billy relaxed and, once again, succumbed to Seneca's desires. He was overwhelmed by the burning passion that grew between them. It was like a spell that controlled him. They nestled in each other's arms and made love.

CHAPTER 4

RESCUE

The small shuttle plane flew north over shallow seas of seaweed and islets. "Can you fly to the east? I'd like to check out the coastline," Doc asked the pilot.

"Sure, Dr. Smith." The pilot guided the plane to the left and dropped his altitude to about seven hundred feet. A minute later they flew over a stretch of beach. "How's that, Dr. Smith?"

A large crab crawled from the water onto the white sand. "Perfect. Hey, look at that!"

"What is it?" asked Maggie.

"It's the biggest damn crab I ever saw. It's a species unlike anything I ever saw."

"Now we know where to come for a filling sea food dinner. Look at the claws on that thing," she remarked.

"You'll have fun catching one of them. That's got to be at least twenty feet across," said the pilot.

"Sounds like a job for Billy and his friends," kidded Doc. "If there's a way, they'll figure it out." The three of them laughed.

Penny heard Billy's name mentioned up front and paused between kisses. Jarret noticed immediately. "I'm here now. Don't worry about him," he said confidently.

Penny gazed at his youthful face. "Enjoy it while you can," she teased and kissed him with a ravenous desire.

For the next half hour, Doc and Maggie scanned the beaches, hoping to get a glimpse of other strange creatures. With none to be seen, the pilot turned inland. A short while later, they approached the city. The plane made two passes over the camp by the airport.

Doc searched the compound below. Oddly, there was no one in sight.

"Did you see anyone?" asked Maggie anxiously.

"No, not a soul."

The plane veered away and headed toward the city. Once they were lined up with Market Street, they began their descent. The plane passed over the post office and pulled up.

"What's wrong?" asked Doc.

"It looks like they've taken up residence at the post office. I saw a car and some people there."

"Well, that's good news."

The plane circled and touched down smoothly on the street a short distance from the post office. Penny immediately ceased playing with Jarret. "Fun time's over, Corporal. I have to deal with my issues now," she explained firmly.

"What about later?"

"Don't push it. We'll see how things go."

The Smiths exited the plane first followed by the pilot. "Do you think they saw us?" asked Maggie.

"If not, we could walk it."

"We really need to warn them about the portals. The alien soldiers could return anytime now."

Maggie stared back at the plane. She wasn't happy with Penny's behavior and didn't hide it. Doc paced about, impatiently waiting for the Expedition to appear. He noticed Maggie's concern and preferred that she stayed out of Penny's business. He wouldn't interfere, however, if she did.

When Penny got out of her seat, Jarret grabbed her arm. "Wait for me. I'll escort you," he said anxiously.

Penny rolled her eyes and warned, "Look, Jarret, I don't need any more problems than I've got. Now, I told you the deal."

Jarret accompanied her to the hatch. "So how will I know when you're ready to be mine?"

"Look, Jarret, you and I can be friends, but I can't promise you anything more than that."

"That's okay, Penny. I'm a patient man. I know I can win you over eventually."

"Please, Jarret, I don't want you to win me over. If things change, you'll know."

Jarret gambled on a parting shot. He pulled Penny close to him and kissed her passionately. Penny was red-faced, knowing that the others witnessed their behavior.

— X —

One of the men raced toward the Expedition, waving his hands. "Hey, Doc Smith's back! The plane just landed across the field," he shouted.

"What impeccable timing they have," quipped Sam.

Jerry exited the post office with John and Seamus. "What's our plan for rescuing Billy?" he asked eagerly.

"We'll take two vehicles. Jerry, you go with Sam. Take the flatbed and pick up Doc's group," ordered John.

"We'll meet you at the spot where Billy disappeared. We won't be long," replied Sam. He and Jerry hurried to the flatbed truck and drove off.

John and Ronnie boarded the Expedition and sped away from the post office. When they arrived, Ronnie hurried out of the SUV and opened the rear lift gate. She grabbed a thick coil of rope and tossed it on her shoulder. Randy took the end of the coil and tied it to the trailer hitch. Ronnie hurried to the edge of the embankment and tossed the coil over the edge. Immediately, she slid down the rope.

"I guess I'm next," Randy grumbled and skillfully slid down the rope.

"Not so fast, young lady. I'm coming, too," shouted John. He descended the rope right behind her. Seamus waited by the vehicle for the others to arrive.

When Ronnie reached the bottom, she saw the marks in the sand where Billy landed. She looked around and saw bloody pieces of flesh strewn about the area. "Oh, no!" she sobbed. Her eyes filled with tears.

Randy joined her and cried, "This can't be Billy!"

John arrived and saw the girls' distress. He picked up a piece of the meat from the sand and inspected it. He burst into laughter at the distraught girls. "It's either moose or elk. I thought you two girls were hunters," chastised John.

"Nice, Ronnie! How embarrassing?" complained Randy.

"Shut up! I thought ..."

"The eulogy for the animal is over. Let's figure out how we're going to find Mr. Brock," said John sternly. He promptly found Billy's tracks leading upstream. "Billy!" he shouted several times but there was no response. He surveyed the terrain around the stream. "It appears he's headed for higher ground. I don't think traveling upstream will get him back to the post office, though," concluded John.

"So, what next?" asked Randy.

"We know he's alive, so let's go back and wait for the others. We'll let them know where we're going in case something happens and they need to find us. I think this is going to take a while."

They climbed back up the embankment and caught Seamus sleeping in the driver's seat. Randy reached inside the Expedition and honked the horn. "Jumping Jesus! You nearly gave me a heart attack," yelled Seamus. "Did you have to do that?"

"Gotcha'," said Randy playfully.

— X —

Doc paced back and forth until he saw the flatbed speeding toward them. "There they are!" he exclaimed.

Penny discretely moved away from Jarret and stepped ahead of the others. She recognized Sam and Jerry in the truck. "Where's Billy? I can't believe he didn't come to greet me," Penny whined.

"Maybe he's busy," suggested Maggie sarcastically.

"He'll never change," Penny complained.

The truck pulled to an abrupt stop in front of them. "We're in a hurry. Billy's had a terrible fall. The others are searching for him as we speak," said Sam excitedly.

Doc motioned the others to get on the flatbed. "Just go easy on the bumps, Sam. There isn't a whole lot to hang onto back here," implored Doc.

"What did Sam say about Billy?" Penny inquired, annoyed.

"Billy's fallen down somewhere and the others are searching for him. Don't get excited, Penny. You and I both know that Billy has a penchant for surprises."

Jarret noticed the concern on Penny's face. "I assume that Billy is the other man in your life," he commented.

"Other man in my life! What are you talking about?"

"Come on, Penny. I'm young, not dumb."

What if Billy is gone for good? If he is, I do need a man in my life, thought Penny.

Maggie noticed Penny's deliberate silence and suggested to Doc, "I think Penny's growing up. She isn't the innocent naïve girl we knew before."

"What makes you say that, dear?"

"I believe she's playing both sides of the fence, if you know what I mean."

"Oh, boy. I can hardly wait to see what comes from this."

Sam parked the flatbed next to the Expedition. Everyone hopped off the truck but Penny. She tried in vain to conceal her feelings for Jarret from the others.

"Did you find him? Is he okay?" asked Doc anxiously.

"No, but his tracks lead upstream. He may be injured but he's well enough to travel. We're going to search for him but it's gonna take some time," Randy explained.

"Anyone else going with us?" Ronnie asked.

Randy noticed Penny standing alone by the flatbed. "Hey, Penny, you coming with us?" she asked.

Penny was surprised by Randy's offer. "I don't know. I don't have a weapon to use and I might get in the way," she replied sheepishly.

"Don't worry. Seamus has been busy while you were gone." Randy reached inside the Expedition and pulled out the lightest and smallest of four swords. "Here. This is for you. We're going to teach you how to use it. Soon you'll be on the hunt with the rest of us."

Jarret decided it was time to make his presence known. He approached Randy and attempted to pluck the sword from her hand. "Wow, look at this beauty!" he remarked.

Randy pulled the sword back from him. "Who's the kid?" she asked cynically.

"This is Jarret Kincaid. He's a Marine from the research facility."

"Just a kid who's wet behind the ears, I'll bet," taunted Ronnie.

John interrupted the girls, "I'm moving on. We're wasting precious time." He descended the rope, followed by Seamus and then Ronnie.

Randy looked back at Penny. "Last chance. Come with us, Penny. "It's about time we explored together," she offered.

Penny panicked and thought, *I wanted a reason to join Billy and the girls in their adventures.* She realized that she had no recourse but to join them. She was concerned about Billy but she had no idea what to expect from him when she saw him. "Okay, you talked me into it," she said reluctantly.

Jarret interjected, "Hey girls, I'm coming, too."

Randy couldn't resist a chance to have fun with a youngster in uniform. She was sure he wasn't prepared to deal with females like her and Ronnie. Besides, she didn't care for his macho attitude. "Are you sure you're allowed to hang with us? We might give you a bad reputation or something," she teased.

"Well, Miss Randy, I'm sure you'll need my help. I'm trained for this kind of situation."

"Right, little boy. You're a lean, mean killing machine. See you at the bottom." Randy gave Penny some instructions on handling the rope during her descent. When she finished explaining, she dropped over the side and descended the embankment.

Penny looked back at Jarret and shrugged her shoulders. "I guess there's a first time for everything. Here goes nothing." She descended the rope slowly but steadily.

Jarret followed after her, but he wasn't so lucky. When he reached the halfway point, he became tangled in the branches. Randy saw him snag on the bushes and yelled to him, "Kick to your left and push away from the branches."

"I can't. I'm caught," he cried.

"You're not trying, soldier boy!"

Penny reached the bottom and looked up worriedly. "Can you help him? He's just a kid," pleaded Penny.

"Yeah, I guess he needs it. I'll be back." She climbed up the rope until she reached Jarret. He was too frightened to move. "Hold on, soldier boy. We're going for a ride!"

"What are you gonna do? You'll make us fall!" Jarret shouted frantically.

Randy pushed off the rocks and swung both of them away from the branches. At first, they remained entangled, but on the second try, the branches pulled from the slope and fell harmlessly below. Jarret looked relieved as he clung tightly to the rope. "Are you okay now, soldier boy?" Randy asked.

"Yes. I'm fine, but I'd appreciate it if you didn't call me that." Randy descended the rope adeptly. Jarret descended much slower but reached the bottom several minutes later.

"Thanks, Randy," said Penny gratefully.

"No problem. We'll make a real Marine out of him yet."

Penny grew silent and walked away. Randy's curiosity bugged her as she pondered what the relationship was between Jarret and Penny. "I sense that there's a little more to this than just acquaintance," Randy whispered to Ronnie.

"We'll find out soon enough."

John and Seamus hiked upstream ahead of the others. Randy and Ronnie dropped back next to Penny, determined to find out was up with her and Jarret. "Penny, didn't you tell me before that you took some martial arts classes?"

"Yes, I did. I took Karate for six months. I don't think I was very good at it, though."

"Don't worry. You'll learn how to use your sword and your Karate skills simultaneously."

"Do you really think you can teach me?"

"Sure. Ronnie and I have been involved in martial arts competitions for years. John and Seamus taught us some sword techniques for combat, too. I can teach you some of the things that they taught us."

"That would be great. I'd really appreciate it."

"What about me? Don't I get a sword?" asked Jarret.

"We'll place your order today, and it'll arrive by mail in four to six weeks," replied Ronnie sarcastically.

"That's not funny! Don't I get one?"

"Sorry, pal. They don't grow on trees. Besides, we don't even know you."

"Let's go, children! We've got a lot of territory to cover. Save your energy," chided Seamus.

The ground turned muddy and soft as they entered the bog. Seamus advised everyone, "We're in a marsh so there's likely to be quicksand. Watch your feet that you don't step into any of the sand pits."

"Yes, mother," teased Randy.

John noticed several tracks around a wet sandy patch with a large branch sticking out of the muck. "Look there. It seems that Billy got caught in the quicksand."

The others gathered near him and studied the tracks. "John's like a bloodhound. Look at him go!" quipped Ronnie.

John looked back at the trees and pointed out, "There are two more sets of tracks leading from the trees down to the sandpit." He circled around the quicksand and spotted more tracks.

"Over there! Three sets of tracks leading away from here. It appears that two people might have rescued Billy."

"That's nothing. I could have done that," Jarret sniped.

"Sure you can, soldier boy," Randy taunted

"Don't distract John right now," said Seamus irritably.

"He's just showing off," mumbled Jarret.

Penny grabbed Jarret's ear. "If you know what's good for you, you'll shut your mouth," she whispered.

"Sorry, Penny."

Seamus and John stepped up the pace to reduce the friction between the girls and Jarret. They proceeded vigorously until sunset when John selected a spot on the side of the mountain to rest for the night. Everyone dropped their gear and gratefully rested. The brisk pace sapped their energy and kept them quiet for a while.

Ronnie stared across the valley at the mountainside. "Isn't that where our cloaked buddies disappeared at the end of the fight?" she inquired curiously.

"Yes, I believe it is. He might still have friends around here, so be alert," warned John.

"Then I guess we'll have to kill them, too," said Randy callously.

Each of them settled in for the night. John set a two-hour schedule for night watch. He and Seamus slept in a sitting position against a large rock. Penny and Randy lay flat on the ground, using their jackets for pillows. Jarret paced back and forth until he got on Ronnie's nerves. "Hey, kid! Can't you sit down?" she complained.

"No," he replied sarcastically. "I'm anxious for some action."

"Now what kind of action would that be?" she questioned him, annoyed by his arrogance.

"You know, fighting."

"Have you ever killed anybody before?"

"Well, no."

"Have you ever fought anyone before?"

"Uh, no."

"Then I suggest you listen and learn. You're surrounded by a lot of experience and most of us have already had some action."

"What did you ever kill, Ronnie? You're a woman."

"This woman could kick your spoiled little ass."

"I'm serious. What makes you the expert around here?"

"If you must know, I'm a tournament champion for three consecutive years for rifle and pistol marksmanship. I studied and designed weapons for several years. Randy, on the other hand, is a martial arts champion. She's won several tournaments. Those two Englishmen are from the seventeenth century. They were the King's elite warriors."

"No way!"

"Yes, and they have an enormous amount of experience when it comes to fighting. Penny's boyfriend, Billy, has been on OJT but he's accumulated more kills than anyone so far."

"So, Billy is Penny's boyfriend."

"Yeah, and to my knowledge, they're still an item."

"So, are you saying that Penny is off limits to me?"

"I think it would be wise of you to cool your jets until you get to know everyone. In the meantime, get some sleep. Your shift will be coming up soon enough."

"I can go a long time without sleep. I'll be fine."

"Just give me some peace and quiet, will you please?"

Jarret lay down next to Penny despite Ronnie's warning. Randy stood the next watch, followed by Seamus, then Jarret. When it was Jarrett's turn to stand watch, Seamus was uncomfortable trusting the young stranger with their safety. He kept an eye on him.

Jarret became bored and looked at his watch. *Nothing's going to happen out here. I might as well get some sleep, too. They'll never know.*

Seamus thought about his world and how he would never see it again. Fortunately, he didn't have any family left behind. The life of a king's elite guard left little time for relationships. He gazed at the moons above and then the sound of a footstep in the mud caught his attention. He reached for his sword and recognized the shape as one of the minions. It crept towards Jarret while he slept.

Seamus quietly slid his sword from its sheath and slipped into the trees. He circled behind the creature and saw no sign of any others. The minion grabbed Jarret by the neck and covered his mouth. It pulled him backwards into the trees, right into Seamus' grasp. In one swift motion, Seamus slit the creature's throat and broke its grip from Jarrett's neck. Jarret fell to the ground gasping for air.

Everyone awoke from the sound of Jarrett's coughing. Seamus dragged the minion's corpse into the clearing and dropped it where all could see.

"Nice work, soldier boy," chastised Ronnie. Jarret was embarrassed by his foolhardiness and said nothing.

"It's one of the soldiers. Where did he come from?" Penny asked worriedly.

Seamus corrected her, "It's not a he. Take a good look at the face."

Penny leaned closer, expecting to see something that resembled a human face. She gagged and turned away from the minion's grotesque face. A yellow, bile-like substance oozed from the minion's throat. "Oh, my God! What is that thing?" she remarked in disgust.

"They are soldiers of some sort."

Seamus admonished Jarret, "Lesson number one, young man: never sleep on watch. Many an army has fallen because of such a heinous act."

Ronnie was quite disturbed that Jarret jeopardized their safety. "How can we trust this kid? He's supposed to be a soldier, yet he's undisciplined. It's the typical male ego interfering with common sense," she complained.

"I guess we won't be getting anymore sleep tonight. Maybe we should just get an early start," suggested Randy.

"Does anyone have a problem with that? It seems that we're all wide awake now anyway," inquired John. Everyone was in agreement. They gathered their things and ventured upstream. The darkness restricted their movement through the dense forest.

When the sky brightened, John halted the group for breakfast. Seamus started a small fire and hung a pot of water above it. The girls sat together and ate bread and fruit that Ronnie brought with her from the compound. Jarret kept his distance from the group, still humiliated over his failure to protect them.

Seamus tossed some leaves into the boiling water and waited patiently until the smell of fresh brewed tea filled the air. He removed the pot from the fire after its contents steeped for several minutes. He filled a mug and sipped from it. "Tea anyone?" he offered.

Randy reached for the cup and took a hearty sip. "Billy told me about your tea. He highly recommends it," she remarked.

"I guess I should try some, too. How about you, Penny?" asked Ronnie.

"Sure, I haven't had a good cup of tea in a while."

Ronnie sipped from the mug and offered it to Penny. She sipped from the mug and called to Jarret, "Do you want to try some?"

Jarret took a seat next to her and drank from the mug. He maintained his silence around the group. *I have to make it up to them somehow,* he contemplated.

Penny liked having Jarret next to her. She felt like she had a man she could control, unlike Billy. *If he could keep his mouth shut more often, I could learn to like him a lot. Imagine the perfect man, one who has nothing to say,* she thought playfully.

Each time Penny looked up, she felt as though Randy was watching her. She grew uncomfortable and wondered if Randy suspected what she was up to. *Maybe I should wait until we find Billy before I say anything else to Jarret. Randy and Ronnie are Billy's friends and they may not appreciate the fact that I might be over Billy. Am I over him? Maybe I'm just being greedy,* she considered. Penny cast a glance at Jarret. Something about him made her tingle inside.

CHAPTER 5

ANCIENT EVIL

The first rays of sunrise broke through early morning cloud cover. Billy awoke and climbed atop a large boulder. He was amazed at the beautiful forest that extended infinitely. Seneca emerged from the trees with fruits and berries for breakfast. She sat beside Billy and fed him some juicy red strawberries.

Billy held Seneca's hand and placed his arm around her shoulder. He felt so many things changing inside him and, while he didn't understand how Seneca could change him, he liked what he was experiencing. He felt Seneca's emotions as if he was connected to her. Billy could smell things that he never smelled before. The birds and squirrels had a scent. The creatures that passed through the area earlier left a scent. Every scent was like a signature and the forest was full of them. "This is incredible! My senses have grown keener, Seneca. You really did change me," he said elatedly.

Seneca smiled in acknowledgement of his satisfaction. Billy grasped Seneca's wrist gently as she attempted to feed him. She was startled by the move and pulled away. "What's wrong, Billy?"

"I know there's something else that you aren't telling me."

"Please, Billy. Not now."

"If we're going to trust each other, you need to tell me everything."

"Please, Billy, I don't want you to blame me for what has happened."

Billy was puzzled by her response. "Why would I blame you? What have you done?" He grew impatient with Seneca's indirectness but then remembered how his intolerance and thoughtlessness strained his relationship with Penny. "Seneca, have you done anything that would injure us?"

"No, I haven't."

"Then I promise to hear you out and I won't judge you," he assured her.

Seneca was remorseful. "I'm grateful that you understand the importance of our trust in each other. This is difficult for me but I'll start from the beginning where things first went awry." Billy waited patiently as she summoned her courage. "My people exist in a world of magic. The land was divided into three regions and twenty sections. A wizard managed each section. Cassius; my cousin, Rena; and myself ruled the three regions. My parents, King Bryn and Queen Myra, ruled the land. The wizards spent much time together, and collectively their power made our land strong and prosperous. Unfortunately, with prosperity comes greed.

The wizards waged a war against each other, summoning all forms of evil to fight for them. My cousin was taken prisoner and we were forced to flee for safety. Many of our people pledged allegiance to whoever the strongest wizard was at the time. Soon, our people were fighting each other. As the battles grew more intense, the wizards summoned stronger entities of evil."

"Did you have anything to do with summoning these evil things?" asked Billy.

"No, I was a young girl when this began." She opened her deerskin flask and took a sip of water from it. "Individually, no one wizard had enough power to take control of the land, so they formed groups. There was one wizard, though, who bargained for immortality and ultimate power with a demon witch. He sacrificed members of his family, one at a time to satisfy this witch."

"That's pretty barbaric!" remarked Billy.

"The minions came into our villages and took our people captive. We tried to defend ourselves but they were protected by evil magic. With the good magic gone, plagues and terrible monsters ravaged the land. The wars waged for years."

"What kind of monsters?"

"They came from other lands and left when the destruction was complete."

Billy saw a tear stream down Seneca's cheek and sat down again with her. Seneca took a deep breath and continued, "The evil wizard, Ruger, was my uncle. He took my father, King Bryn, my mother, Queen Myra and my two sisters to his castle where he sacrificed them to his demon. Cassius and I escaped to hide in the mountains with other refugees from our villages. The demon's lust for our souls was so great that she forced Ruger to send his minions after us. She needs our souls to break the magical bonds that imprisoned her and to regain her powers.

"I believe there are only two of her cohorts left – Ruger and Pirocles," concluded Billy.

"That's right. Ruger made the pact with the demon for immortality. He is the remaining Mideonite that we need to fear. Pirocles is just a stooge and can't do anything by himself. If Ruger delivers Cassius and me to the demon, he believes he will receive eternal life from her, but our souls must be taken on the night of the full moons. If the pact is not fulfilled, the demon must wait twenty years. The full moons are in five nights."

"And what if this demon does get your souls?"

"No one will be safe if she is freed with her powers intact."

"What were the tentacles all about?" inquired Billy.

"As a punishment for not delivering us to Diomedes, she turned Ruger and his disciples into hideous creatures. The tentacles in Ruger's mouth enter the brain of his victims and draw out their life force. In doing this, he gains the knowledge of his victims."

"But how did Ruger bring me and my friends here to this planet? Is he that powerful?"

"I'm not sure. Our priestesses told us that an outsider would cause Ruger's demise. That outsider must be you, Billy."

"I doubt that. I will do what I can to help you, though," he replied humbly.

Billy sensed someone close by. Seneca sniffed the air alertly and noticed as well. "Ruger reached the future by way of a time path," a man spoke from behind the trees.

"Who are you? Show yourself," ordered Billy.

"I'm unarmed and I have no intention of hurting you." The bushes shook and a man wearing a brown cloak stepped into the clearing.

Billy recognized the cloak as one like the Englishmen wore when he first met them on the plateau. He recalled that John mentioned a stranger named Xerxes. The figure pulled its cloak back, revealing the albino face of a man with no facial hair.

Seneca moved closer to Billy and communicated telepathically with him. "Do you know this man, Billy?"

"In a roundabout way. I think he's on our side," replied Billy telepathically.

The stranger invaded both of their thoughts with his own telepathic thoughts. "I am Xerxes and I am telepathic as well. You are correct that we are on the same side, although I hardly expected to find worthy allies in this world."

"Xerxes, where are you from? I heard from a friend that you came from the future," inquired Billy.

"Ah, you know of me. I'm from another location, where my people monitor the galaxies and maintain stability among the many planetary races. We established paths to various planets that required frequent but subtle intervention by us. We are, in essence, the guardians of the universe."

"So how was Ruger able to access these paths?" asked Seneca.

"An evil witch named Diomedes was placed into exile. Her power was limited until Ruger made contact with her. She tricked him into performing acts that would restore some of her powers. To help Ruger achieve her goals, she revealed to him the location of one of our hidden paths. Ruger stole a device for manipulating time and space along with a device to power it, but he did so in a reckless and catastrophic fashion. Everything he learned came from Diomedes. What Ruger doesn't realize is that when Diomedes' power is restored, she won't need him anymore. She will usurp his power and kill him. My mission is to stop them both and restore the balance of the universe that he has upset."

"What do you mean by 'the balance of the universe'?" asked Billy.

"Ruger's actions have affected much more than you can imagine. Other civilizations have been affected like yours, and worse. Whole planets have been destroyed and things will continue to get worse if we don't stop him."

"Do you have a plan, Xerxes?"

"The guardians have set traps for Ruger in some of the paths. In the meantime, I will attempt to force him to use those paths. Sooner or later, we'll get him"

"What can we do to help?" asked Seneca.

"Do not allow yourselves to be captured. Your brother, Seneca, has been captured and is alive. He is the bait to lure you into Ruger's clutches."

Seneca's eyes grew wide with excitement. "If he's alive, then we must rescue him!" she exclaimed.

"No! It would be foolish for you to be captured before the full moons."

Billy was overwhelmed by the entire episode. He now understood why Seneca was reluctant to tell him about Ruger. Xerxes pulled his cloak over his head and walked toward the trees. "Xerxes, wait! What should we do?" Billy called out.

"I will meet you in two nights where the three rivers merge to the north of us. Until then, avoid Ruger and his army at all cost." Xerxes disappeared into the trees.

Billy and Seneca were dumbfounded. Things were more confusing than ever. Seneca stared blankly at the trees where Xerxes disappeared and tears rolled down her cheeks.

"What's wrong, Seneca?" asked Billy.

Seneca sniffled and wiped her tears from her face. "I feel like this is all my fault. My uncle caused all of this."

"He isn't your uncle anymore. He's become something terrible and you certainly didn't cause any of this to happen."

When Seneca looked into his eyes, Billy embraced her and kissed her. Immediately, he felt the fire inside of him growing again. His thoughts were interrupted by a strange sensation. Seneca noticed his distracted look and became concerned. "What's wrong, Billy?"

"I sense something dangerous. We'd better get moving."

"That's strange. I didn't sense it. What was it?"

"I'm not sure. It felt like something probed me like tiny electric fingers against my skin."

"I wonder if the traits I gave you are sharper in combination with your human traits. Perhaps your senses are better than mine. That's very good."

"We'll worry about that later," Billy responded. "Let's get moving."

As Billy and Seneca hiked through the dense forest, he wondered if his friends would look for him. They would surely have a tough time catching up with him at this pace. For once, he had an advantage on the girls.

"What are you thinking, Billy? You've been awfully quiet."

Billy blushed as he expected that Seneca knew his thoughts. "Didn't you read my thoughts?" he asked.

Seneca was bewildered. It seemed that she could only read his thoughts when he directed them to her. "No, Billy. I guess your thoughts are shielded unless you direct them to me," she replied.

Billy realized that it hurt Seneca to lose the open telepathic bond. They shared everything until this latest change developed. He knew it would be difficult to share each other's emotions and feelings like before. "Seneca, when will these changes stop happening to me?" he asked, curious.

"I don't know. No shape-shifter has ever shared traits with a human before."

"How did you know that they would work with me?"

"I didn't."

"Don't you think that I deserved to know that before you altered my body?" he asked defensively.

Seneca bowed her head and walked alone. She was embarrassed and had no way of knowing what Billy was thinking about her?

"Answer me, Seneca!" Billy shouted.

"It was for your own good!" she exclaimed, distraught.

"No, Seneca, it was for your own good."

It hurt because she knew he was right. She kept her distance from Billy and cried. Without a doubt, she damaged her relationship with Billy. If he left, she'd be alone to pursue Ruger.

They walked quietly for much of the day. Both Billy and Seneca felt awkward and searched fruitlessly for the right words to break the ice. By late afternoon, storm clouds rolled in and the wind picked up. Lightning flashed along the mountaintops and thunder echoed through the valley. A light drizzle fell on them.

Billy broke the silence and asked, "Do you know where we can find shelter from the storm?"

"Yes, I do. There's a cave up ahead on the left. We can stay there for the night."

Seneca grabbed Billy's arm and stared sadly at him. "Billy, I'm so sorry," she said apologetically.

Billy disregarded it and suggested, "Let's find the cave before we get soaked."

The rain turned torrential and the winds blew at gale force. Once they arrived, Billy hurriedly collected branches from the mouth of the cave and started a small fire using dead leaves for kindling until the wood dried off. The cave was chilly and drafty.

Seneca sat down in the rear of the cave and shivered. Tears streamed down her cheeks. Billy felt bad for being cross with her. He sat by the fire and thought about all the good things that happened between them. When he looked at her, he recalled how he was falling in love with her. He opened his thoughts to her, allowing her to feel that same emotion.

Seneca smiled and moved next to him. She snuggled up to him and kissed him. Soon they became lost in a fireball of passion. Billy felt their worlds merge into one again. The spiritual happiness that he enjoyed with Seneca was better than the physical pleasure he experienced with her. He soon forgot his anger. The two slept comfortably through the night, nestled in each other's arms.

When morning came, Billy awoke first. The rain fell heavily outside the cave. Billy felt the cool breeze on his face and wished the fire still burned for warmth. He glanced at Seneca and again marveled at her beauty. Seneca opened her eyes and smiled at Billy. He slid beside her and wrapped his arms around her. "Seneca, there are some questions bothering me. I have to know the answers to them."

Seneca sat up, concerned about what he would ask. "Is this real between you and me or is it part of your experiment? And if it is, what happens to us when this is over?" he inquired, concerned by what would come later.

Seneca held Billy's hands in hers. "It's become real, Billy. At first, you were just a weapon we could use against Ruger. When I met you, I could tell you were one to be trusted. You were a perfect candidate to be endowed with our traits. Since you weren't aware of that, your feelings were genuine. I've never met a male who could show me true feelings. The biggest disadvantage of being a shape-shifter is that we cannot shield our thoughts from each other. That is also the reason why we haven't been able to defeat Ruger."

"Do you think we can defeat him?" asked Billy.

"I never believed that Ruger could be beaten. I expected that I will fight him to the death and that would be the end. As for you and me, I never thought about what will happen when this is over because I don't expect us to survive."

"But if we are victorious, what then? Would you go back to your people or stay with me? You have obligations to your people."

"What do you want, Billy? What should I do?"

"I don't know. You mean a lot to me, but I don't know what we're destined for."

"Why don't we wait until we have to decide? I want to enjoy your companionship while I can." Seneca wrapped her arms around his waist and nestled against him.

"Seneca, is there anyone special in your life in Firenghia?" asked Billy.

"No. In fact, I have until my thirtieth year to choose a mate to rule with me or I forfeit my position to the next elder's firstborn. Ruger could have been king, but he forfeited his title at an early age when he elected to become a wizard. He felt that he had more power that way. When he killed my parents, the kingdoms became divided. Cassius and I were titled king and queen of our respective territories. My cousin, Rena, was entitled with the third. We had no control of the territories but we hoped that someday we could restore the land to what it once was. I guess it was only a dream."

"Does it bother you that you have to choose a mate?"

"No, but I want to be happy with whomever I choose. If anything, I have born more responsibility than any Firenghi will ever bear."

"I promise, Seneca, whatever the outcome, you will always be special to me. If you go back to Firenghia, there will always be a place in my heart for you."

A series of grunts outside the cave caught their attention. "Stay here," whispered Billy. He crept to the cave's entrance and peered outside.

Several minions waited beside the entrance and struck Billy with their clubs. He staggered and fell unconscious to the ground. Seneca approached the entrance to the cave and saw the minions gather around Billy's fallen body. She rushed to help him but three of the minions clubbed her repeatedly until she fell to the ground, unconscious as well.

CHAPTER 6

DRAGONS

"Time to move on. Billy and his companions are traveling at a brisk pace for some reason," said John.

"How far are we are going? I mean, are we sure that Billy even went this way?" inquired Penny.

"It seems that he made up his mind to travel upstream for whatever reason."

"Billy must have a reason for what he's doing. He knows we'd search for him," explained Randy.

"Yeah, but sometimes Billy's curiosity sometimes gets the better of him," remarked John.

Jarret overheard and commented, "Sounds like this Billy is a handful."

"If you're lucky, someday you might be half the man he is," Randy replied defensively. Penny wondered why Randy reacted so and what she meant. Perhaps there was something to Billy's relationship with the girls.

The afternoon passed without incident until they emerged from dense foliage near the water. They stumbled upon the corpses of apes and minions, scattered about the clearing. "Look at all the bodies! It must have been one heck of a fight," exclaimed Ronnie.

"I fear that Billy may have been involved in this battle. Hopefully he wasn't a casualty," remarked John.

"I see three sets of human tracks near the water," said Seamus excitedly.

John looked across the stream and scanned the shore. "Seamus, take Jarret across the stream and search the other side of the bank," he ordered. "See if you can find where they went ashore."

"If he crossed, I'll find his tracks," Seamus assured him. "Let's go, junior."

"My name is Jarret, not junior," replied Jarret indignantly.

"Whatever. Let's go."

Randy heard a grunt from the trees. "Did you hear that?" she asked warily.

"Hear what?" replied Ronnie.

"I heard something in those trees."

"I heard something, too! Let's get out of here," said Seamus nervously. He and Jarret waded across the stream to the other side. Ronnie, Randy, Penny and John worked their way up along the sandy banks. They moved upstream until Seamus located tracks on the other side.

"I found tracks!" Seamus shouted. A loud howl filled the air followed by a barrage of rocks.

"Get across the stream, now!" ordered John urgently.

Six apes appeared at the edge of the forest and hurled rocks at them. The four of them leaped into the water and swam quickly until they safely reached the middle of the stream and waded. The stream was slow moving and the water was warm, lapping gently at their necks.

"I guess they're still irate over their last battle," remarked John.

"They ought to be grateful they're still alive. I could have shot them all," said Ronnie.

"I wish they all died," complained Penny bitterly.

They reached the other side of the stream and climbed onto the bank. "Can we rest for a few minutes?" asked Penny.

"Not yet," said John. "We're too vulnerable here."

Seamus and Jarret followed the tracks ahead of the others. Seamus asked Jarret, "How much do you know about tracking?"

Jarret thought for a moment and then answered, "Not much, I guess. There isn't much use for it in the Marines."

The mixture of the wet sand, clay and soil made the tracks very distinct. "See how deep the tracks are in the soil. Feel how dense it is and you'll get an idea whether they walked or ran."

"You can tell that?"

"Sure. There are other ways, too: the amount of moisture, the angle of the impression, the spacing between the tracks. You learn after a while to recognize these things."

"Thanks, Seamus," replied Jarret gratefully. "I really do appreciate the lesson."

When they came upon the next clearing, Seamus and Jarret spotted something peculiar. Lying at the base of a tree were two pink strands of flesh that looked like ribbons. "What are those things, Seamus?"

Seamus picked them up and examined them. He knelt on one knee and examined several tracks that were partially erased. "These things look like tongues from some strange creatures. I've never seen anything like them before." He looked to his left a short distance and noticed more tracks. "There's another set of animal tracks and some human tracks. The human tracks continue upstream."

The girls caught up to them and noticed the different tracks. "Who do you think could be out here with Billy?" asked Randy.

"You never know with him. It's obviously not a tiger this time," quipped John.

"I don't think we're too far behind him. These pieces of flesh are still moist," said Seamus confidently.

Later in the day, the weather soured. Dark gray clouds filled the sky and the wind picked up in intensity. "We'd better look for shelter before the rain starts," said Ronnie.

"We'll need to go toward the mountains to find shelter," replied John.

Four flying dragons swooped in from high above them. Jarret looked up and saw them. "Take cover! Flying creatures at two o'clock!" he exclaimed.

"Now there are dragons chasing us! Oh, I hate this friggin' place!" groaned Ronnie disgustedly.

"Get under the trees! They'll have difficulty reaching us there," ordered John.

The first of four flying dragons swooped down upon them. The creature looked like a large, green elephant with magnificent wings. It had a sharp pointed snout and its mouth was filled with sharp teeth. Its ears, curled and pointed, resembled short horns protruding from its head. It had four sharp claws on the end of each of its four powerful legs.

Seamus eyed the dragons and hollered, "The soldiers are riding the dragons!"

"Holy Father in heaven! These are demons from hell," uttered John.

"If they bleed, they die!" Ronnie declared boldly.

After two futile attempts at them, the first dragon turned back up to the sky. Ronnie took out her pistol and noticed water dripping from the barrel. She frowned and stowed it in her jeans again, knowing it was dangerous to fire a wet gun. She stepped out from the shelter of the trees and waited with her sword drawn as the second dragon swooped in.

"What are you doing, you nitwit? Get back here!" shouted Randy.

The dragon descended into the clearing and snatched at her. Ronnie dove to her right and rolled away. She quickly got up and jabbed at the dragon's flank. It was a short jab and didn't cut deeply into the beast's side, but she did wound it.

The dragon unleashed a deafening roar. It lurched sideways and bounced across the ground, before hitting a tree. Ronnie dove and lay just behind the dragon's right wing. The soldier fell to the ground from the impact. It scurried to its feet and lunged at Ronnie.

Penny instinctively rushed at the minion from behind and drove her sword into its back. It froze in an upright position before falling to the ground. She stood over the dying creature and stared as if in a trance.

Ronnie leaped upon the dragon's back and grabbed the reins.

"You're gonna get killed on that thing!" yelled Randy frantically.

"This is the only way to fly!" replied Ronnie sadistically

The dragon spread its wings and took flight with Ronnie on its back. She was amazed that it wore a muzzle with spikes and buckles on its head. *So that's how the riders control the dragons. Each pull of the reigns inflicts pain on a particular area of its head. When I land, I'll have to make some changes,* thought Ronnie. She tugged on the reigns and tested her control of the dragon.

Amazed at how gracefully the dragon reacted to her control, she quickly adapted to the riding gear and guided the dragon across the sky. She steered the dragon behind another and maneuvered above it. Her dragon instinctively reached down with its claws and plucked the soldier off the dragon's back. She steered the dragon into a wide turn and veered toward the other two.

When she tugged at the reigns, the dragon released the soldier. She watched it fall helplessly to the ground until its dragon swooped in and devoured it. Ronnie guided her dragon behind the next one and repeated the drill. Again, her dragon plucked the unsuspecting soldier and left it freefalling to the ground. Just as the other dragon did, it plucked its rider from the air and devoured it. "Now, where's that last dragon?" Ronnie scanned the sky and then the ground. She spotted the dragon hovering above her friends. The dragon tried relentlessly to reach them through the trees.

Penny still remained frozen, still in shock by the dead soldier's corpse. She never killed anything before and just stared with her eyes focused on the lifeless figure in the clearing. Randy pulled her back to the shelter of the trees and slapped her face. "Snap out of it, Penny!" she yelled.

Penny finally turned her attention to Randy and stammered, "I killed it."

"Penny, you did what you had to do." Randy escorted her away from the dragon and sat her down by a large tree. She saw Jarret standing idly behind a tree and suggested, "Hey Jarret. Why don't you do something useful and keep an eye on Penny."

Jarret sat next to Penny and placed his arm around her. Everyone else was occupied fighting the dragon, and since he didn't have a sword, he could only watch. Penny stared blankly at the corpse, oblivious to everything else around her. Jarret was never one to pass up an opportunity. "I'll get you out of here, Penny," he whispered to her.

"I killed it. I killed that thing," she muttered tearfully. Jarret stood Penny up against the tree and held her close to him.

Seamus looked back at Penny and Jarret. He saw the look on her face and knew she wasn't right. Seamus rushed at Jarret and grabbed him by the collar. Angrily, he pulled Jarret away from Penny and threw the youngster to the ground. "You miserable wretch. You call yourself a soldier. You're a bloody disgrace. Stay away from her."

Jarret backed away and hid in the bushes. Penny resumed her fixed stare at the corpse. When Seamus returned to the battle, Jarret realized it was time to leave. He suffered enough humiliation at the hands of these people and they would never accept him as one of their own. He pondered his dilemma and thought, *What if I escaped and took Penny with me? They wouldn't have time to search for her boyfriend and us at the same time. That's it! I'll take her with me.*

Ronnie brought her dragon down upon the last dragon and plucked the rider from the beast's back. This time, the soldier was tossed on the ground. Both dragons lunged at the fallen soldier and devoured it. Within seconds, nothing remained of the soldier but shreds of black leather. Ronnie landed her dragon and immediately removed the muzzle from its large head. The dragon had several deep cuts in various spots around its head. Ronnie tore off a piece of her sleeve and made a bandage for the dragon's head. When she finished, she rubbed the dragon's neck.

The brown dragon stood nearby and stared at Ronnie. She wondered if that dragon would be as receptive to her touch as this one was. She cautiously approached the brown dragon and removed its muzzle. It had numerous gashes around its head from the muzzle, too. She tore her other sleeve off and bandaged the dragon's wounds.

The other two dragons landed in the clearing. They stared ominously at Ronnie. The area became crowded as the large, winged beasts hoarded close together. The latter two dragons were beautifully colored. One of them was bronze and the other was teal. "How about some help? I'm out of sleeves," shouted Ronnie.

"No way," John and Seamus replied in unison. "Dragons were never our forte. You, on the other hand, are doing just fine," continued Seamus.

"I'm coming. Hold your dragons," said Randy, who was never one to be shown up. She warily approached the two remaining dragons. Removing each one's muzzle, she bandaged their wounds with her sleeves.

The dragons lowered their wings and their heads onto the ground. They closed their big eyelids and fell into a slumber. Light drizzle had now become a steady rainfall. The dragons didn't seem to mind as they rested.

The green dragon extended its wing for Ronnie and perched it against a tree. Ronnie giggled when the dragon snored loudly. "I do believe it's giving us shelter," she remarked. Ronnie and Randy walked confidently underneath the wing and waited.

John and Seamus reluctantly approached the dragon. Seamus paused and looked back for Jarret and Penny. They were nowhere to be seen. "That dirty scoundrel! He's fled with Penny," exclaimed Seamus.

"What do you mean he fled with Penny? Did I miss something?" inquired Ronnie.

Seamus told them of Jarrett's behavior and how he reprimanded him.

"I have an idea but I have some work to do, first." Ronnie took the muzzles and removed the spikes from them. She cut a few sections of leather out and loosened the buckles by a notch.

John watched curiously and admired Ronnie's handy work. "What were you thinking when you jumped on that dragon's back? Are you out of your mind?" he asked.

"It was one of those things I might never get another chance to do. You know how Randy and I love a good thrill. I couldn't resist the opportunity."

"What do you think about Penny and this Jarret character? Obviously, you have something in mind."

"We can't do anything until the storm passes, so we might as well get comfortable. I'm sure they won't get far. Knowing Pvt., I mean Corporal Kincaid, he's hoping to find Billy ahead of us and redeem himself. If Penny sees him do it, he'll score points with her."

"He'll do what?"

"Never mind. It's just an expression."

The rain continued into the night. Fortunately, the air was warm and the dragons slept peacefully. Everyone stayed dry underneath the green dragon's wing. "This is a good place to rest. I don't think we'd get very far in this storm," admitted Seamus.

"You were damn lucky," chided John.

"Come on, John. You should know me by now," replied Ronnie.

"I'm learning."

"I have some fruit left to eat but that's it," announced Randy.

"I could use some meat. Tomorrow we'll hunt."

"That sounds good to me," replied Seamus.

"Ditto," added Ronnie. John and Seamus stared at her with a confused look.

"Ditto is an expression for 'me, too'," she explained. The two men understood after a moment's pause.

"What if your dragon pets smell food and wake up? They won't try to eat us, will they?" inquired Seamus nervously.

"I wouldn't worry about it. They'll be fine."

By sunrise, the rain ended and one sun broke through the early morning clouds. The dragons awoke from their slumber and set out to hunt for food.

Seamus was the first to awaken. He noticed that the dragons were gone and shook Ronnie. "Yo, girl! Your dragons have flown the coop."

"Don't you know anything about animals? They're looking for breakfast," explained Ronnie pompously. "Then they'll be back."

"How do you know?"

"Where else are they going to go? They ate their former masters, so they can't go back to where they came from. Dragons aren't stupid creatures, you know."

"When did you become an expert on dragons?"

"Women's intuition."

Randy and John heard their voices and awoke. They stood up and stretched. "We have to find Penny and Billy soon," Randy urged them, concerned.

"We're going to ride on the dragons. They'll help us find Jarret, Penny, and Billy," replied Ronnie.

John gawked at her in surprise. "I don't think so. I'm not going anywhere near those creatures. Didn't you see the way they ate those soldiers? They're dangerous," he complained.

Seamus chimed in, "I prefer to stay on the ground. We can meet you later upstream."

"I guess Randy and I are leading the aerial assault."

Randy coughed faintly. "You want me to ride on a dragon?" she asked, surprised.

"Are you afraid, too?" Ronnie challenged her.

"No, it's not that. I just wasn't expecting it. Besides, I should stay here and protect the boys." Ronnie folded her arms and glared at her in disappointment.

"Fine, I'll do it! But only if I get to ride the bronze one," Randy requested.

"He's all yours."

"I have never met anyone, man or woman, as insane as the both of you," Seamus uttered in disbelief.

"That's us, Seamus. You should know that by now. You boys continue upstream and we'll fly recon for a while. We'll join you later for lunch," said Ronnie confidently.

Ronnie looked up and saw the four dragons circling above. "Just in time. See that, Seamus."

"Yeah. Yeah."

The green dragon landed first and approached Ronnie. She placed the new muzzle gently on the creature's head. It tensed at first but when Ronnie climbed on without tightening the buckles, the dragon relaxed. The brown one landed next, followed by the bronze one. Randy carefully placed the muzzle on the bronze dragon and climbed on top.

"Last chance, boys!" Ronnie beckoned.

"No, thanks, Ronnie. We'll see you upstream," said Seamus.

When Ronnie tugged on the reigns, the green dragon spread its wings and took flight. Randy imitated Ronnie's actions and her dragon took to the air behind Ronnie's dragon. The other dragons followed behind them as well.

Ronnie guided the dragon high above the mountaintops and through the few remaining clouds in the sky. She was amazed at how effortlessly the dragons could float across the sky. When she crossed the second mountaintop, she spotted the soldiers' camp. Randy saw it as well and waved to her in acknowledgement.

While Ronnie descended lower and circled over the camp, Randy searched the area on the mountainside and spotted more soldiers. She flew in closer for a better look. A small band of soldiers approached the camp, carrying Billy and Seneca, who were tied to wooden poles.

Randy descended lower to about a hundred feet above the ground. When she passed over the soldiers, she recognized Billy by his clothes. Ronnie swooped in behind her, curious as to what she found. She spotted Billy immediately. Her dragon swung above Randy's and she motioned by hand for Randy to follow her.

The two circled around and quickly pounced on the unsuspecting caravan of soldiers. The dragons feasted on some of the soldiers, while the others fled into the trees and hid. The third and fourth dragons descended on the camp and sent the soldiers into a mad dash to the forest for shelter.

Ronnie and Randy climbed off their dragons and rushed to Billy's aid. Billy was badly beaten and unconscious. His arms and legs were tied tightly with vines to the wooden pole, leaving blotches of blood dripping from the wounds.

How does he keep doing this? He finds women in the strangest places, Randy pondered as she tended to Seneca. She cut her loose and helped her to her feet. Seneca was also badly beaten and had difficulty standing. Her ankles and wrists had swollen welts from the vines. She recoiled in fear when she saw the dragons.

"Don't worry. They're on our side," Randy said calmly.

"Is Billy okay?" Seneca asked weakly.

"I hope so. Let's get the two of you out of here."

"We have to get to the three streams and find Xerxes," Seneca mentioned in desperation. "If we miss him, it could be the end for all of us."

"Who is Xerxes?" asked Randy, curious.

"He's a friend. We need his help."

"Let's get Seamus and John. They're going to fly whether they like it or not," Randy told Ronnie.

"I agree. Help me get Billy up on my mount."

The two girls lifted Billy onto the dragon's back, and then Randy hoisted Seneca onto her dragon. "Hold on tight. I'm new at this," Randy informed Seneca.

"Oh, dear," murmured Seneca.

The dragons took flight, one after the other. Randy was in awe of the dragons. She enjoyed the breaths of fresh air high up in the sky. It was like a newfound freedom. Seneca was groggy and said nothing during the flight.

Ronnie led the search along the stream for John and Seamus. It didn't take long for her to spot the men from the air. She guided her dragon down to the ground along the banks of the stream.

John and Seamus watched the large beasts glide gracefully toward them. "Seamus, my friend, I have a feeling that we are going to ride on those dragons whether we like it or not."

"I believe you're right. I see that they found Billy, although he isn't looking too well."

Randy assisted Seneca in dismounting, then hurried to Ronnie's dragon and helped pull Billy down. They laid him gently on the ground and examined him. John pulled Billy's shirt up and exposed some purple welts on his chest. "It appears that Billy may have some broken ribs. We'll have to move him carefully."

Seneca communicated with Billy telepathically. "Billy, are you okay? I'm here for you. Your friends are here for you as well. Please talk to me."

Randy saw the concern on Seneca's face. She wondered how they met and what their relationship was. Her curiosity led her to break the ice with introductions. "By the way, I'm Randy. That's Ronnie over there and these two men are John and Seamus. What's your name?"

"I'm Seneca. Thank you for rescuing us."

"How did you and Billy meet?"

"My brother and I rescued Billy from quicksand in the marsh."

"What's this about the three streams and Xerxes?"

"We must stop Ruger, Diomedes and their army of minions before it's too late. Xerxes is the key to defeating them. That's why we must meet him at the streams."

"You and Billy are in no shape to travel," cautioned Ronnie.

"We must. It's important that we get there as soon as possible."

"Did you say Xerxes?" asked John anxiously.

"Do you know him?"

"Yes, I do. He spent much time with my men and me after we arrived in this world. He's the reason that we're alive today."

"The two of you are getting on the dragons, whether you like it or not. We have to find Penny, Jarret and Xerxes. There's no time to waste," Randy said adamantly.

Billy regained consciousness groggily. Seneca and Randy propped him up and gave him some water. "I was so worried about you. I thought I lost you," said Seneca anxiously.

Billy noticed Seneca's severely bruised body. "Gosh, those bastards really did a number on us. Are you okay?"

"I'm pretty sore, but we'll heal fast. We're lucky your friends came along when they did."

"Seneca, can you ride a horse?" asked Ronnie.

"Of course."

"Good, then you'll have no problem with the brown dragon. You'll take Billy with you. Randy and I will take the scaredy-cats."

"I resent that remark. I was never trained to ride dragons," whimpered Seamus.

"Well, I'm sorry I forgot to include you in my class. Remember, this is new to me, too," sniped Ronnie.

"Fine, let's go before I change my mind."

— ⧗ —

Jarret led Penny upstream in the shelter of the trees and rocks that lined the banks of the stream. Penny was in mild shock and not quite coherent. Jarret didn't know what to do about it and only knew that he had to get her as far away from the others as possible.

They entered a clearing near the base of a mountain and paused for a rest. Penny stared past Jarret and her eyes bulged with fear. Jarret turned and saw a strange dinosaur resembling a T-Rex with a crocodile-shaped head plod through the trees. By the time it reached the center of the clearing, it saw them. Penny recalled that Billy named it a Crocosaurus.

Jarret was astonished at the size of the creature. It lumbered toward them with huge strides. Jarret pulled Penny to a cave near the base of the mountain. Penny couldn't take her eyes off the beast as they approached the cave. "Come on, Penny! We can make it," urged Jarret.

They reached the cave as the creature closed on them. Jarret pulled Penny into the dark cave and tumbled face first to the ground. Penny tripped and fell on top of him. The Crocosaurus rammed its head into the cave's entrance and struggled to reach them. It roared furiously as it repeatedly tried to fit its big head through the narrow opening.

The ground shook and the walls trembled from the force of the collisions. Rock and soil fell from the cave's ceiling each time the creature's head struck the cave. Saliva from the dinosaur's mouth splashed across the gravel that made up the cave's floor. The stench from its breath was sickening.

Penny crawled desperately away from the entrance as far as she could go. She huddled against the wall of the cave. Jarret picked up stones from the cave floor and hurled them at the creature's head.

"Leave it alone! It will go away," shouted Penny.

The dinosaur paced around the clearing several times, then disappeared into the forest. "Are you okay?" Jarrett asked.

Penny laughed hysterically despite her tears. "I'll be okay but no thanks to you, you bonehead. We almost became dinosaur lunch." Jarret was relieved to see Penny smile but worried about her reaction to him.

"Do you remember what happened?" he asked nervously.

"No. I mean yes. I remember stabbing one of those horrible soldiers in the back. I was so scared. Then that big lizard out there scared the living daylights out of me."

Jarret was embarrassed over their predicament. "How did you know it would go away?" he inquired.

"That's the same type of beast that attacked our camp. It gets frustrated easily. It'll give up and leave for a while but it always comes back."

"Oh, great," muttered Jarret. He flicked on a lighter and surveyed their surroundings. He immediately noticed the burnt wood and ash remains from a small fire. He knelt down and placed his finger in the ashes.

"Looks like somebody had a fire in here. The ashes are still warm, too. Maybe your friend, Billy, was here."

"It doesn't matter. At this rate, we'll never catch up with him," she replied. Penny sat down on the ground with her back against the wall. Jarret sat next to her and placed his arm around her. To his surprise, she didn't pull away. Instead, she pulled him toward her and kissed him. Jarret was overwhelmed with excitement as the two of them fumbled through each other's clothing. "Penny, are we doing what I think we are doing?" he asked nervously.

"Just shut up and enjoy it. After all, this is what you wanted, isn't it?"

"Yeah, but …"

Penny cut him off in mid-sentence and rolled on top of him. She had an urge to make love to someone like never before. It seemed like the ideal time to release a lot of sexual tension. Unfortunately, Jarrett's stamina wasn't quite what she expected. Jarret lost his focus and rolled onto his side. "What's the matter?" she asked.

"Uh, nothing," Jarret replied sheepishly.

Penny pulled him on top of her. "Then come on. What's stopping you? Come on!" she urged.

"Uh, maybe this isn't a good idea," Jarret answered, humiliated once more. Penny shook her head in disbelief. This wasn't how she expected a knight in shining armor to perform. She thought for a moment and then realized what had happened. Jarret wasn't able to control his excitement. "Never mind, Jarret. You blew it. This was your big chance," Penny responded disgustedly.

"Please don't tell the others about this. I'll do anything you want."

"Oh, will you. I'm going to hold you to that."

"I really mean it. Nothing has gone right for me with your friends," he pleaded.

"I want your word that you'll treat my friends with respect and stop trying to impress them."

"Oh, I know I'm going to regret this," Jarret griped.

Penny sat up and folded her arms. "Well?" she asked impatiently.

"Alright, I promise."

— X —

While flying along the stream, Ronnie spotted the Crocosaurus loitering at the side of a mountain. She motioned for Seneca and Randy to look below. Seneca recognized the cave as the one that she and Billy were ambushed in. She pointed to it and gestured for the others to follow.

Ronnie understood and flew low enough to get the creature's attention. The other dragons followed her and hovered above it. The dinosaur was intimidated by the dragons and fled into the forest. The dragons landed a short distance from the cave in the middle of the clearing. Seneca helped Billy down from the dragon's mount.

Randy anxiously slid off the dragon and hurried to the cave, hoping to find Penny. When she entered, she was shocked to find Jarret and Penny sitting naked on the cave floor. "Penny, what in the hell is going on? Jarret, you rat fink!" exclaimed Randy.

"Randy, it's not like it looks! Honest," said Penny defensively.

"Will the two of you please get dressed so we can get out of here?" ordered Randy as she turned away.

Penny was humiliated. "Give us a minute and we'll be out," she requested humbly.

"It looks to me like you've had your minute," chided Randy.

Penny glanced at Jarret and uttered, "You can say that again."

"You promised …" said Jarret unhappily.

Penny dressed hurriedly and complained, "Look what you've gotten me into. Fortunately, Billy isn't here to see this."

Randy barred the others from entering the cave. "Everyone's okay. They'll be out in a minute."

Billy waited patiently by the dragons with Seneca. He called to Randy, "Did you find Penny?"

"Oh, yes. She'll be joining us shortly."

Ronnie asked John, "How did you feel riding on the dragon? Were you comfortable?"

"Surprisingly yes!"

"Do you think that you and Seamus could take one of the dragons?"

"I think so, as long as it doesn't eat me."

"You'll do fine. I'll take rat boy and Randy will take Penny."

Penny and Jarret hustled out of the cave with guilty looks upon their faces. Penny became pale when she saw Billy waiting outside. "Billy, I didn't know you were here," she blurted, now thoroughly embarrassed.

Billy was disappointed in her reaction and replied, "Yes and I'm glad to see you, too, Penny. How about a 'hello' or 'I missed you, Billy'?"

Penny was humiliated and stared down at the ground in shame. She couldn't look Billy in the eye. Billy sensed that Penny and Jarret had become more than just acquaintances. His keen sense of smell told him that Penny and Jarret wore each other's scent but didn't have relations.

Penny suspected that Billy knew what happened. Unfortunately, the more she thought about it, the more she revealed to him. Finally, guilt overtook her and she asked him, "You know, don't you?"

"Yeah, I do. For what it's worth, I missed you."

Penny noticed how badly bruised Billy was. She forced a smile and replied, "For what it's worth, I missed you, too. What happened to you?"

"Oh, me and Seneca got caught in a gang fight with a bunch of Ruger's minions."

"Minions? What are they?"

"The soldiers are minions to Ruger."

Penny stared in disbelief. Billy hugged her and led her over to the dragons. She was surprised that Billy didn't explode on her. She would have felt better if he had.

Seneca helped Billy up onto the dragon while Penny watched curiously. Billy sat on the dragon as if he were on a mighty stallion. Penny was stunned that her friends flew on the dragons like this. She touched Billy's leg affectionately and walked somberly over to Randy's dragon. She climbed up behind Randy and wrapped her arms around her tightly.

Penny felt awkward and tried to think of something to break the silence. "How did you learn to control the dragons?" she asked.

"It's like riding a horse. The soldiers already had them trained. We just commandeered them," explained Randy. All four dragons took off in unison and sailed high above the mountains.

Penny's mind wandered through the earlier events and what the consequences would be. *That should be me with Billy. Oh, what have I done?* she thought, feeling dejected.

The dragons flew for an hour before Seneca spotted the three streams. She gestured for the others to land in the clearing. All four dragons landed on the north bank. The clearing was wide enough for all of them to stretch their wings comfortably. Nearby was a cave, partially hidden in the rocks. It was an ideal spot to make camp.

A voice rang out and startled them, "Well, it's about time! I had given up hope that you would make it."

John saw the man and exclaimed, "Xerxes, my friend! How are you?" The two men embraced.

Seamus anxiously approached the robed albino man and shook hands with him. "I didn't expect to see you again, especially here."

"Isn't this a case of twisted fate? Who would have imagined all of us here together for the most important mission in the history of the universe?" Xerxes quipped. The others surrounded the men and waited anxiously for an explanation.

"How long are we staying here? The dragons need a rest, as do the rest of us," said Ronnie.

"We can stay until morning. There's plenty of room in the cave," answered Xerxes.

The two suns set and a cool breeze blew across the clearing. The dragons slurped mightily from the nearby stream. The last time they drank, they slept steadily through the rainfall. No doubt, they would sleep again.

Seamus started a small fire near the mouth of the cave. John and Ronnie went to the stream to fish for food. John taught Ronnie how to snare the fish from the water using a spear. Billy lay down in the rear of the cave and was fast asleep. Seneca lay next to him and placed her head on his lap. She, too, slept. Penny, of course, took note and couldn't take her eyes off of them. They appeared so peaceful together. *Why can't that be me? Maybe I need to do something to let Billy know that I still want him,* she thought as she became irritated.

CHAPTER 7

THE EVE OF BATTLE

Everyone sat around the fire, wondering where their fate would take them. "How reliable are the dragons, Ronnie? They could be a major contributor to our plan," asked Xerxes.

"Just tell me what you want them to do."

"They could create the diversion we need. Billy, Seneca and I will enter the portal to hunt down Ruger. The rest of you will need to keep the minions away from the portal until we return. I'm sure they'll try to follow us, so you'll need to get position in front of the gate with the dragons."

"Do you have any idea what you'll find on the other side of the portal?" inquired Randy.

"I expect to be in Ruger's castle," replied Xerxes confidently.

"And what is the point of doing this?" asked John.

"We must recover the portal control unit and its power source, and then destroy Ruger and Diomedes."

"Who's Diomedes?"

"She's the demon witch that Ruger is about to turn loose on us. She's using Ruger to escape her prison. Once she's free, no one is safe."

"Do you have a plan for dealing with Diomedes?"

"I won't know until I see what form she has taken. If she is in a physical form, she can be killed but not through normal means. If she appears in a spiritual form, she cannot regain her power from Ruger but she can leave her chamber using a soul as a medium."

"This is kind of spooky," said Randy nervously.

"Yeah, this devil and spirit stuff sounds like witchcraft and devil worship," remarked Ronnie.

"That's a good term for it - devil worship," said Xerxes somberly.

"What happened to the dinosaurs and the Neanderthals? This crap's out of my league," complained Seamus.

"Can't we just attack Ruger's castle on foot? Do we have to use this portal?" asked Penny.

"The portal is the only way to get there. The castle is protected by a magic barrier that is another realm."

"Is this the mission you spoke of on the plateau?" asked John curiously.

"Yes, it is. I never expected to involve you in it, though."

"I have an idea, Xerxes," said Randy. "I'm sure that the dinosaur will return in the morning if the dragons are away from the cave. The creature is very territorial. I'll bet we can lure it up to the camp and turn it loose on the minion army."

"How would you do that?"

"If we capture some bait, we could dangle it in front of the creature. It'll chase the bait all over the place."

"That might work. The portal is well defended, as you would expect, so we can use any and all help."

"One more thing," added Xerxes. "I want each of you to understand the importance of what we are undertaking tomorrow. We must succeed at any and all costs." No one spoke as they pondered the significance and the peril in what was to come.

Maybe I should join them. I do want Billy to know I still care, considered Penny. She was about to approach Billy when Ronnie and Randy intercepted her. "Penny, I didn't have a chance to thank you for saving my life. Randy told me what you did for me when the dragons attacked. Thanks a lot," Ronnie responded humbly.

Penny was surprised. "I I didn't do anything special. It was a reflex," she stammered.

"It took a lot for you to kill that miserable rodent. I know it isn't human, but I realize it's the first time you've ever killed anything."

The incident came back to Penny. She convinced herself that it never happened but now she remembered every detail vividly. The thought of killing the minion made her nauseous. She recalled the bone-crunching sound and the sick feel of flesh splitting as she plunged her sword into its back. A lump formed in her throat and suddenly she felt weak. "I, uh, I just reacted. I didn't know what I did until after it fell to the ground."

"Well, you did fine. You'll learn that sometimes you have to do things in order to survive. You passed your first test." Ronnie left them to continue their conversation.

"Randy, can I talk to you about something?" she asked uneasily as she summoned her courage.

"Sure, what is it?"

"Back at the cave. I …"

"Penny, that's your business. I was surprised, that's all."

"No, that's not what I meant. When you have a dangerous encounter or escape a life-threatening situation, does it ever make you, uh …?"

"Turned on? Absolutely! Why do you think Ronnie and I are so addicted to all this excitement? Out here, there's a plethora of it. There is nothing more satisfying than cheating death. Is that what your cave incident was about?"

"Well, yes. I kind of lost control."

"Did you quench your fire?"

"Are you kidding? We never got that far. Jarret was a little bit too eager and I guess you could say the moment passed him by. Please don't repeat it, though."

"That's funny! So, the kid needs some practice."

"Are you mad at me for doing that behind Billy's back?"

"That's between you and Billy. For some reason, I think he'll understand."

"Thanks, Randy. That means a lot to me. What do you know about the new girl?"

"Not much; only that we rescued her and Billy from the minions. Billy was unconscious then and hasn't said much since. He appears to be in a lot of pain."

Penny approached Billy and sat by his side opposite Seneca. She leaned against his shoulder and drifted off to sleep.

Jarret kept his distance from the group, and reeled from embarrassment. Ronnie felt sorry for him and called out, "Hey, rookie. Come over here."

"What do you want with him?" asked Randy.

"Oh, I don't know. I'm sure we can think of something."

"What's up, Ronnie?" Jarret asked somberly.

"Shut up and sit down. You've got a lot to learn if you're going to stick around here." Ronnie lectured Jarret for over an hour on ground rules and codes of behavior for their new world.

Randy was amused and listened nearby. When Ronnie finished her lessons, she made a promise to Jarret: "If you can behave yourself, I'm sure you'll find that it's well worth your while. When you hang out with Randy and me, it's never boring."

Jarret was elated to be accepted by Ronnie. "I promise you, I'll make you proud of me. You'll see."

"I'm sure you will. Now get some rest."

Billy awoke and wasn't quite sure where he was. He was more confused than ever when he saw Penny on his left and Seneca on his right. Seneca sat up and rubbed her eyes. Billy looked at his watch. The reflection of moonlight illuminated the hands, which indicated that it was nearly midnight. The long days made it difficult to use a twelve-hour watch so Billy had to do a little math to interpret the time. *Add an hour and sixteen minutes every four hours and it'll be close to real time in this world,* he recalled Doc telling him.

Seneca awoke and asked, "How are you feeling, Billy?"

"A bit sore, but I think I'll be fine."

"I was so worried about you. I thought you were dead."

"It seems that I have a habit of doing that to people."

"I see you have a friend," she said curiously.

"Yeah. She and I have some things to work out about our relationship."

"Were the two of you mates at one time?"

"No, we never quite got that far."

"Do you have feelings for her?"

"Yes, but they're pretty complicated. I couldn't begin to explain."

"Then don't try. I would rather share you than lose you."

"I appreciate that, Seneca, but I'm used to monogamous relationships. More than one only leads to trouble. I know this is a different world, but I haven't adjusted to it yet."

"Sometimes it's good to let things happen by themselves. You'll see."

"Thanks, Seneca. Maybe I will."

Penny stirred and snuggled against Billy's shoulder. He instinctively pulled her close to him.

"I'm going up to the ledge above the stream," Seneca informed him. "It's a beautiful night to watch the moon and the stars."

"I'll be up in a little while," replied Billy.

Seneca smiled coyly and said, "I'll be waiting." She walked out of the cave and left them alone.

Penny opened her eyes and gazed at Billy. She had so much to say but didn't know where to begin. Billy tried to ease the tension and greeted her, "Hello, stranger. It's been a while since we've been alone like this."

"Hi, Billy. Did you mind me sitting with you and your friend?"

"No, not at all."

"I hope I wasn't intruding."

"No, it's okay. Seneca's pretty cool."

"I'm sorry about what happened in the cave with Jarret."

"Don't be sorry. Sometimes we learn from things like that."

"There was this rush of excitement from being chased by the monster and then being cornered in the cave. I lost control and ..."

"Penny, it's okay."

"But I'm afraid that I hurt you."

"Penny, in the old world, nothing exciting ever happened for us to let our emotions grow. I guess we kind of suppress a lot of our feelings there. Out here, we're all learning to grow in a different way."

"So where do we go from here?"

"That's up to you. Seneca and I have a loose relationship. We've been good for each other. She understands where you and I stand and she doesn't have a problem with it."

"Where do we stand, Billy? I want us to try again. I really want a future with you. I won't compete with Seneca but I will try to be there for you." Penny pulled him close and kissed him, gently at first, then passionately.

Billy knew that this was what he wanted, but Seneca was right. In this world, things are different. "Why don't we join Seneca up on the ledge? It's a lovely night, moons and all."

"Billy, the last time we spent a night under the moons, I fell in love with you. I can't imagine what could happen next."

Billy was elated with her response. "You never know. Let's go up and I'll introduce you to her." Penny helped Billy to his feet. His ribs were still very sore and forced him to hobble. They hiked up the narrow path to the ledge on the side of the mountain. Seneca perched on the edge with her feet dangling over the side. Billy and Penny sat down beside her and looked across the treetops.

The night air was filled with sounds of many strange creatures. Billy started the introductions: "Seneca, this is Penny. I didn't have a chance to introduce the two of you earlier."

"Hi, Penny. It's good to finally meet you."

"Hi. It's nice to meet you, too."

After a few awkward moments of silence, Billy asked, "Seneca, I've been wondering. Is it possible for me to project my thoughts over a distance, perhaps back toward my city?"

"I don't know. As a Firenghi, I don't have that ability, but your body has developed some new traits that I can't explain. What were you thinking about doing?"

"Well, there's a saber-toothed tiger that rallied other tigers to save my life when we fought the Mideonites in the city. I wondered if I could summon the tigers to help us again."

"You'll have to try that one yourself. I'll be really impressed if you can do that."

"It was just a thought," he confessed sheepishly.

"Why don't you lie down over there and relax. Penny and I should have our own little chat."

Billy wasn't comfortable with the situation but he wasn't in the mood to argue. He was still exhausted and the night air was comfortable. He lay down against a log and gazed at the stars. When he looked across the valley toward the largest of the mountains, he wondered what was happening in the minion camp. He pondered the battle that loomed ahead.

It would be a bloody battle and there was likely to be casualties. Even with the dragons for support, his friends would be in jeopardy as well as himself. Billy stared in the direction of the city and considered, *How do I address a tiger? How will he know I'm looking for him? Maybe if I try to project images to him, he'll understand what I need him to do.* Billy projected his location and where they were going. Then he projected a battle with the minions. Soon, he lost his focus and fell asleep. His body's accelerated healing process sapped him of his strength for a short time.

Seneca and Penny sat quietly for several minutes, staring at the sky. Seneca cast a glance at Penny and sensed her unease. "Penny, I want you to know that we can be friends. I don't want to take Billy from you and he's aware of that. There will be no competition."

Penny was surprised by her remark and asked, "You and Billy don't have a relationship?"

Seneca smiled coyly and asked, "Has he told you anything about me?"

"No, we haven't had much time to talk since your rescue. I want to be a part of the things that Billy likes to do and if you and the others are part of it, then I'd like to share in it, too."

"I'm a little different from you, Penny. I'm not quite human like you are."

"What do you mean 'a little different'?" Penny inquired, curious.

"It's a bit complicated."

"I can see that your eyes are different but other than that, you seem just like me."

"I'm a Firenghi," revealed Seneca. "We are a race of shape-shifters."

"Wow, a shape-shifter! You can change into different creatures?"

"Yes, I can but only one creature. Billy was quite surprised since he met my alter-shape before he met me. When we first met, the only thing we had in common was our fight against Ruger and his army of minions. Things changed and then I guess I changed too."

"How do you mean?"

"Billy and I had relations because I needed to pass on some of my traits to him. These were necessary for him to combat the evil ones. Then, I developed feelings for him and things changed quite a bit. We've handled them so far, but I don't know what the future holds for us. If we don't stop Ruger and his army, we won't have to worry about the future."

"So how do you feel about me in regards to Billy?" asked Penny. "I guess you know about our rocky past."

"I don't know about your past with Billy but we can develop feelings together if it is in our best interest."

"Do you mean like the three of us in a relationship?"

"Yes, if it's good for us. It doesn't have to be a physical relationship. As I told Billy, things are different in this world compared to your world. I would be happy to share in a relationship with the two of you."

"What has Billy said about this?"

"We discussed it but I didn't ask him to make a choice. I wanted to discuss it with you before any of us makes a commitment. Sometimes, it's better when you don't have to choose. Just let things happen and see how they end up."

"I'm more interested in the part about the traits that you gave him. Tell me about them."

"It's really quite simple. At first, I wasn't sure if it would work since we never encountered any of your species before. If female shape-shifters have an exchange of bodily fluids whether it's through a kiss, relations or blood transfer, their traits transfer quite rapidly. Up to now, this was only done among our own kind. Our clans each have their own traits because of this."

"What does this have to do with Billy?" asked Penny, now with great interest.

"Billy was very lucky in his previous meetings with Ruger but now it's become personal. Ruger will stop at nothing to kill him. Billy has done what no one else has been able to do: survive against Ruger."

"You mean Billy's had more than one encounter with Ruger?"

"Yes, he has."

As the evening wore on, Seneca described everything that happened to Billy since their relationship started. Penny was amazed and had many questions. They talked well into the night. Seneca tired and suggested, "I believe it's time for me to rest. I'm still not feeling very well."

Penny gazed into Seneca's eyes and said, "I've never seen eyes so beautiful. They make you so attractive."

Seneca brushed her hand across Penny's cheek and said, "I know what you're thinking, but I don't know that you could inherit my traits like Billy did. I don't know of any Firenghi females who ever passed them to another female Firenghi, let alone a human."

"Then there might be a chance that you could pass your traits on to me?"

"I really don't know. Are you that interested in gaining some of Billy's new qualities through my traits?"

"Yes, I am. What new qualities did he inherit from you?"

"He has telepathic abilities that work primarily with others who have this trait. It's limited in reading the thoughts of those who don't have it. Some of Billy's traits seem to have mutated from those of shape-shifters. His senses are vastly improved, but he has some gifts that I've never seen. It seems that he's still undergoing changes and develops a new gift every day."

Penny again stared into Seneca's eyes. "I'm interested in you and your traits. I feel myself changing and maturing in so many ways of late. I've had so many years of sexual frustration and lack of confidence. I feel as though all that has changed and I'm not afraid anymore."

Seneca cradled Penny in her arms and kissed her. Penny lay on her back and pulled Seneca onto her. She and Seneca kissed and nestled against each other. Penny felt desires that she hadn't imagined before. Her head spun with passion and excitement. Her blood felt as though it would boil. Seneca paused for a moment and studied Penny's face. Penny looked up at Seneca and craved more. She rolled on top of Seneca and kissed her again. Her emotions were out of control and her body trembled from head to toe.

Hours later, Penny regained her composure. She opened her eyes and gazed at Seneca. "Are we just exchanging traits or is there more to this?"

"I'm a lot like you. All my life, I've been running from Ruger and the horrors he's bestowed on my family and friends. I never had time to be close to anyone. This experience has been a welcome and liberating feeling. I think Billy may have his hands full with the two of us." The two kissed passionately once more. They lay next to Billy and slept for the remainder of the night.

CHAPTER 8

MINION CAMP

Morning arrived with sounds of thunder and flashes of lightning. Billy awoke first and saw the girls on either side of him. He wondered what the two conversed about after he slept.

Seneca awoke and sat up. "How are you feeling, Billy?"

"I'm still sore but nothing like yesterday. How about you?"

"I feel great. I slept well," Seneca replied and smiled. Penny rubbed her eyes and awoke.

"Good morning, Penny," Billy greeted her.

"Good morning, Billy."

"What did you girls discuss last night?"

"All kinds of stuff," replied Seneca. "I think Penny's pretty well caught up on things." Billy was curious as to what she meant by that.

Penny sat up, grinning shyly. "Good morning, Seneca." Seneca smiled coyly at her. Billy noticed and suspected something wasn't right. A loud clap of thunder interrupted the conversation.

"We ought to get back to the cave before we get soaked," suggested Seneca. She and Penny left together.

Billy stood with his hands on his hips and complained aloud, "What the hell is going on? They're up to something." He walked down to the cave and met Randy at the entrance.

"Well, Billy, what brings you to this side of town? You don't want to associate with us anymore?" kidded Randy.

"I'm sorry, Randy. You wouldn't believe what's happened to me."

"Try me."

"Maybe later. I'm a little queasy this morning."

"I'll hold you to that."

"Thanks, I appreciate it." Billy entered the cave where everyone ate breakfast.

John tossed several pieces of wood on the fire. "Good morning, Billy. How are you doing today?"

"I'm not sure yet. Better than yesterday, though."

"You seem to be healing quite rapidly. I'm amazed."

"It seems that way. Thank you for coming after me."

"It wasn't easy catching up to you."

"I know. We were pursued by just about everything that you could imagine."

"So were we. Well, it's good to see you on your feet."

"Thanks again, John." Billy went to the rear of the cave. He noticed that Penny and Seneca sat together by the fire. Billy sat down across from the girls. His curiosity got the better of him and he couldn't wait anymore. "Okay, girls. So, what was the consensus last night? I'm sure your conversation was quite interesting." Seneca and Penny giggled.

"When it becomes necessary, you'll find out," joked Penny.

"Not even a clue, huh?"

"Nope," Seneca replied playfully.

Billy had a feeling that this new union between the girls was bad news for him. Once again, the females had the upper hand on him. First, it was Ronnie and Randy double-teaming him at every turn. Now it's going to be Seneca and Penny.

Randy neatly skinned five birds that she and Seamus caught earlier. Seamus filleted and cooked the poultry like a skilled professional. "What kind of bird was it? It looks really weird," asked Billy.

Seamus replied dryly, "It's an edible bird. If you don't like it, don't eat it."

"Just curious. Of course, I'll like it." Billy was surprised to hear that kind of sarcasm from Seamus and wondered if it was fear that made him so.

The girls were quite cheerful and talkative as they lined up for their meal. John laid the slices of poultry on slabs of wood that simulated plates.

No one minded the inconvenience. Billy noticed how upbeat Penny was around Seneca. He sat by himself and watched the girls happily chatting. He could read Penny's thoughts as she stared admiringly at Seneca. It dawned on him that the girls had taken more than a casual liking to each other. Then he realized that he could read Penny's thoughts, unlike the previous day. *My, how Penny is growing up. She isn't the naïve little girl I once knew. But why can I read her thoughts? Maybe this is something new.*

Penny stopped talking and looked over at Billy. She excused herself from the conversation and approached him. Billy thought nothing of it as she kissed him on the cheek. Her next comment nearly took his breath away with surprise. "That's right, Billy. I'm not the naïve little girl you once knew. And yes, I have grown up."

"But, but how did you ..."

"Do you think you're the only one around here who can read minds?"

Billy was speechless. Penny hugged him and returned to Seneca's side. The two girls promptly resumed their conversation. Billy's mind raced in a hundred different directions as he tried to make sense of what just happened. *How did she read my mind? That means she had to ...!*

Billy suddenly realized that he was at a distinct disadvantage with both of the women having the ability to read his thoughts. Things were not starting out very well this morning. Seneca used her telepathy to inform him, "I told you not to worry. Things tend to take care of themselves."

"Seneca, that's not what I had in mind!" Billy shouted.

Everyone looked at Billy in surprise. He forgot that the others weren't aware of their telepathic communication. He walked over to the girls and knelt down. Seneca replied coolly, "Don't worry, Billy. She's going to do fine."

"What are we talking about here? How about me? Maybe I'm not fine with this."

"She'll prove to be a valuable ally in our cause as much as you and I are. Be patient."

"But Seneca, what did you do with her last night?"

Seneca became annoyed with Billy's behavior and said defensively, "Well, Billy. I think that's personal. Don't assume you know everything."

Billy shook his head in disbelief. He wondered secretly if Seneca might be using both of them for her own personal gain. At least he still had the ability to cloak his thoughts when he remembered to.

Xerxes called for everyone's attention. They gathered around the fire and listened attentively. "The rain has complicated things a little but our plan is still a go. It'll be difficult because of the weather, but we'll make the most of it."

"What's our goal?" asked Ronnie.

"Our main objective is to get into the portal as soon as the entrance is cleared."

Seneca informed Xerxes, "Penny will be joining us. She also has telepathic powers. I think she can help us."

"But I see she's a novice," Xerxes remarked. "Perhaps she isn't ready."

"You'll be surprised how fast she progresses."

"Very well then. I understand that shape-shifters are a curious lot, so I won't question your judgment."

"Seamus and I will hunt for bait to lure the dinosaur up to the portal," said John. "The dragons will follow up with their attack after the beast enters the camp. If that doesn't work, we'll hold off and regroup for another attack at nightfall."

"Is there anything we can do in the mean time?" asked Randy.

"I'd like for you and Ronnie to scout the area around the portal and see what kind of defenses they have," replied John.

"It's not exactly flying weather out there," complained Ronnie.

Randy added, "Yes. It's a bit chilly and we're not exactly dressed for the occasion."

"We need you girls to do this. This whole mission could be riding on the results of your flight."

"I understand. We'll take care of it," said Randy somberly. Ronnie and Randy left the cave and approached the dragons.

"Perhaps, we can fly above the clouds. Maybe that'll get us out of the rain," suggested Ronnie.

"It's a low ceiling. Let's try it."

They noticed Jarret standing quietly by the trees. "Why don't you take G.I. Joe for a ride? After all, you are his teacher."

"Now, be nice, Randy. You might want to participate in my class one day." The girls giggled.

Ronnie motioned for Jarret to join her. He anxiously approached the dragon from the front. Ronnie felt the dragon arch its back and a loud hiss came from its mouth. "Jarret, stay where you are. He thinks you're a threat to him." She slid off the dragon's back and gently rubbed its forehead. She whispered softly into its ear. It relaxed its back and nuzzled its big head against her.

"Come around to the side. Never approach a dragon from the front."

"How do you know so much about dragons, Ronnie?"

"I don't, but I'm sure they're just like horses."

"Then you really didn't know what you were talking about when you told me to stand still. If you were wrong, the dragon would have eaten me!"

"Stop whining, he wasn't going to eat you. He was just warning you. Now get on before I change my mind."

Jarret complained sarcastically, "I can't trust you about anything. You're a nut case."

"So what? I'll make it up to you."

"Ronnie, you don't have a history of mental illness or anything else in your family that I should know about, do you?" asked Jarret sarcastically.

"As a matter of fact, I do - on my mother's side."

"Never mind. I'm sorry I asked."

The two girls piloted their dragons through the driving rain and disappeared into the clouds, followed closely by the other two dragons. John, Seamus and Xerxes watched from the cave entrance in awe. "It's interesting that the dragons travel in a group like that," commented John.

"I never expected to see humans flying on them," replied Xerxes.

"They still make me nervous. I always worry that they're saving me for desert," complained Seamus.

"Don't worry, Seamus. They'd only spit you out, you salty old dog," joked John. The three men laughed heartily before splitting up. Xerxes sought out Billy and the girls for their briefing. John and Seamus gathered some things and hastily set out into the forest to trap their bait.

Billy, Seneca, and Penny sat together at the rear of the cave. He was upset with the girls and wasn't in a talkative mood. Xerxes approached them and immediately sensed the tension among them.

"Okay, you three, what's the problem?"

"It's okay, Xerxes," replied Seneca. "Billy's just surprised by some changes I made without consulting him. We'll work it out."

"Why don't you tell him what you've done?" replied Billy angrily.

Xerxes chided Billy, "I'm not interested in what the girls have done. My only concern is that we succeed in our mission. If you behave like this, I'm concerned that you'll jeopardize the mission. Now, I'll ask again. Is there a problem?"

"No, I guess not," answered Billy sheepishly

"Are you sure?"

"Yes, Xerxes, I'm sure."

"Good. Here are my intentions: We'll take up a position just outside the minion camp near the portal. We have to get as close as possible without being spotted. I expect that John will provide enough distractions that we can sneak through the portal without detection by the minions. The others will attempt to secure the area in front of the portal. That's where the dragons will help us. They'll prevent the minions from ambushing us from behind. Remember, our priority is to get into the portal. Don't stop, regardless of what happens to the others. If you do, their fate will be for naught."

"This doesn't sound very encouraging, Xerxes," Billy commented somberly.

"Look. I'm not going to lie to you. This is a long shot at best. There could be a lot of casualties and none of us may survive. If we fail, everything we know and love will perish at the hands of Diomedes."

"What happens on the other side of the portal?" inquired Seneca.

"I expect that we'll encounter some of Ruger's minions and I'm sure the other side of the portal is located near or in Ruger's castle. I believe that Diomedes' chamber has been maneuvered there as well."

"Xerxes, I still don't understand how someone can just move things around through time and space like this," Billy remarked.

"There are spheres that contain a material foreign to your world. Each sphere has a small valve on it that allows oxygen, which is the catalyst for this material, to enter. The more oxygen that enters the sphere, the more powerful it becomes. This sphere powers a portal control unit or PCU that opens paths through time and space. For every path that's created, adjustments must be made to the sphere and the device to balance the network. Ruger, under Diomedes' directions, has stolen both a sphere and a PCU. He has made many mistakes in his attempts to use the device. One of these mistakes is what placed you here."

"Can these mistakes be undone if we get the device back?" Penny inquired.

"Perhaps. I won't know for sure until I determine the extent of the damage he's caused throughout the universe. But first, we must recover the sphere and the PCU."

"The universe!" exclaimed Billy. "How powerful is this device?"

"You have much to learn and unfortunately time is not on our side," explained Xerxes. "When we get to the other side, we'll split up into two pairs and search for the sphere and source. If the sphere is powered down, the network will collapse and we may not be able to return. If we capture the PCU first, Ruger will surely shut down the sphere. The only way we can overcome Ruger is by surprise. We don't have the luxury of using magic like he does so be wary and be careful."

Seneca offered, "I'll go with you, Xerxes. I think it's the smartest way to pair up."

"How will we know what this PCU looks like?" asked Billy.

"It's an electronic assembly with a series of buttons and two small panels," revealed Xerxes. "It's usually worn on the wrist."

"I guess we'll know it when we see it," Billy relented.

"You should get some rest," advised Xerxes. "Once we enter the portal, it could be a long time before you sleep again." Billy put his frustration aside and calmed down.

"I'm not ready for this," fretted Penny.

"It's alright to be frightened, Penny. We all are," said Seneca sympathetically.

"Billy, in case we don't make it through this, I don't want my last moments with you to be sad or angry," said Seneca. Billy reached out to both girls and hugged them. They sat down and quietly pondered what waited ahead.

— X —

Ronnie's dragon descended first, through the clouds toward the mountaintop. The feel of the wind blowing through her long, black hair made her feel like a warrior princess riding proudly on her dragon. This was the feeling she always dreamed of. *Now if only Jarret was my warrior king. Oh, well. No dream is perfect*, she thought to herself.

The riderless dragons split up and circled above them. Randy's dragon banked wide to the right and approached the camp from the opposite direction as Ronnie's dragon. She was uncomfortable flying alone on the dragon and wondered if she should have taken Seamus with her. The thrill of flying on a dragon was never something that she imagined, or cared about for that matter.

Jarret enjoyed himself. He had the best of both worlds at his feet. He had his arms around the waist of a lovely brunette and the thrill of a lifetime riding on a dragon. He never expected an adventure like this in the Marines but here he was, a young man in uniform, going where no Marine had ever gone before. *If things ever go back to normal, I'm going to find that recruiter and tell him what he missed*, Jarrett thought to himself.

Visibility was limited so they were forced to pass quite low over the camp. Jarret saw something that resembled a gate. "Hey, Ronnie. Is that the portal we're looking for?"

Ronnie steered closer until she had a better view. "I believe it is. Will you look at that?"

The portal was majestic in appearance. It was a thick gold ring mounted on top of a stone base with seven steps leading up to a small platform in front of the ring. Inside the ring was an orange mist that swirled in circles. The portal was guarded by a dozen of Ruger's minions. Seven large canopies sheltered other minions in the camp near the portal. Smoke billowed out from under each of the canopies from the campfires.

Jarret studied the size of the canopies and calculated the number of minions that might be sheltered under each canopy. "Ronnie, I think there's close to a hundred and seventy-five of those minions down there. There couldn't be more than twenty-five under each canopy and still have room for a campfire as well."

"Good estimation, Jarret. I couldn't agree more. Let's get out of here." Ronnie waved Randy off on the next pass and pointed back toward the cave. Randy veered her dragon in a tight circle and followed. She was anxious to get out of the rain and reach the warmth of a fire.

— ✕ —

Seamus asked John, "Do you have any idea how they're going to defeat Ruger and his minions when they find him?"

"No, I don't. All Xerxes wants us to do is get them into the portal. I'm not sure what they'll do on the other side if they encounter more troops."

"I guess our job is easy compared to what they'll deal with."

"And that, Seamus, is why we must succeed. We have to give them the opportunity to get to Ruger and his demon."

— ✕ —

Ronnie piloted her dragon through the clouds to the ground. Randy emerged shortly behind on her dragon. The two set down a short distance from the cave. Ronnie, Randy and Jarret hurried to the cave to escape the cold rain.

Ronnie met with Xerxes while Randy and Jarret proceeded directly to the fire to warm up. Xerxes waited anxiously as they approached. Jarret couldn't help staring at Randy's shape through her wet shirt and jeans. She immediately took notice and teased, "See something new?"

Jarret was embarrassed and stammered, "No, I'm sorry. It's just that you and Ronnie don't act like girls, but then I see you like this and I realize that the two of you are ladies."

"Why thank you, Jarret. There is an intelligent young man inside that uniform."

"I guess I'm learning," remarked Jarrett humbly.

Ronnie finished her discussion with Xerxes and turned her attention to her friends. "What are the two of you babbling about?" she asked.

"Jarret was admiring my figure through my wet tee-shirt."

Ronnie stared disappointedly at Jarret and asked, "Did you do that, Jarret?"

"Uh, yeah. I did."

"What about my figure? Mine's nicer than Randy's?" Both girls giggled as Jarret blushed from embarrassment. Xerxes chuckled to himself and walked away. Never before had he met two women like Ronnie and Randy. Ronnie moved closer to Jarret and glared at him. "Remember, young man, you're my student. You keep your eyes on me if you expect to learn anything." Jarret nodded obediently.

— ⧗ —

Later in the afternoon, John and Seamus returned with a wild pig tied to a wooden pole. "Who's making lunch today? I'm famished," said John.

Seneca emerged from the rear of the cave and volunteered, "I'll get this one. I hope you don't mind a fruit and vegetable meal."

"Not at all. I'll eat anything at this point."

Seneca took a small sack and disappeared into the woods. She was very good at collecting fruits and vegetables since it was the way of life for her people. She returned a short while later and placed a large quantity of berries and fruits on a flat rock. Seneca pulled a short knife from her tunic and skillfully diced the food into tiny pieces. Billy emerged from the cave and watched in awe at the skill and speed she displayed. "The way you handle that knife, I wouldn't want you mad at me."

"I think it would be far worse for you if I were angry and in my alter-shape," she warned and stared him down.

"I get the point," he relented.

Seneca scooped berries and fruit onto the slabs of wood and served everyone. Xerxes tasted the meal and remarked, "Nice job, Seneca. This is very good."

"Thank you, Xerxes."

"Where did you learn to blend them this way?" asked Ronnie.

"These berries and fruits are abundant in my world. I practiced for a while to learn how much of each to acquire a certain flavor."

When they finished eating, John asked Ronnie, "Would you take one of the dragons and scout for our beast?"

"Sure will. If he's out there, I'll find him."

John then asked Randy, "Would you secure the bait to one of the dragons and please, don't let them eat it?"

"No problem."

"I hope our dinosaur has an appetite today. I could have made a fine meal of that pig," remarked John.

"It's not too late," said Billy.

"Forget it. The pig is spoken for," joked Seamus.

John surveyed the cloudy sky and quipped, "It's a fine day for a battle."

"Are you serious? This is lousy weather," replied Billy.

"I think you'll find that it significantly improves our chances of overtaking the enemy."

— ⧗ —

Ronnie took off on her dragon and circled over a large area in search of the beast. After several passes, she spotted the Crocosaurus creeping slowly through the trees. She directed the dragon into a dive and soared passed the creature's head. The creature unleashed a deafening roar that sent reverberations throughout the jungle. It picked up its pace and pursued Ronnie's dragon.

Ronnie was careful to maintain a safe distance between her dragon and the dinosaur but after a short while, the Crocosaurus lost interest. She returned to the camp to rendezvous with Randy and landed her dragon near the cave. "Show time, people," she announced. "The beast is on its way."

Ronnie grabbed Jarret by the arm and said, "Come on, rookie. We have work to do." She pulled him out to her dragon while the other dragons waited for a rider. Randy emerged from the cave and hopped on her dragon. She took off and immediately felt the added weight of the pig dangling below. Ronnie's dragon flew ahead toward the dinosaur. They found it fairly close to the cave. Randy took over the task of luring the monster up to the Mideonite encampment. She waved to Ronnie and glided down toward the dinosaur. Ronnie circled once more and headed back toward the cave.

— ⧗ —

John said a quick prayer for a victory against the minions. Seamus and Xerxes bowed their heads and listened attentively. When John finished, the three of them left the cave and mounted the third dragon.

Billy, Penny and Seneca rode on the fourth dragon. They quickly caught up with Ronnie and followed her to the minion camp.

The rain eased up but thick fog rolled in and covered the lower regions of the mountain. The minion camp was just above the layer of fog, about two-thirds the way up the mountainside. Randy had difficulty keeping the dinosaur behind her. Visibility decreased and the creature tired. Each time Randy circled closer, the dinosaur grew more reluctant to follow her. She flew lower and dangled the boar dangerously close to the dinosaur's snout.

— X —

The dragons landed high on the mountain above the minion campsite. Billy, Penny and Seneca dismounted and dispersed into the woods. Ronnie ordered Jarret to go with them and help out.

Billy found a good location for them to monitor the portal from. Now, they would wait anxiously for their opportunity to get past the minions and enter the mysterious portal. He eyed the minions meticulously, hoping that somewhere in their routine was a flaw that would enable them to access the portal. Jarret sat idly by, wondering what was happening. He still didn't understand what the portal and the minions were all about.

Seneca had an uneasy feeling about Billy, particularly since he cloaked his thoughts from her. She and Penny didn't have the ability to cloak their thoughts like he did. "What are you thinking, Billy?"

Billy hesitated for a few minutes before answering, which made the girls all the more suspicious. "You'll know when I know. Just keep your eyes on the portal."

Seneca reminded him, "You know what Xerxes said, Billy. We aren't supposed to do anything until the attack starts."

"We may only get one crack at the portal," Billy reminded them. "I'm not going to waste an opportunity."

"Don't you ever stop?" Penny chastised him. "Can't you just follow orders for once? You always have to have things your way." Billy's face reddened and he glared at Penny.

"She didn't mean it like that, Billy," Seneca interceded. "We're worried about you."

"How timely? Let's save the theatrics for later. Some of us have things to do."

Penny looked at him pitifully and said, "You can be such an ass, Billy."

Billy tuned her out at that point. He wasn't in the mood to play games with the girls. His objective was to get Xerxes and Seneca into the portal no matter what. What happens to Penny and him was secondary. Jarret chose to avoid the argument all together. He stayed in the background and waited quietly. In some ways he respected Billy's resistance to the girls and hoped to do so with a little more tact than Billy.

Xerxes joined them and asked, "Are you ready?"

"Yes, we're ready," replied Seneca.

"No problems?" he asked, hoping that their issues were behind them. Penny replied, "None. We're good."

"Be ready to make a break for the portal when I give the word." Xerxes peered through the bushes and patiently watched the trail for any sign of the dinosaur.

— X —

Randy lost sight of the dinosaur again and turned the dragon around. She feared that she lost the creature for good. After another pass, she came in lower, but the fog made it difficult for her to see. She started to pull up, but the dragon jerked hard, nearly throwing her off. It squealed loudly and crashed to the ground. Randy was thrown into the trees. She coughed repeatedly and blood seeped from her mouth.

The Crocosaurus seized the boar in its mouth. When it realized that it had a bigger prize before it, it dropped the boar from its frothing jaws and rushed at the dragon. The dragon rose up on its hind legs to confront the dinosaur. The two monsters fought fiercely and fell to the ground. They rolled about and flailed at each other with claws cutting and teeth gnashing.

Randy lay still near the trees where she fell. She could hear the creatures battling nearby, but couldn't move. Her biggest fear was that she had let her friends down. She muttered weakly, "God help us all."

The two creatures battled upright again and crashed into the trees. Randy watched helplessly as a large tree fell in her direction. She closed her eyes and made her peace. This was surely her final moment. Holding her breath, she expected the tree to smash the life out of her. After several seconds, nothing happened. She slowly opened her eyes and saw that the trunk of the tree had stopped a few feet above her. She tried to move but her right hip and leg were broken. She tried to slide out from underneath the tree, but the pain was too much.

Tears ran down the side of her face as she reminisced about her life. She recalled how her marriage ended so painfully. For months she suspected her husband of infidelity, only to find out he was dying. When she discovered the truth that he had been seeing specialists, it was too late. He wanted to spare her the grief but he died the morning after she discovered that he had terminal cancer. Randy never got over the guilt of adding to his misery in his waning hours. She failed to be there for the one she loved when he needed her most. Now she failed again at another critical time. Life seemed so unfair to her. She closed her eyes and waited for the end.

— X —

Ronnie grew impatient and climbed on her dragon. "Where are you going?" asked John.

"To check on Randy. Something is wrong."

"Be careful."

"I will."

John kissed her.

Ronnie smiled and thanked him. She tugged on the reins and the dragon spread its mammoth wings. The wings flexed twice and the dragon was in the air.

From the other side of the camp, Xerxes muttered, "It's hopeless. We'll never get past all of them. The dinosaur should have been here by now."

"There's got to be a way," replied Billy. "What if we rush the portal? Maybe it works like a two-way highway. Perhaps we'll be safe once we get inside."

"Yes, but we'd only be safe from minions coming out."

— X —

Ronnie guided the dragon along the trail toward the cave. About halfway there, she saw Randy's dragon and the Crocosaurus battling amid the trees. She panicked as she searched the ground for Randy. After three passes, she landed the dragon nearby and searched on foot. Her dragon waited uneasily for her to return.

"Randy, where are you? Randy!" The noise from the creatures' battle was deafening. Trees fell during the battle, while dirt and stones flew through the air. Randy imagined that she heard Ronnie calling her but dismissed it as hallucination. *I wish she were here. I miss her. I miss all of them,* she thought tearfully.

Ronnie scurried around the battling creatures and ducked into the trees. "Randy, can you hear me? Where are you?" Randy opened her eyes and listened. The sound of Ronnie's voice was much clearer.

I'm really losing it now. Her voice almost sounds real, thought Randy.

Ronnie climbed onto a fallen tree trunk and walked along the length of it. She browsed through the branches and spotted Randy lying in the brush underneath. "Randy, are you okay?"

Randy was startled when she realized that Ronnie was really there. "Ronnie, I'm hurt. Please, help me."

Ronnie climbed down off the tree trunk and said, "I'll have you out in a minute." She took Randy by both arms and pulled her from under the tree. "Can you walk?"

"No, it's my leg and my hip. I think they're broken."

"My dragon is nearby. I'll get you there." Ronnie lifted her again and wrapped her arm around Randy's waist. After several attempts, she managed to pull Randy to the dragon. Randy moaned as Ronnie lifted her onto the dragon's back.

"I'm sorry, Ronnie. It hurts so bad."

"Don't worry about it. You'll be fine." Ronnie quickly set the dragon in flight and flew toward the post office.

"How could this happen? I let everyone down," Randy uttered sadly.

"Thank God the tree stopped before it hit the ground or you'd be history."

"I can't make it," cried Randy.

"I'm going to get you back to camp. Don't quit on me," urged Ronnie.

"We have to lure the creature up to the minions' camp."

"No way!"

"Please, Ronnie, try for me."

Ronnie knew how much it hurt Randy to fail even if it meant her death. "One pass and then we head back to the compound," she said reluctantly. Randy's head fell limp against Ronnie's back. Ronnie steered the dragon back to the battle.

Both of the creatures tumbled to the ground. The Crocosaurus saw the opportunity and bit into the throat of the dragon. A loud snap and the dragon's neck was broken. Ronnie guided her dragon past the Crocosaurus' head. It galloped after them toward the minion camp.

Randy's face was ashen as blood continued to trickle from her mouth. Tears streamed down Ronnie's cheeks, as she feared losing her best friend.

When the Crocosaurus was close enough to the minion camp, Ronnie turned the dragon back toward the post office. Randy looked back and was relieved to see the dinosaur enter the minion camp. They hadn't failed after all. The Crocosaurus sent the minions scurrying for the trees. Small numbers of them fought the dinosaur with their spears and clubs, but they were quickly devoured.

Ronnie tugged desperately on the reins. The dragon sensed her urgency and flew faster than Ronnie believed possible. When they approached the post office, Ronnie guided the dragon straight toward the field. This time there would be no circling to slow down.

The dragon came in hard and fast. The landing was rough and the dragon nearly tumbled while attempting to stop itself. Ronnie held the reins tightly with one hand and Randy's arms with her other.

Jerry watched in amazement as the dragon landed with both girls on its back. "Help!" he shouted. "Hurry, everyone!"

Nigel and Krill rushed out of the building. They were stunned to see a full-sized dragon perched in front of the building. Even more astounding was the sight of Ronnie and Randy riding on it. Ronnie delicately lowered Randy off the dragon to Jerry. "I've got to get back to the battle. Take care of her."

"Don't worry, Ronnie. I'll make sure."

A doctor and two nurses emerged from the post office. As soon as they saw Randy's condition, they took her from Jerry and carried her inside.

"Has the battle started?" asked Nigel excitedly.

"Yes, they're attacking the minion camp as we speak."

Sam suggested, "I'll take Jerry with me and get more weapons from the police arsenal. We'll meet you there?"

"We'll need all the help we can get. There's a whole army of those creeps up there. Close to a couple hundred."

"Nigel and I are going with you!" said Krill.

"Get on, then! The bus is leaving." The two men carefully mounted the dragon behind Ronnie. She tugged on the reins and the dragon lifted off into the sky.

John and Seamus circled the camp with their dragons several times before peeling off. Despite the Crocosaurus' attack, there were never less than a dozen minions near the portal. John worried about Ronnie and Randy. He searched the sky uneasily but saw no sign of them.

Seamus shouted from his dragon, "Look, John! It's the dinosaur!"

"Circle around again," ordered John.

— X —

Seneca asked, "How are we going to get past the minions? They won't leave."

"I thought you girls had everything figured out. I guess there are still some things I can do," remarked Billy sarcastically. Penny glared at him. Billy sprang up from behind the rocks and rushed toward the portal.

"No, Billy! Come back!" Penny screamed.

"I hope he's got a plan," said Seneca, concerned.

"Whatever he's up to, get ready to follow him!"

When Billy was twenty feet from the portal, the minions saw him. They rushed at him with a variety of primitive weapons. Billy drew his sword and dueled with them. As the number of minions grew around him, he retreated to the other side of the portal. They swarmed around him as he dueled with them.

"He's done it! Let's go," shouted Xerxes. When they reached the unguarded portal, Seneca and Xerxes slipped through unnoticed.

Penny and Jarrett went to Billy's aid instead and attacked the minions from behind. The minions forced Billy on the ground, but Penny wounded two at the rear of the pack and quickly got their attention. Jarrett picked up a club from a fallen minion and struck two minions in their heads and killed them. Billy retrieved his sword and attacked again.

The minions realized that the three of them had no place to go. They surrounded their three captives and toyed with them.

— ⏳ —

Sam parked the Expedition in front of the armory. He searched the area suspiciously before entering the building. He and Jerry entered the armory and followed a long hallway to steel double doors. "Open Sesame," kidded Sam. He turned the handle but it didn't open.

"How about that? I thought I left it unlocked."

Jerry watched curiously and wondered what Sam had up his sleeve. Sam put a key in and turned it. The lock clicked loudly and the doors opened. "That's more like it. Come on in," said Sam.

They entered a large bay full of weapons, field gear and ammunition. He pointed to a crate near the door. "This one here should do."

The two men grabbed the handles of the crate. As they lifted it, someone screamed from behind the shelves and scared the daylights out of them. "Yee-hah! Sam's back!" shouted Martin.

"Jumpin' Jesus!" exclaimed Sam. "You nearly gave me a heart attack."

"We knew you wouldn't let those things get you."

Sam was surprised to see his missing partners. "Marty! Brent! I thought you guys were dead."

"No, we had to hot leg it out of there," answered Brent. "They sent a few trackers after us but we took care of that."

"Where are the other guys?"

"They didn't make it," replied Marty somberly.

"What's going on, Sam?" asked Brent.

"We're about to engage in another war with our costumed friends. This one's bigger than the last one. Now help us load up the truck." Marty and Brent picked up a crate and carried it out to Sam's Humvee.

"What do you want to pack for this party?" asked Brent.

"Take your pick. I want to make a big impression, if you get my drift. Mortars would be a good start, though." The men gathered a variety of weapons and munitions from inside the station and placed them inside the vehicle.

— ⏳ —

Billy, Penny, and Jarret stood with their backs to each other. "This isn't the way I expected things to end," complained Billy. "I thought we'd die from something a little more exciting than these ugly things." The minions jabbed at them with their spears and swords. Billy swatted at them repeatedly but they kept a safe distance from him.

"Don't you have any more surprises? You're usually pretty good with them," replied Penny sarcastically.

"I've used up my quota for one lifetime. How about you? You seem to be full of them." Penny ignored him and focused on the minions.

Eight tigers attacked the minions on the other side of the camp. Half of the minions left Billy's group and rushed toward the tigers.

Ronnie spotted her friends from up on the dragon and guided it downward. Seamus and John approached from the opposite direction with their dragons. Billy's ploy was the distraction they were waiting for. They came in low and allowed the dragons to carry out their attack on the minions. "Look!" shouted Ronnie. "The Crocosaurus is attacking, too!" Nigel and Krill were amazed at the creatures involved in the attack.

The dragon swooped in and slashed at several minions. The second dragon followed the same path. The strafing continued for several passes until the dragons tired. They peeled off from their attack and flew back to the cave.

"What are you doing, Ronnie?" asked Krill. "Why are we leaving?"

"It's not me. The dragons are tired."

John saw the dragons departing. His dragon turned and joined the other three. They didn't consider that the dragons would need to rest at some point. They expended a lot of energy during their flight and flew for a while.

The tigers raced towards Billy while the Crocosaurus wreaked havoc at the other side of the camp. The minions were distracted enough that Billy cut down two of them while Penny wounded another. Jarret grabbed a spear from one of the fallen minions and took down two more. The path cleared to the portal. "Penny! Jarret! Go for the portal, now!" ordered Billy.

Six minions quickly cut them off. Billy lunged at them and fought fiercely. One of the minions wounded Billy's left arm with the end of its spear, then knocked him to the ground with the shaft. As it prepared to bring its spear down into Billy's chest, one of the tiger's dove on the minion and tore out its throat.

"Penny! Jarret! Go for the portal, now!" shouted Billy as he lay on his back. Penny and Jarret reluctantly fled into the portal. The tigers reached the portal area and chased the remaining minions into the forest.

The ground shook near Billy. As he rolled to his feet, he saw the Crocosaurus chase a group of minions toward him. He rushed into the portal and avoided the onslaught.

— X —

The dragons set down near the cave and the men dismounted. "What in the hell is going on? Why is this portal thing so damn important?" asked Nigel.

"That thing is a transportation portal through time and space. That's what this whole mess is all about, explained John. "That's why you and I are here with people from the future and creatures from the past."

"What about the others?"

"It looks like Xerxes and Seneca got into the portal. I couldn't tell what happened to Billy, Penny and the kid."

"Did you say Xerxes?"

"Yeah, he's here, too. This was the big deal he was involved in."

"So, what happens with the battle now?" asked Nigel.

"We're going back to the portal without the dragons. We have to be there when the others return to protect them from the minions."

The tigers broke off their attack and disappeared into the forest. The remaining tiger, Brutus, hesitated in front of the portal and stared suspiciously at it. In a single leap, he entered the portal and disappeared into the orange mist.

CHAPTER 9

RUGER'S CASTLE

Seneca and Xerxes emerged from the portal into the middle of a huge hall. Torches, randomly placed around the chamber, provided dim lighting and cast eerie shadows across the musty, ebony block floor. At one end of the chamber were two sets of stairs that led to either side of a landing above them. Underneath the landing was a large tunnel with torches that lined the left wall. At the other end of the chamber was a dark hallway. Along the far wall of the chamber were seven wooden doors. There was a wide set of steps in the middle of the right wall which had a faint red glow inside.

Xerxes approached the stairwell and peered down the tunnel. He noticed the faint glimmer of flames on the ceiling. Seneca was uneasy and stood close to Xerxes. "I can feel Ruger's presence. He's close," whispered Seneca.

"Yes, and so is Diomedes. This is the worst possible situation. I'll cloak our presence."

"I didn't know you're a magician."

"I'm not. It's only a method we use for cloaking. That's how we are able to perform our work without being noticed."

Xerxes and Seneca descended a long flight of stone stairs to a large cavern filled with columns of fire. Sweat dripped from Xerxes' naked brow as he stepped behind a large boulder. He saw Ruger and a huge shape whose colors blended in with the fire. Seneca peered over his shoulder and saw them, too. "There's Diomedes and Ruger," whispered Xerxes. "Let's get closer and see what they're up to."

Xerxes and Seneca crept along the rock wall, careful to stay hidden from Ruger and the demon witch. Seneca was appalled at the sight before her. Diomedes was seven-feet tall with two curled horns protruding from her head. Her eyes were like those of a snake and her mouth shaped like a wolf's. When she spoke, a forked tongue darted from between her lips. She was muscular and stood hunched over. Behind her was a tail about four feet long, which ended in a club of bone. Around her neck, she wore a necklace made from corpses' limbs strung together with a blood-soaked rope of tendons. Around her waist was a belt with the heads of several of her victims.

Seneca looked closer at the heads and shuddered in horror. The heads were those of her family members that Ruger sacrificed many months ago. She gagged and fought to keep from convulsing.

Xerxes squeezed her arms firmly and warned, "Focus, Seneca. If not, you'll be joining them. Remember why you are here."

Diomedes cornered Ruger and screamed at him in her raspy, guttural voice, "You didn't stop the outsider."

"No, Diomedes, but we're close."

"Where is Seneca?"

"She's coming, Diomedes. I promise."

"And why haven't you brought Cassius to me?"

"I told you, I need him alive to lure Seneca here. When she arrives, they'll both be yours."

Diomedes approached him. "I think you've outlived your usefulness, Ruger. I don't trust you."

"But, Diomedes, we have a pact! It will only be a little bit longer."

"I don't think so. Come to me, Ruger."

"But you need me, Diomedes. You can't kill me!" pleaded Ruger as he retreated from the witch

"You fool, Ruger. I don't need anyone. I may not have all my powers back but I am strong enough to make the transformation and leave this cursed place."

"But what about eternity? You promised me!"

"Oh, yes. Your body will live for eternity but you won't!" Diomedes roared with laughter and stalked Ruger. He retreated toward the steps with her close behind.

"Diomedes, give me just a little more time. I sense a disturbance at the portal. Perhaps this is the moment we've been waiting for."

"It had better be for your sake, Ruger."

Ruger fled from the cavern by way of the steps. In his haste, he failed to notice the shadows of Xerxes and Seneca across the reddish surface of the cavern floor. He hurried across the chamber to the portal and entered the swirling orange mist. An eerie feeling passed over him as he sensed that he wasn't alone in the portal. He searched warily but could only see the mist in front of him and the sand at his feet. He worried that someone could cross in the other direction without his knowledge. Knowing that his army was camped on the other side, Ruger was confident that no one entered the portal.

"We have to get out of here quickly," whispered Xerxes.

"Then what?" questioned Seneca.

"I'm not sure. I didn't think Diomedes could leave her cavern, yet." They rushed up the stairs to the chamber and saw no sign of Ruger.

"He must have gone through the portal," muttered Xerxes. "Let's try the hallway. Maybe we can find the sphere before he returns." They hurried down the hallway and discovered another chamber.

A soft whistling sound broke the silence. Xerxes wondered if it was just the wind or if it was Ruger's magic at work. He pulled Seneca into a small, darkened vestibule, ever so wary of a trap.

— X —

Billy felt as though he walked through a fog. He became nervous as an ionized mist surrounded him. His feet glided effortlessly on the sand-like path. He kept an eye for Penny and Jarret but there was no sign of them. Perhaps that was how the portal worked. Crossing the portal took a while and Billy had no idea how much time elapsed. His head was full of thoughts about what waited on the other side.

Penny and Jarrett exited the orange mist and were in awe of their new surroundings. The ebon stone chamber and torches were a stark contrast to their world. A few moments later, Billy arrived behind them. He was glad to leave the orange mist behind. He immediately focused on the surroundings and used his telepathy to seek out Cassius.

"What is it, Billy?" asked Penny.

"Cassius is somewhere nearby. I sense Diomedes at the bottom of those stairs. Xerxes and Seneca are nearby as well."

"How do you know?" asked Jarret.

"I can sense them, but it's very faint. I think Ruger is using something to interfere with our communication."

"What do you want to do first?" asked Penny.

"I know that Cassius needs our help. Let's find him first. Seneca and Xerxes know what they have to do." Billy approached the first wooden door and opened it. Inside, he could see only darkness.

Penny pulled a torch from its rusty bracket on the wall. She jumped in fright as the cobwebs danced across her wrist in the breeze. She shoved the torch at Billy, happy to be rid of it. Billy led them down a flight of stairs to the doorway of a small room. He strained to see into the dark room. Even the light from the torch struggled to penetrate the blackness inside.

"There's something evil here. I can feel it," fretted Billy. Penny and Jarret huddled together like two frightened children.

Billy entered the room and drew his sword. He poked at a layer of thorny vines on the table. They grew out of a decomposed corpse on the table. He noticed some movement underneath the vines and his curiosity pushed him to probe with his sword. Lying under the vines was a rotted corpse, filled with maggots. The head was opened and the brain was removed. The eyes hung out on the cheekbones. The front of the skull had two large holes where the nasal cavities would be.

Gasping, he turned his face to the wall and vomited. Penny and Jarrett saw the corpse and they, too, gagged nauseously.

— X —

When Ruger exited the portal, he was alarmed at the sight before him. His army was in disarray and corpses littered the entire area. He bellowed a blood-curdling scream and ripped the head from the nearest minion's shoulders. He flung it in anger at the small group of minions huddled near in the trees. After barking several orders, he paraded through the remaining mass of soldiers.

The Crocosaurus caught sight of him and lumbered in his direction. Ruger clapped his hands together above his head and uttered an incantation. A bright flash of light filled the air and momentarily blinded the creature. A loud roar erupted, then the earth trembled as the dinosaur tumbled to the ground. After three tries, it righted itself on its feet and roared defiantly at Ruger as if to give a final warning before it disappeared into the forest.

The minions cleared a small perimeter close to the portal of corpses. They stacked the bodies on a pile near the edge of the clearing and set them ablaze. The sky filled with black smoke and the stench of burning corpses.

Satisfied that things were again under control, Ruger entered the portal and returned to his castle. Once again, he had the feeling that he wasn't alone. He emerged from the portal and looked about the chamber but saw nothing. He noticed one of the wooden doors had been opened. "Ah, I have guests. This time they'll not escape me."

His confidence was suddenly rattled by Diomedes' raspy voice; "Ruger, I want them now!"

Ruger was stunned to hear the voice echo across his chamber. He saw Diomedes perched at the top of the stairs. "How did you get there, Diomedes?"

"Both of the children are near. I feel my powers growing. I want them now!"

"I know, Diomedes. They are here. Guard the chamber while I seek them out."

"My powers are limited and I am mortal, you fool."

Ruger impatiently retorted, "You're the mighty one, Diomedes. Use your strength. They are mere mortals."

"I don't like your tone of voice, Ruger."

Ruger thought it wise not to instigate Diomedes further. "I'm sorry. It's fatigue."

"I don't care! Get them now!"

Ruger quickly left the chamber and mumbled, "One day, I'll see you die, you miserable bitch."

— ⊰ —

Jarrett approached the corpse and reached for the chin. When he turned the skull, he saw something small and dark disappear into the throat area. His curiosity pushed him to lift the chin higher. A small black creature, resembling a wingless bat, darted out from an opening in the neck area and bit into Jarret's wrist. He writhed in pain and shook his arm. "Billy, help me!"

The creature wouldn't release its hold on him. Blood trickled from his wrist and created a small pool on the dank floor. Penny was mortified and stumbled backwards against the wall. She let out a brief cry and covered her mouth. A skeleton fell from its shackles on the wall and became a cobweb-covered pile of bones on the floor.

"What the hell is with you two?" complained Billy. He grabbed Jarrett's arm and held the torch against the tiny creature. "Hold still. This might hurt," he warned. The worm-like creature sizzled for several seconds and released its bite. When it fell to the floor, it exploded in a small blue flame. Jarret clutched at the wound on his arm.

"Let's get out of here. Cassius isn't in here," said Billy grimly.

Jarrett and Penny anxiously followed Billy up the steps. Penny slammed the big door behind them. Concerned, she asked, "Are you alright, Jarrett?"

Jarret shook his arm several times and winced. "My arm feels like it's on fire," he said tearfully. Billy inspected the wound on Jarrett's arm. There were four short black appendages hanging from the bite wounds. "I've never seen anything like this. I'm going to pull them out before infection sets in."

Jarrett sweated profusely. His arm was already turning red. Billy grappled with the first appendage and tugged on it. He ordered, "Penny, keep the torch ready. This thing is pulsing."

Billy pulled the string out until it caught on something. He could see a plug shape just under Jarrett's skin. "Okay, Jarrett, this is gonna hurt, but it's got to come out."

"Just get it out! It hurts so bad," pleaded Jarret. Billy yanked hard on the string. There was a loud scream but not from any of them. At the end of the appendage was a ghastly little head with glowing green eyes and tiny fangs. Billy held it over the fire until it popped and disintegrated.

"Oh, how horrible!" cried Penny.

"One down, Jarrett. I'm going for the next one."

Tears streamed down Jarret's cheeks but he didn't make a sound. Penny wanted to console him but she was terrified of the tiny creatures. Billy repeated the process until all four of the little creatures were removed. Jarrett grew weak and delirious. He was soaked in sweat from head to toe. Billy lifted him to his feet and helped him up the stairs.

When they returned to the main chamber, Billy closed the door and instructed Penny, "I want you to stay here with Jarrett. You'll be safe until I get back."

"But Jarrett needs help now. We can't wait."

"Then take him back through the portal. Perhaps Doc can help him. I don't know what else to do for him."

A loud raspy voice echoed through the chamber, "I don't think you'll be going anywhere."

Billy held the torch up and stepped forward. "Diomedes, I presume," he said callously.

"Yes, and you are?"

"Going to kill you, you bitch!"

"I hardly think so, you fool."

Billy drew his sword and stalked the demon. He read Diomedes' thoughts and each time she attacked, he struck at her with his sword and wounded her. Diomedes became incensed when she saw the lacerations that Billy inflicted on her.

"So, you can read my thoughts. I underestimated you, human, but I can play games too!" Diomedes hissed and jabbed at Billy with her claws. Her long, serpentine tongue struck at Billy and forced him to retreat into the corner. Billy faked a stroke at her head and kicked her in the chest. She stumbled back awkwardly as Billy lined up his sword with her throat.

Diomedes spat into Billy's eyes before he could deliver the lethal strike. His eyes burned and he screamed in agony. He tried to focus on Diomedes' next move but the pain in his eyes distracted him greatly. She grabbed him by the neck and threw him against the wall. Billy fell to the ground, but seized the opportunity to wipe his eyes with his shirt. The pain lessened and his vision soon cleared.

Diomedes was nearly upon him and reached for his throat. This time Billy drove his sword into Diomedes' armpit. She wailed and retreated. Billy felt confident as he gained the advantage but Diomedes cloaked her thoughts. Before he could make his next move, Diomedes lunged at him, catching him off guard. She pounced on him and pinned him helplessly on the ground.

"Now, it's time for you to die," she proclaimed triumphantly. She sat upright on Billy's chest and raised her arms in the air. Two large flaps opened on her chest to reveal a large mouth. Diomedes leaned forward and thin, slimy tentacles emerged from the cavity, like hungry red tongues searching out their prey.

Billy gasped from the weight of Diomedes on top of him and was helpless to struggle against her. Penny screamed hysterically. She drew her sword and rushed at Diomedes. With all her might, she drove her small sword into the witch's back.

Diomedes stood and howled in pain. The walls shook and the ceiling echoed from her shriek. She turned and faced Penny. Her eyes reflected her anger. The tentacles quickly retracted into her cavity and the chest flaps closed.

Penny was frantic and now had no weapon to fight with. Diomedes flailed helplessly at her back but was unable to reach the sword. Penny retreated until she was cornered. "Billy, help me!" she pleaded as she sobbed.

The sound of Penny's voice gave Billy renewed strength. He retrieved his sword and rushed at Diomedes from behind. Once again, Diomedes opened her chest flaps. She raised Penny by her throat. Penny choked and kicked frantically. The tentacles again emerged from the hideous mouth and wrapped themselves around her legs. Diomedes was about to feed on Penny when Billy struck at her arm with his sword. Penny fell to the ground, as did Diomedes' quivering arm. A vile, yellow fluid seeped from the severed arm.

Billy struck at Diomedes' knee, cracking several bones in her leg. Diomedes fell to the ground, shrieking in pain. The tentacles released Penny and retracted. She got to her knees but Billy struck at her head with all the strength he could muster. The chamber echoed with a loud crunch. With a surprised look in Diomedes' eyes, she and Billy stared at each other for several long seconds. Then, as if in slow motion, Diomedes head rolled off her shoulders and fell to the floor. It was followed by the loud thump of her lifeless body crashing to the ground.

Billy warily retrieved Penny's sword from the carcass and returned it to her. He took Penny's hand and helped her to her feet. "You saved my life, Penny. Thanks."

"Please, let's get out of here. Diomedes is dead and we need to get help for Jarret."

"I can't. I have to find Cassius. Take Jarrett back with you. Find Doc and tell him what's going on. If anybody can help us, he can."

"But what about you?"

"I'll be fine."

Penny gazed adoringly for a moment at Billy before tending to Jarrett. She remembered that quiet moonlit night with Billy. It seemed so long ago. "Be careful, Billy."

"I will."

Penny helped Jarret to his feet and took him to the portal.

Billy waved to them as Penny and Jarrett entered the orange mist of the portal. He glanced back at Diomedes and was startled to see her body disintegrate into a puff of red smoke. He tried the other doors but each one led to an empty dungeon. When he opened the last door, he found Cassius chained to the wall.

Cassius looked so frail as he hung limply from the wall. Billy slashed at the shackles with his sword until they broke. Cassius crumbled to the ground with a groan. Billy dragged him to the main chamber and sat him up against the wall. "Cassius, it's me, Billy. Can you speak?"

"Billy, is it really you?"

"Of course, it's me. I'm going to get you out of here."

"No. You must help Seneca. She needs you, Billy."

"But, Cassius "

"It's too late for me."

"Cassius, no! We're all getting out of here." Cassius slipped into unconsciousness.

Billy wept for him. He remembered him as a magnificent specimen of a man. Now, Cassius was reduced to a mere bag of bones. His nose was deformed with two large cavities from Ruger's tentacles. Ruger had slowly sucked the life out of Cassius, barely keeping him alive. Billy moved

Cassius to the steps and propped him up against the wall. He fretted about what he should do next. Should he seek out Seneca and Xerxes or take Cassius back through the portal?

Something furry rubbed against him and frightened him. Billy stumbled backward until he hit the wall. He drew his sword, prepared to fight. When he saw Brutus in front of him, he was relieved. "Brutus, you scared the living hell out of me!" The tiger growled and sat on the ground.

Billy couldn't believe his luck. He patted the tiger across its head and scratched behind its ears. He considered that Brutus could protect Cassius while he searched for Seneca and Xerxes. He pulled Cassius into a vacant room and called Brutus inside, using his telepathy to communicate with the tiger. He wanted Brutus to stay with Cassius until he returned. Brutus strode to the nearest corner of the room and lay down on his side.

Billy left the door slightly ajar and headed up the steps to the hallway. He crept slowly and watched for any sign of Seneca and Xerxes or Ruger.

— X —

Seneca and Xerxes could feel Ruger's power weaken.

"Billy must have killed Diomedes! Ruger's lost some of his power," said Xerxes excitedly.

"So, he'll be easier to catch?"

"No, Ruger is a caged animal and we are still in his domain. He'll resort to drastic measures now. Besides, Diomedes may not be gone for good."

"Can you reach Billy with your telepathy? I've tried but I can't connect with him."

"I can barely sense him. Ruger's magic is blocking us out. We'll hide until Ruger shows up. I'm sure he knows we're here by now."

Seneca and Xerxes treaded through a dark tunnel toward the glow of a single torch. They entered the stairway at the end of the hall and ascended it. At the top, they entered a chamber with five doors and another hallway similar to the first chamber. In the middle of the chamber was a wooden table with a battered, silver chest on it. Xerxes pushed Seneca behind burgundy drapes into a closet where they waited for Ruger's appearance.

"Xerxes, why don't we open the chest?" Seneca asked, curious. "Maybe it's the key to finding the source."

"The chest is protected by a spell," explained Xerxes. "If you touch it, you'll suffer a horrible fate. I know Ruger all too well."

Soon enough, Ruger entered the chamber and went to the chest. He held a short stick over the chest and mumbled strange words. He placed the stick on the table and opened the chest.

Ruger removed two candles and a small bowl from the dilapidated cabinet in the corner. He then lit the candles and placed them on either side of the chest. He reached into the bowl and uttered another incantation.

Xerxes whispered, "He's got a hand full of spiders and he's putting a spell on them."

Never before had Seneca actually witnessed someone perform black magic like this.

Ruger tossed the spiders onto the floor. A ghostly green gas rose from each of the spiders as they scurried about the floor. They fanned out in a circular pattern.

"Shouldn't we attack him now, Xerxes?"

"No, not yet."

"Why not?"

"I don't see the device on his arm."

Ruger retrieved a golden skull from the cabinet and placed it on the table. He raised his hands up high and recited strange incantations. The eyes of the skull glowed bright red and a narrow column of fire rose from the chest to the ceiling. The smell of burnt sulfur filled the room.

Ruger sang out more incantations and sparks flew from the fire, striking each of the spiders. The sparks burned brightly on the floor and soon grew into new columns of fire extending into the air. Ruger continued his chant and the columns of fire took shape.

Seneca and Xerxes watched in horror as the spiders were consumed by the flames and changed into thirteen of the most horrible creatures they ever saw. The creatures were part spider and part demon. Each had long curled claws and beady black eyes. The torsos were shaped like a human's but they were covered with a black resinous substance. The creatures crouched over onto eight disjointed legs and drooled foamy, white saliva onto the floor. The pools emitted a horrible stench that was nauseous. When the transformation was complete, Ruger commanded them in a strange language. The creatures immediately dispersed in different directions. Ruger returned the skull to the cabinet and closed the cover on the chest. He extinguished the candles and departed the room.

Xerxes whispered, "He didn't restore the protective spell on the chest. I don't like this. It could be a trap."

Xerxes and Seneca waited patiently until the room and hallway became silent. They left the closet and trailed Ruger. When they turned the corner into another hallway, Ruger and his creatures were gone. Xerxes and Seneca were frightened and became panicked.

"I think we've just been trapped," uttered Xerxes sadly.

Ruger appeared behind them. "Well, it's nice of you to join me. I've been waiting for you, Seneca, for a long time."

"Uncle, how could you do this to your family? You've become a monster."

"It was a small sacrifice for immortality and, thanks to your meddling, I must wait a bit longer. That being the case, you will pay dearly for interfering."

"Give up, Ruger, before we are all destroyed by your greed," warned Xerxes.

"You will be my prisoners until I am ready to deal with you. Meanwhile, there is still one more of you that I must deal with. Come with me."

"We won't go anywhere with you!" Seneca replied defiantly.

The snarls from six of Ruger's creatures startled them from behind. "If you choose to stay, then you'll have to deal with my pets. It's been a while since they've tasted fresh blood."

Seneca and Xerxes reluctantly followed Ruger down the hall. The floor was covered with a plush red rug. They passed through a doorway, shrouded in burgundy drapes, to another chamber. At one time, the castle belonged to Seneca's parents who were king and queen of the land. The drapes and carpet were but a few remnants from that magnificent era.

Ruger pointed to a bench in the corner and ordered them to sit. When Seneca sat down, her wrists and legs were immediately snared and held by thorny green vines. Xerxes also sat and, before he could react, the vines imprisoned him as well. The vines covered their entire bodies until they looked like ivy statues. Seneca cried out in pain as the vines penetrated her skin and took root inside her body. Xerxes tried valiantly to fight the spell of ivy but to no avail.

Ruger laughed madly with delight as he watched them struggle. His laughter echoed down the hallway. Seneca screamed as the vines tightened around her neck and mouth, restricting her from making any sound.

Billy heard Ruger's laughter and cringed. He knew that he must have captured Seneca and Xerxes. He followed the tunnel until he sensed something evil. He doused the torch and ducked into an open doorway. Two grotesque, eight-legged creatures shuffled past without noticing him.

Billy was grateful for his keen senses. Not only could he sense the creatures coming, he could see them in the dark. He drew his sword and crept behind the creatures. With one swipe of the sword, he split the first creature in half. The second creature lunged at him, only to have its head split open as well. The bodies quivered and burst into flames.

Billy jumped away from the flames. "Son of a bitch!" he shouted. "Black magic again." He leaned against the wall and took a deep breath. His strength waned, but he continued down the tunnel and ascended spiral stairs to another hallway.

Torches lined both sides of the hallway all the way to the end. The floor was covered with a thick red carpet lined with gold frills. Billy felt Ruger close by. At the end of the hallway, he saw two burgundy curtains made of thick velour. He passed the curtains and entered a smoke-filled room. A chilly breeze stirred the smoke and cleared the center of the room. "Doesn't this guy ever stop?" Billy grumbled.

The last of the smoke cleared, revealing Ruger's presence. Billy stepped back and searched for other creatures. There were none. "So, we meet again," taunted Ruger. "I believe we have a score to settle."

"Cut the crap, Ruger. I've had enough of your nonsense."

"You haven't learned, have you, silly boy?"

Billy drew his sword and pointed it at Ruger. "I don't think that's a good idea," said Ruger arrogantly. "Do you see those ivy-covered figures in the corner?"

Billy looked at the two shapes and realized it was Seneca and Xerxes. Seneca struggled to use her telepathy to communicate with Billy but she was weak and the vines fought to control her mind as well as her body.

"Go ahead. Take a closer look at your friends," ordered Ruger.

Billy projected a message to his friends: "I'll be back for you."

He chided Ruger, "You expect me to believe that those lumps of vines are my friends. Save it, Ruger." Billy approached Ruger with his sword drawn. He followed Ruger's thoughts as he approached him.

Ah, Ruger is summoning more of his creatures. I'll play along, he thought. Billy stalked Ruger to the far corner of the room. Through Ruger's thoughts, he knew two creatures were behind him. Ruger smiled at Billy and assumed a prone position. "You win, my friend. I'm out of tricks. Do with me as you please."

Billy was prepared when the first creature lunged at his back. He spun and buried his sword into its chest. He pulled the sword out and struck at its head, decapitating it for insurance. The head rolled harmlessly across the floor and exploded. The second creature lunged at Billy and bit into his leg. Billy severed its head and watched the creature incinerate before his eyes. The pain in his leg spread and became intense. He charged at Ruger but a sudden rush of red smoke blinded him. When his vision returned, Ruger was gone.

"Damn you, Ruger! I'll get you yet," Billy shouted angrily.

The smoke faded from the room and Billy could see again. He went to the vine-covered figures and attempted to free his friends. "I'm here, Seneca and Xerxes. I'll have you out soon."

The barrier for their telepathy disappeared. "Forget it, Billy," said Seneca feebly. "The vines are rooted into our bodies. You can't pull them away without hurting us."

"What should I do? How do I free you?"

"Kill Ruger and the spell will be broken," responded Xerxes. "But first you must find the PCU. It's imperative."

"I know you'll save us, Billy," Seneca replied tearfully.

"Don't give up on me. I've rescued Cassius and I'll be back for you." Billy reached between the leaves and touched her arm. He could feel the vines penetrating her skin and the pain she was experiencing. He left the room and stormed down the stairs at the end of the hallway. At the bottom, he encountered four more of Ruger's creatures.

The first two fell over each other in their haste to reach him. He easily disposed of them with two strokes of his sword. The remaining two learned quickly from their peers' mistakes. The first creature darted past him with a half-hearted swipe from one of its bony legs. As Billy retreated from its range, the second creature lunged at his leg and bit into it.

Billy felt another surge of pain rush up his leg and into his hip. He rammed the sword through the creature's head and into its throat. He fought a lengthy battle with the remaining creature before he killed it. Exhausted from the battle and bleeding, he collapsed on the floor.

Billy looked up at the burgundy curtains that hung in the doorway, then at his bloody leg. He pulled down one of the curtains and tore it into shreds. He used one of the shreds to make a bandage for his leg. Billy tried to locate Ruger by entering his mind and reading his thoughts. It seemed almost too easy and Billy was wary of a trap. He saw Ruger standing in front of a different portal than the one he crossed previously. Ruger entered the orange mist with the silver chest and labored to cross it.

Perhaps his magic is weakening because of Diomedes' fate, Billy thought. *I've got to follow him.* He suddenly recognized the location of the portal. He remembered the burgundy curtains in the room upstairs. "That sneaky bastard never left the room after all," Billy groaned, frustrated. "He must be weakening if he's resorting to illusions instead of magic."

Billy returned to the room and rushed into the orange mist. As he raced along, he realized he couldn't risk being caught in the portal if Ruger shut it down. He couldn't see Ruger and worried that this might be another illusion.

As he continued down the orange path, his legs grew heavy and he dragged his feet through the orange sand. *The other path was much easier and shorter,* he thought. *Maybe he's already closing the portal.* The path swayed and Billy felt nauseous. He hurried faster but the orange mist slowed him down even more. The path shrank and Billy felt panic taking over.

The shrinking dimensions of the portal forced him to his knees and he was barely able to move. As hard as he tried, his energy was spent. He closed his eyes, expecting to die as he made one last lunge in desperation. A few seconds later, he tumbled out of the portal and fell flat on his back. Everything turned to black and Billy remembered nothing.

— X —

Penny stumbled from the portal while clinging to Jarret. He was unconscious and she was overcome with fatigue. She looked up and saw that Ruger's minions surrounded them. Two of the minions spouted streams of wet silk that quickly bonded to Penny and Jarret. She stared for a moment at the hideous creatures in horror, and then collapsed onto the ground.

CHAPTER 10

REINFORCEMENTS

Doc paced nervously while Isaac and Spencer waited for him to make a decision. Isaac and Spencer were both tall, thin teenagers with dark skin and short hair. The two men were anxious to participate in the action. They watched on a daily basis as Billy and his friends went on exciting adventures and hoped that this day would come.

Isaac asked, "Dr. Smith, do you mind us coming with you? We don't know anyone, but we can help just as much as the others can."

"No, as a matter of fact, I'm glad to have you with us. We should have gotten more people involved from the beginning in these excursions. I hope it isn't too late."

Spencer asked curiously, "For what, Doc?"

"There are a lot of strange things happening and we're trying to get to the bottom of it."

"We're ready when you are," Isaac replied enthusiastically.

Wills arrived and informed them, "Supplies are packed on the flatbed and ready to go." All the men climbed on the truck and Doc drove them to the spot where Billy fell down the slope.

Doc surveyed the area and inquired, "The minions' camp was located on the second mountain, wasn't it, Wills?"

"That's what they said. Billy thought that it was about a third of the way up the mountainside."

"Now, if I know Billy correctly, he would have gone up to the minion camp just to see what those things are up to," suggested Doc.

"His curiosity always gets the better of him," replied Wills.

"I think we can drive most of the way by heading north through the city. That would save us a whole lot of time instead of tracking him on foot."

"That'd be a lot faster than climbing down this wretched slope, too."

Doc turned the truck around and headed for the city. The flatbed truck drove through the ruined city and turned up Market Street. When they reached the last side street before the forest, a Humvee sped in front of them and narrowly missed striking them.

"Yikes!" yelled Isaac from the rear of the truck.

"That was Sam!" said Doc excitedly.

The Humvee stopped next to them and Sam hopped out. Jerry sat in the passenger seat and Sam's partners sat in the back. "Fancy meeting you here," he quipped.

"Where did you learn to drive? You're supposed to be a cop," kidded Doc.

"Not anymore. No harm, no foul."

Doc looked at Sam's two companions and asked, "Who are your friends?"

"Oh, just a few co-workers. We were separated during the last conflict. That's Brent and the other fellow is Martin."

Doc shook hands with the men and asked, "Do you know where you're going?"

"Not really," replied Sam.

"Follow us. We'll get you there."

Sam climbed into his Humvee and followed the flatbed into the mountains. There was a well-worn path leading through the forest and up the slope of the mountain. The minions made little effort to conceal their trail.

"This must be the main route that the soldiers used to travel in and out of the city," surmised Doc. "They must have used wagons or carts. Look at the ruts in the ground."

"What happens when we run into these soldiers?" asked Spencer.

"Hopefully Sam has enough weapons that we can handle them."

When the vehicles began their descent over the first mountain, their path was partially blocked by the carcass of a dragon. Doc stopped the flatbed and eyed at the dragon.

Sam drove along the side of the road and passed the creature. "Geez, Jerry! Will you look at that? Have you ever seen anything so big?" remarked Sam.

Jerry replied uncomfortably, "As a matter of fact, I have. More than once, if you must know."

"So, you're intimate with these wild things?"

"Yes, and not by choice."

Doc drove closer and stopped by the carcass. He was stunned to see a real dragon with wings since he always believed them to be mythical. Doc and Maggie got out of their vehicle to examine the carcass.

"This could be Randy's dragon. It must have been one heck of a battle," Doc commented.

Maggie looked saddened and mentioned, "I hope the doctors can help her. She's gonna need it."

Sam studied the head of the dragon. He noticed the leather reins. "What's that thing on the dragon's head?" he pondered aloud.

Doc examined the head more closely. He felt the leather reins that dangled from the dragon's head. "This is truly amazing. It's a muzzle with reigns on it. I guess that's how the girls flew on the dragons! But who made these reigns?" he queried.

Doc and Maggie climbed over the dragon's carcass and studied it further until Sam grew impatient and honked the horn. As they climbed into the cab of the flatbed truck with Spencer, Doc wondered if they would encounter more of these creatures. He maneuvered the vehicle around the fallen tree and continued up the path.

"I wonder what happened to that dragon?" inquired Spencer.

"If I didn't know better, I'd say that Randy was somehow ambushed by a dinosaur," replied Maggie.

"But what in the world could she have been doing to get into a mess like that?"

"You never know with them. They are always into something crazy."

"Randy wasn't looking too well back there," remarked Doc.

"We could fly her back to the observatory where Joe Miller's people could take care of her," suggested Maggie.

"That depends on our success with the minions."

The trail was marked well by the minions' tracks and the truck had little difficulty scaling the second mountain. When they reached the halfway point of their ascent, though, the trail disintegrated into a narrow, rut-filled gap.

Doc stepped out of the truck and surveyed the rough terrain. "This is where we get out and walk. I figure we'll reach their camp in a few hours," he announced to everyone. They locked up the vehicles and hiked up the broken path. Sam kept his gun pointed ahead while Spencer and Isaac guarded the rear.

Two dragons glided over them. "I wonder if Billy's friends are on those dragons," Spencer commented excitedly.

Doc watched intently from the edge of the embankment. "It appears so." Spencer looked relieved as the second dragon gracefully landed beyond the trees. "It looks as if there are two people riding on the back of the dragon. It could be the Englishmen."

Brent carried a wooden crate with rope handles. Doc, Jerry and Brent helped Martin carry the guns and ammo up the trail until they reached a clearing in front of a cave.

John exited the cave and greeted them, "Well, well. What brings you to this side of town, Dr. Smith?"

"We came to save your hides."

"What the hell is happening out here?" asked Jerry excitedly.

"You'll find out soon enough."

A large shadow passed over them. Jerry recognized the familiar figures on the third dragon. It was Ronnie, Krill and Nigel. After two passes, the dragon landed.

"Good God!" muttered Doc. "Everyone's flying."

"This is war, Doc! We're waiting for Billy's group to return from the other side of the portal."

"Can you take us to the portal?" asked Doc anxiously. "I've got to see it."

"Sure. We're heading there now," answered John.

"What about the weapons and ammo?" inquired Sam.

"Bring them along. I'm sure we'll need them. We have to gain control of the area around the portal and the minions are rooted in right now."

"What do you mean minions?" asked Doc.

"Xerxes said that the soldiers are minions of an evil wizard. He's responsible for all our problems."

"Where's Billy now?"

"He went through the portal."

"How'd he get there?" Doc asked anxiously.

"We were able to distract the minions long enough so Billy's group could get through but if they try to get out, they'll be captured."

"Well, let's kick their minion asses out of here!" exclaimed Doc.

A few hours later, they reached the edge of the forest near the minion camp. John eyed the minions near the portal. He saw Penny and Jarret tied up in a white blanket. "Damn! They've captured Penny and the pest!"

The minions carried Penny and Jarret into a tent. Through the opening, they watched the minions prop their friends up against one of the supports. "How can we rescue them, John?" asked Jerry.

"Right now, their lives aren't in danger. We may have to wait until Billy's return before we can get them out of there."

"Maybe we should try to warn Billy that the minions are at the portal's entrance."

"No, not yet. We'd have to risk sneaking someone past the sentries at the gate. It would take another diversion to do that."

"Do we know how many of those things are out there?" inquired Sam.

"I'd say less than a hundred are left," answered John.

"Then I'll prepare a special package for our friends. I'm sure we have just what the doctor ordered. No pun intended, Doc."

"Go for it, Sam." Doc enjoyed Sam's witty sense of humor. It helped ease his tension.

— X —

Ronnie ran her hand along the thick scales of the dragon's neck. She spoke softly into the dragon's ear, "I don't expect you to understand me but I'm asking you to fly again for me." The dragon turned its head to Ronnie and emitted a sigh from its large mouth. She rubbed the creature's snout and placed her head against it. "I know you're tired. It's okay." She removed her hand from the dragon's head. The dragon stood upright and spread its wings. The other dragons unleashed mighty roars and stood erect.

"Nigel! Krill! Get on a dragon. We're back in business," Ronnie shouted excitedly.

"Not again. I hate this," complained Nigel.

"Me, too," replied Krill miserably. "I'd rather be at the minion camp fighting with the others."

The fog lifted and the rain ceased. All three dragons glided across the sky toward the minion camp. Ronnie flew her dragon over the minion camp and scanned the grounds. She steered her dragon toward the portal to monitor the minion army. The others followed in formation. They glided in and mercilessly thrashed at the minions. When they landed in front of the portal, the minions quickly dispersed. The dragons devoured many of them.

John saw the dragons touch down near the portal and shouted elatedly, "Let's go! The dragons are back."

Sam anxiously distributed firearms to everyone and some small packages to his boys with explicit instructions. Brent and Martin took the parcels and disappeared into the trees.

Doc and Maggie hurried to the tent to rescue Penny and Jarret. The others secured the area in front of the portal. Sam and Brent attacked the minions with grenades and C-4 explosive packages while Martin took out many of them with his mini-gun. The others used pistols to take down more of their foes. When the fighting ceased, the remaining minions fled down the trail in a panic.

"It's a shame the rest of those things are getting away," complained Isaac.

"Don't be so sure of that," replied Sam. Two large booms were heard from a short distance away. The sound of a mini-gun firing a steady stream of bullets followed the earth-shaking blasts.

Sam giddily remarked, "It's always nice to have the right tools for the job." Isaac, Spencer, and Sam slapped their hands together in a high-five.

Doc and Maggie entered the tent and cut the white, silk blanket away from Penny and Jarret's bodies. Doc noticed the injury to Jarret's arm and inspected the wound more closely. "Is it bad?" asked Maggie.

"It looks like he was bitten or pierced by something poisonous."

Maggie sat Penny in an upright position. "Penny, it's me, Maggie. Say something."

Penny mumbled a few incoherent phrases and trembled. Her eyes opened wide and her jaw dropped in surprise. "What are you doing here, Maggie? I thought I'd never see any of you again."

"Relax, dear. It'll be alright."

Penny hugged Maggie tightly and sobbed, "Oh, Maggie, it was terrible. We have to help Billy, Xerxes and Seneca."

"What happened to them?"

Doc interrupted, "Penny, where is Billy? Who are Xerxes and Seneca? Has anyone crossed through the portal?"

"We all went through the portal. Jarrett needs help so I brought him back. Is he alright?"

"He's in bad shape, Penny."

"Can't you do something for him?"

"I don't think so. He's got a better chance with the doctors."

Doc called to Krill, "Can you take the boy back to the post office. He needs medical attention, badly."

"But what about Billy?"

"We'll worry about him."

Tears streamed down Penny's cheeks. She couldn't believe Jarret could be seriously injured from something so bizarre. "Billy killed Diomedes and is hunting Ruger," Penny explained. "We didn't find Seneca and Xerxes, though."

"What's all this about?" asked Doc.

"We've got to help Billy, first," insisted Penny.

"Penny, you're in no shape to go back."

"I'm going. I've got to help him."

Maggie offered, "I'll stay here with Penny. Now stop wasting time."

Penny looked up at her pleadingly but Maggie said firmly, "They'll find him. You need to stay here with me."

Doc instructed Sam, "You secure the area. We'll be back as soon as we find them." When he eyed the portal meticulously, his heart beat fast with excitement. He took Maggie by the hand. "I'm going to travel into a wormhole to either another world or another dimension. Can you believe it?" he said nervously.

Maggie squeezed his hand and pushed him forward. "I can believe anything at this point, she remarked."

Doc entered the portal, followed closely by Isaac and Spencer. Maggie and Penny watched them disappear into the orange mist and the sweeping sands.

John, Ronnie, and Nigel piloted their dragons into the sky and scanned the area for minions. Seamus and Sam stood guard by the portal. "If they aren't back in an hour, we're going in after them," said Sam adamantly.

Seamus argued, "They distinctly told us to stay here. We need to protect the portal."

Sam paced back and forth nervously while they waited. "I can't just sit here and wait."

"Maybe you can't, but I can."

Sam chuckled and replied, "I like you, Seamus."

CHAPTER 11

SPELLS

Billy wasn't sure how long he lay there for, but when he opened his eyes, he was surprised to find himself inside the Neanderthals' cavern. He remembered the large fire and the many tunnels that led to the surface. Nearby was the wooden pen he rescued the female prisoners from a few weeks earlier. *What in the hell kind of maze is this? How do the Neanderthals fit into this?* he thought. Billy grew worried when he saw no sign of Ruger or the Neanderthals. The cavern was deserted. He wondered if the Neanderthals saw Ruger as a god. *That would explain his relationship with them, but where are they now?*

Billy felt stronger and his leg healed thanks to Seneca's traits. She was right about making him better-suited to face Ruger. He stared at the fire meticulously. Something about the fire bothered him. It always burned brightly but there was no evidence of wood to fuel it.

Billy searched the area and found no firewood. He picked up a stone, and threw it at the base of the fire, expecting ashes to scatter. Strangely enough, nothing happened. He picked up another stone and threw it harder, but there was still no disturbance in the ashes. Billy held his hand close to the flames and felt nothing. He took a deep breath and plunged his hand into the flames. He cringed and waited for the burning sensation to overtake him, but nothing happened. "What the hell is going on here?" he exclaimed.

Billy stepped nervously through the imaginary flames and found a stairwell carved in the hard rock. At the bottom of the steps was a tunnel. He descended the stairs and followed the dark tunnel. In the distance, he saw an eerie glow and heard howling in the distance. At the end of the tunnel, he found another cavern illuminated in a bright yellow glow.

Billy sneaked into the cavern and hid behind a boulder. From there, he observed Ruger amid the Neanderthals, muttering incantations before a large statue of Diomedes. "Holy shit!" he whispered to himself. The statue was eerily life-like and began to ooze blue smoke from the mouth until it enveloped the statue. The smoke cleared and the statue came to life.

Billy was mortified to see that Diomedes still lived. "I killed her already! What do I have to do to finish her off permanently?" he uttered to himself.

Diomedes raised her arms and howled the most blood-curdling roar that Billy heard yet. The Neanderthals dropped to their knees and bowed to her. Diomedes' chest plates opened wide and she plucked one of the Neanderthals by the neck with her tentacles. She fed the helpless creature into the carnivorous cavity within her chest. The Neanderthal screamed and kicked feebly until it was completely devoured.

Diomedes belched and spoke sarcastically in her raspy voice, "I prefer the flesh of humans to these things, Ruger."

Ruger replied, "Don't worry, Diomedes. There will be more. I believe you owe me for bringing you back."

"I'll consider it when you bring the Firenghian children to me. Ruger and Diomedes stepped through the kneeling mass of Neanderthals and departed through a different tunnel. As soon as they disappeared from sight, the Neanderthals fled from the cavern. They rushed up the tunnel toward the imaginary fire, howling in fear.

Billy was suddenly alone in the cavern. He followed Ruger and Diomedes through the tunnel by focusing his telepathy on them and reading their thoughts. At first, he had difficulty, but he persisted until he finally reached into their minds. Immediately, he felt something probe his mind. He quickly withdrew his focus from them and tried to shield his thoughts. "Damn! They know I'm here now."

Billy followed the tunnel and passed through another portal. He stepped into to the chamber with the stone table in the middle and hid behind a wooden cabinet. Ruger and Diomedes stood together in front of a small sphere, with their backs to Billy. The sphere's blue glow reflected off a silver base, leaving strange flashes across the walls.

Billy watched curiously as Ruger placed his hands strategically around the orb. He turned a small knob and the sphere flashed brilliant orange and yellow colors. "Do you know what you're doing, Ruger?"

"I would appreciate your patience, Diomedes. I'm working on it. Did you know we have a visitor?"

"Get the portal open now. I'm losing my patience."

"Yes. Yes. Just like a woman. Some things never change."

Diomedes grabbed Ruger by the throat and her chest plates twitched. Ruger squirmed and gagged as Diomedes clutched his throat tighter.

"Do you have any more smart remarks before I consume your wretched body, Ruger?"

"I beg your forgiveness, Diomedes. It was a thoughtless slip of the tongue. I promise you; it won't happen again." Diomedes dropped him to the ground and sneered at him.

Ruger muttered something under his breath and rubbed his throat. He regained his composure and stared at the wooden cabinet. "Come out and show yourself."

Billy shuddered when he realized that Ruger was looking at him. "I'll tell you one more time, come out and show yourself," ordered Ruger. Billy drew his sword and stepped from behind the cabinet. He approached Ruger and Diomedes, prepared to do battle.

"You haven't learned yet, have you? Well, I think this will change your mind." Ruger raised his arms and faced the wall. An image of Seneca and Xerxes covered with the vines appeared.

"We've been through this," countered Billy. "Show me something I don't know."

"Now, listen to their cries."

Billy watched helplessly as the vines tightened and constricted around his friends. He could hear Seneca's frantic cries. "You see, my friend, in about six hours, they will be completely consumed by the vines. What remains to be seen is how much pain they will endure in reaching that point.

"Ruger, you bastard! I'll kill you!"

"I hardly think so and to make sure, I have something special for you."

Ruger raised an arm and opened his hand. A small white ball appeared in his palm. He threw the ball at Billy and watched with delight as the ball exploded into a white mist. It engulfed Billy and formed a bubble around him. Inside the bubble, the mist became solid. Billy was paralyzed like a doll in a case.

"It's about time you took care of this problem, Ruger," grumbled Diomedes.

Ruger ignored her and sneered at Billy. "Sorry I can't stay to see your demise but we have a world to conquer. You've lost again, my friend." Ruger pointed at the wall and a beam of orange light projected from the PCU on his wrist. In seconds, a new portal appeared. Ruger looked back and taunted, "Enjoy your new home."

Billy was helpless to do anything but watch Ruger and Diomedes enter the portal. A tear fell from his cheek as he witnessed the last chance to save his friends slip away.

Diomedes paused in front of the portal and grabbed Ruger's shoulder. "Ruger, where are Seneca and Cassius? I see you have them both. I want my powers restored."

"I realize that. I'm taking you there now." Ruger cringed at the thought of being devoured by Diomedes. In the back of his mind, he wondered if he could achieve immortality on his own, using the PCU. In addition, he was concerned about whether or not he could trust Diomedes with so much power. *I'm only alive because she couldn't get to Seneca and Cassius herself. At least while she's away from the cavern, she's in a mortal state,* he thought. *Maybe I should let my captives destroy her.*

— X —

Doc stepped from the portal into the main chamber of Ruger's castle. Isaac and Spencer followed closely behind him. "What a rush! I've never felt anything like that," Doc yelled excitedly.

"This is unbelievable," replied Isaac. Spencer was amazed and could only stare in awe of the chamber around him.

"Listen. I heard something," whispered Doc. One of the doors along the wall was ajar. He approached it cautiously and slowly opened it. Brutus quickly emerged and snarled at Doc. "No one move. Stay perfectly still," ordered Doc nervously. He wasn't sure how the tiger would treat him but there was no way he would outrun it. He spotted the injured man in the room and looked at the tiger. Brutus galloped toward the tunnel under the landing. Isaac and Spencer scurried out of the tiger's way as it disappeared into the dark tunnel.

"Come on, fellas. I need your help," requested Doc urgently. "We have an injured man here." The men entered the room and tended to Cassius. They carried his limp body from the room and back to the portal.

"Do you know this poor guy, Doc?" asked Spencer.

"No, but he's probably one of Billy's friends. Let's get him through the portal. Maybe Ronnie can take him back to the compound." Doc hoped that Seamus and Sam still had control of the area around the portal as he led Isaac, Spencer, and Cassius back through it. Although Cassius was reduced to bare bones, he was still a big man to carry. Despite his size, though, they managed to get him through the portal.

Seamus spotted them and shouted, "Come on, Sam! The boys are returning and someone's hurt."

Doc asked anxiously, "Where are the dragons? We need to get this guy back to the compound immediately."

"They're scouting overhead," answered Sam. "I'll hail one of them."

Nigel looked down from his dragon and saw Sam wave to him. He veered the dragon into a slow descent and landed nearby. John and Ronnie followed him on their dragons to see what the commotion was about.

Sam informed them, "Doc's got an injured man. One of you needs to take him back to the compound for medical attention."

Nigel volunteered, "I'll do it. Ronnie and John should stay here."

"We need to give the dragons a break," Ronnie reminded them.

"Nigel, can you check on Randy when you get back there. Then let your dragon rest for the evening."

"Of course."

"There's no sign of the minions," said John. "I think we can give the other dragons a break, too."

As Penny sipped water from a flask, Maggie kept an arm around her for support.

"Are you okay, Penny?"

"I feel a little better. Did Doc find them yet?"

"No. They brought back a stranger who's badly injured. They're going back in again."

Penny pushed Maggie's arm away and got up. "I need to go with them, Maggie. It's important."

"Wait a minute, I'll call Doc over. You can talk to him." Penny sat down on the ground again and waited impatiently.

Maggie informed Doc, "Penny's adamant about going with you."

"Let me talk to her." When Doc returned, he knelt down in front of Penny and placed his hand on her shoulder. "How are you feeling, Penny?"

"I'm fine. I'm going with you, so don't try and talk me out of it."

"Can you tell me what happened in there?"

"There's no time. If I go with you, I think I can find Seneca and Xerxes."

"Penny, you've got to slow down. You're exhausted."

"I'm feeling better. Let's go." Penny got up and walked toward the portal.

Doc frowned at Maggie and said, "I guess she's going." They pursued Penny to the portal.

Penny couldn't help thinking about her relationship with Seneca and how it enhanced her strengths and her senses. She still didn't understand all the changes but she was learning quickly. Her stamina grew and her strength returned.

"Do you know who the injured man is with Nigel?" asked Maggie.

Penny approached the dragon and examined the stranger. "I think that's Cassius, Seneca's brother. I never met him but Seneca told me about him."

Ronnie approached them and interrupted, "I'm going with you, too. You'll probably have to fight your way back and everything out here is secure. If anything happens, the dragons will take care of business."

"Very well, then. Let's get going," said Doc.

Maggie and Penny anxiously approached the portal. Doc grabbed Maggie by the arm and ordered, "Maggie, you stay put."

"No way! I'm going too."

Doc rolled his eyes and muttered, "Doesn't anybody ever listen to me?"

"Stop it, Doc. You're acting childish," chided Maggie.

Doc shook his head disgustedly and muttered, "I can't win with these people."

They passed through the portal and arrived inside the castle. Maggie and Ronnie stared in awe at the chamber around them. Ronnie placed her hand on the wall and felt the hard black stone. "This is amazing. It resembles an eleventh century castle."

"I'm sure it's equipped with dungeons as well," quipped Doc. "So, keep your eyes open."

They surveyed the hallways at either end of the chamber and the landing above them. "Okay, Penny, which way?" asked Doc.

"Up these stairs."

They ascended the ebon stone stairs and followed the tunnel until they reached a hallway. Doc was awed by everything he saw in Ruger's castle. He couldn't get over the architecture used on the walls. He admired the stone carvings of creatures he never imagined before. Maggie was intrigued at the beauty of the red carpet in the hallway and even more impressed by the burgundy drapes at the end. Ronnie and Penny drew their swords and focused on the room at the end of the hallway. Isaac and Spencer carefully guarded the rear.

Doc and Maggie walked between them like excited tourists. Ronnie and Penny reached the end of the hallway first and paused outside the chamber. There was a single curtain in the doorway. Another lay on the ground, torn to shreds. It was dimly lit by a single torch on the wall.

Penny held her hand out for Ronnie to wait. She cautiously entered the room and was horrified by the two vine-covered figures that were Seneca and Xerxes. "Ronnie, look at this!" she shouted.

Penny tried to use her telepathy to communicate with Seneca. After several attempts, Seneca responded weakly, "Penny, there's another portal in the room. You've got to help Billy. He followed Ruger through it."

"Where is the portal? I can't see it." Penny asked frantically.

"Look in the corner next to the door. It's there. You'll feel it."

"How can I help you?" Penny asked with tear-streaked cheeks.

"You can't. Just go before it's too late."

Doc and Maggie entered the room. They saw Penny staring at the vine-covered figures with Ronnie by her side. "What are you doing, Penny?" asked Doc curiously.

Penny replied sadly, "Seneca and Xerxes are under the vines. They're bound by Ruger's magic."

"That's absurd."

"Is that what you call it?" she said sarcastically. Penny searched the walls by the corner. She reached her hands out carefully and felt for anything unusual. Suddenly, she felt the tingle of a portal. "Here it is! It's the other portal! Ruger's cloaked it with his magic." No one understood what she was babbling about, but when Penny stepped toward the wall, she disappeared.

"What are we waiting for? Follow her," urged Maggie. Doc was stunned at this latest feat and hesitated.

Ronnie shrugged her shoulders and said, "Why not?" She entered the portal.

"Robert, this is one of those times you have to think outside the box. Now come on."

They followed Penny through the invisible portal. It was smaller than the other portal. Doc couldn't grasp the reality of passing through a portal into another world and grew irritated when Maggie nudged him from behind. "Maggie, would you please stop."

"Oh, Doc. You're such a stick in the mud."

Doc grumbled aloud to himself, "Don't they ever stop?"

When Penny stepped out of the mist, she froze with fright. The Neanderthals raced in large numbers from the fire and fled into the tunnels leading up to the surface. Doc and Maggie stepped out behind her and clutched at each other in fear.

"What the hell are we doing here?" uttered Penny, baffled.

Ronnie exited next and drew her sword to do battle. "Hold on. They're fleeing from something," said Doc.

"Why are they running out of the fire? I don't understand it," questioned Maggie.

When the last Neanderthal passed them, Penny went to the fire and carefully placed her hand in it. "It's an illusion! This must be a passage into another area."

"I'm not walking into any fire," said Isaac nervously. "This is insane!" Penny ignored him and passed through the fire. Ronnie tested the fire with her hand and followed.

"Why don't Spence and me wait here until you come back?" suggested Isaac.

"It's your choice," said Doc.

Maggie took her husband's hand and they disappeared into the fire. She enjoyed the adventure much more than her husband. "What's wrong, Doc? I thought you liked discovering the unknown."

"I do, but this isn't real. It's …"

Maggie kidded, "It's outside the box, Doc."

"Maggie, I never thought I'd see the day when you ran the show, especially in an environment like this."

Penny and Ronnie hurried through the tunnel. Penny used her telepathy to reach out to Billy but felt nothing. She grew fearful that he might be dead.

"Are you sure you know where you're going?" asked Ronnie.

"They had to come this way. There's no other way out of here."

Doc and Maggie caught up to the girls. They sensed Penny was growing frantic.

"What's wrong, Penny?" asked Maggie.

"Nothing. Nothing at all. That's the problem."

"Come on, Honey," urged Maggie. "We've come too far to stop."

"There's a light up ahead," Penny said, hopeful that it meant something.

"Why are we going in there?" asked Doc apprehensively. "Something scared the daylights out of those Neanderthals and if we were smart, we'd get out of here, too."

Maggie ignored him and forged ahead with Penny and Ronnie. They spotted the chamber ahead of them. "We've reached the end of the tunnel," said Penny nervously.

Doc mumbled sarcastically, "That's really great. I'm so happy."

Penny walked through another portal and entered Billy's chamber. She saw the image in the mist of Seneca and Xerxes still projected against the wall. Then she saw Billy encased in the bubble. She rushed at the bubble and banged the sides but with no success.

Billy's heart leaped when he saw Penny enter the room but he couldn't respond to her. He tried telepathy and eye movement but he was incapable of doing anything from within. His body was frozen in the transparent material. He felt nothing but a cold numbness about him.

Penny punched at the bubble repeatedly before erupting into tears. She leaned her face against the bubble. "Billy, please say something. Tell me what to do," she pleaded.

Maggie tried to comfort her but to no avail. Doc looked around the room for something to strike the bubble with. He spotted the sphere on the table and thought, *Perhaps the sphere controls the bubble.* Doc placed his hand on the tiny valve and rotated it. The glow around them flickered and changed shades. He tweaked the valve and the glow receded. When he thought about what consequences his actions might cause to the portals, he returned the valve to its original position.

Penny recalled the good times she and Billy had. She thought about what Ruger did to Seneca and Xerxes. Everything rushed through her mind at once. "Ruger, you son of a bitch!" she screamed. Penny pounded harder on the bubble. Maggie tried to stop her but she pushed her away.

"He can't have Billy! He can't have him!" sobbed Penny. She tried to focus on Seneca and Xerxes for help.

"Please help me. We've got to break the spell on Billy. Please Seneca. Please, Xerxes."

Billy's heart broke as he watched helplessly. He felt a strange sensation around his body and his eye twitched. *Somehow, the bubble is weakening! Maybe Penny can break the spell,* Billy thought. He focused his telepathic power on Penny's fists. Each time she struck the bubble, it reverberated more. He struggled desperately but it was futile.

Seneca and Xerxes felt the rippling effect of Penny and Billy's concentration. They focused on the bubble as well, although at a distance, but their condition limited the impact of their telepathy. The room grew bright and a large orange portal flashed in front of them. Ruger and Diomedes stumbled from the portal and fell to the ground.

"It's time to get out of here, now!" Doc exclaimed and grabbed Maggie's hand.

"What did you do, Doc?"

"I don't know!"

"Come on, Penny!" shouted Maggie. "We've got to go before it's too late!"

"I'm not leaving Billy!"

"I'm not leaving until Billy's free, either," said Ronnie adamantly. Doc pulled Maggie with him into the tunnel.

Ronnie drew her sword and prepared to fight. She advised Penny, "If you know any tricks, you'd better use them now. I don't know how long

I can stop them." Penny huddled against the bubble and sobbed. Ronnie tarried with Diomedes and kept her away from Penny.

"You've interfered for the last time. Now you'll all die!" bellowed Ruger.

Diomedes swatted Ronnie's sword from her and opened her chest plates. Four tentacles slithered hungrily across the floor and grabbed Ronnie's legs. She fell backwards as she tried to get free. Two more tentacles emerged from Diomedes chest and snagged Ronnie's arms. They pulled her across the stone floor toward the mouth in Diomedes' chest.

Penny screamed in horror as she watched helplessly. She pounded again on the bubble and begged, "Billy, please help us! Please!" Billy was mortified by Diomedes' cavity. He became enraged by his captivity until a surge of energy grew inside him. He tried with all his might to bust free from the bubble. Ronnie's legs were nearly inside of Diomedes as she lay on her back. She swung her sword desperately but couldn't hit the tentacles.

Penny leaned against the bubble and cried, "Please, Billy! I need you. Please help us."

A bright flash filled the room and a large bang shook the chamber. The bubble, which held Billy captive, exploded into a cloud of white smoke. Diomedes tumbled from the impact and lay dazed. Ruger fell against the wall and slid to the ground, stunned from the impact.

Ronnie struggled to free herself from the tentacles but they continued to pull her into Diomedes' chest cavity. Billy emerged from the smoke with his sword drawn. Diomedes looked up long enough to see the flash of Billy's sword crash down on her skull. She lay quivering on the ground with her skull split open. A thick, yellow fluid seeped from the wound and released a nauseating stench. Her breathing became weak, irregular gasps.

Billy struck at the tentacles and cut Ronnie free. The mouth quivered while a forked tongue crept across the floor in search of prey. He struck with his sword again and cut the tongue off. More slimy fluid seeped onto the stone floor. He pulled Ronnie from Diomedes and kicked the tentacles away from them. Ronnie looked like a frightened little girl. Her eyes were teary and her face pale. "I'm so glad to see you, Billy," she blurted.

"Same here. Are you okay?"

"I am now. Where's my sword? I have some payback for these freaks."

Penny spotted the PCU on Ruger's wrist. When Ruger got to his knees, Penny dove on him and planted the hilt of her sword into his jaw.

He lay stunned by the blow. She undid the straps on the PCU and removed it from his arm. She cried out triumphantly, "I've got it!"

Diomedes struggled to her feet. She staggered and crawled toward the portal while fluid oozed from her head. "Kill her, Billy! Don't let her escape," yelled Ronnie.

"I've tried. It won't work."

"So how do we stop her?"

"There's a better way."

"I don't get it!"

"No. Trust me, Ronnie. I have a better idea," Billy responded calmly.

They watched warily as Diomedes stumbled into the orange mist and disappeared from sight. Ruger used his magic to escape again as well.

"Now what?" Penny asked.

Billy went to the sphere and turned the valve until the glow flickered and receded.

When the ball lost its illumination, a loud pop came from the portal, followed by a scream from within.

"What happened, Billy?" asked Ronnie.

"This sphere powers a network of portals," explained Billy. "When the valve is closed, the sphere loses its power and the network collapses. Anything inside the tunnel at that time is probably lost in some kind of void."

"How did you figure that out?"

"Ruger manipulated the valve on the sphere when he opened a new portal. There was a power drain until the network balanced itself. When Doc turned the valve, the network began to collapse. Ruger and Diomedes barely made it back."

"Now all we have to do is finish Ruger, right?" asked Penny.

"I hope so."

Billy looked around the room for Ruger. "Where did he go now?" He tried to locate him using his telepathy but with no success. Billy placed the sphere back on its base and adjusted the valve until the glow illuminated the chamber again.

"Get the sphere and the PCU out of here," ordered Billy. "I need Ruger's silver chest to free Seneca and Xerxes. Ruger needs the contents of the chest to protect him and it's probably the key to his magic. In fact, I'll bet he's going for it now."

"What about Seneca and Xerxes? Can we help them?" asked Penny.

"I don't know but we're gonna try. I think we have to be in the same room with them to break the spell."

Billy led his friends back to the Neanderthals' cavern. They emerged from the illusion of fire as the sound of gunfire echoed throughout the cavern. Isaac and Spencer shot repeatedly at the Neanderthals and tried valiantly to keep them back.

Billy reached his hand across the wall of the cavern in search of the invisible portal. Ronnie fired six shots at the Neanderthals and quickly took down four of them. "I've found the portal. Come on," shouted Billy. He guided each of them into the invisible portal and entered just as the Neanderthals closed on him.

When he returned to the chamber where Seneca and Xerxes were captive, he was surprised that Ruger hadn't arrived yet. He rushed to the chest and opened it. Smoke rose from the chest in a strange yellow plume but nothing happened. Billy retrieved the skull and examined it. He wasn't sure how it worked but he had to figure something out fast.

One of the Neanderthals entered the room from the portal and stalked him. Billy made eye contact with the grotesque creature and backed away.

"This one's mine, Billy!" exclaimed Ronnie.

"No!" Billy replied. "I've got to try the skull. It's the only chance for Seneca and Xerxes."

"That's crazy!"

"Get in the hallway. I don't want any of you to get hurt."

The Neanderthal drew closer to Billy. He backtracked around the table away from the creature. Penny begged him, "Please, Billy! Don't get hurt!"

Billy ordered, "Penny, get out of here now."

The creature rushed at Billy while he held the skull before him. Penny reluctantly retreated from the room. The eyes of the skull glowed red and a bright light flashed. All that remained of the creature was a smoldering mess. Billy breathed a sigh of relief. "Whew! That was easy."

Penny re-entered the chamber and asked excitedly, "How did you do that?"

"All Ruger's toys seem to work off energy and emotion. I have a theory that the skull protects the owner by generating a force equal to the force opposing it."

"You mean that if someone intends to use deadly force, it will retaliate with deadly force?"

"Exactly. Now let's try to free Seneca and Xerxes."

Seneca and Xerxes looked like two large lumps covered with the vines. Xerxes was unconscious and Seneca was about to succumb to the pain. Billy, Penny and Ronnie entered the room and were horrified by their condition. Billy held the skull out before him and imagined that he was inside of Seneca and Xerxes. Nothing happened so he moved closer and tried again. After waiting several moments, still nothing happened. Billy grew frustrated and set the skull on Seneca's lap. He held the plant-like appendage that used to be her hand. He felt heat from the skull and a hissing sound filled the air. He jumped back. The vines shivered violently and retracted from Seneca's skin. They fell harmlessly to the floor and burst into flames.

Billy placed the skull onto Xerxes lap and held his arm. The vines again shook violently, fell to the floor and burned. Seneca and Xerxes looked ashen and drained from the experience. Seneca reached out for Billy and held his hand. "I knew you'd find a way to save us," she said weakly. Penny helped Seneca from her seat and hugged her. "You did well, Penny. I'm proud of you."

"I couldn't have done it without you and Xerxes."

Xerxes awakened but his condition was much worse than Seneca's. He couldn't walk on his own and required their assistance. Billy put the skull in a brown sack and tied it to his belt. He picked up the silver chest and joined the others at the portal.

ESCAPE FROM THE CASTLE

As they crossed the black stone floor, a wisp of smoke rose from a small crack. It continued in a slow stream until it became a bright cloud. To their surprise, Ruger emerged and stood before them. "I hope you didn't think I would just let you walk out of here with my property, did you?" asked Ruger cynically.

Billy motioned for the others to get into the portal. He set the chest down behind him as Ruger ogled them. He mocked Ruger, "Game's over, Ruger."

Isaac and Spencer slipped into the portal, quickly followed by Doc and Maggie. Ruger didn't seem concerned that they departed with the sphere. He pointed defiantly at Xerxes and Seneca. "You can leave, too. Since Diomedes is gone, I no longer require your presence either." With a wave of his hand, the two were thrust into the portal.

Ronnie tried to distract Ruger with a little swordplay but he nonchalantly waved his hand again and a flash of light blinded her. She tumbled backwards and fell to the ground.

"Who's next? Is it you, wretched boy or your clumsy wench?" Ruger pointed at Penny and four vines shot from the wall and snared Penny by her wrists and ankles. The PCU fell harmlessly to the floor.

As Billy contemplated his next move, Brutus appeared from the stairs and stood beside him. Billy's confidence grew with the tiger's presence. "You'll never get away with this, Ruger," declared Billy boldly.

Ruger pointed his finger and a bolt of lightning struck the stone floor near Billy. The floor shuddered violently. A large square section of the floor crumbled and vanished into blackness, sending Billy and Brutus tumbling into the depths beneath the castle.

Ruger laughed at Penny as she screamed hysterically. "Now, I'll have the device and your soul." He greedily reached for the device but a narrow beam of light shot from a dark corner. He clutched his arm and screamed in pain. His hand was obliterated. The vines that held Penny vanished. She helped Ronnie to her feet and retreated through the portal.

Ruger greedily clutched the PCU with his remaining hand and shouted, "Who is it that has trespassed into my domain?" Four metal clad creatures emerged from the shadows near a green portal. They wore dark blue armor and stood over six-feet tall. Everything about them was robotic. Each movement by their limbs was systematic.

Ruger cursed them as he realized he left the green portal open without knowing who or what was on the other side. He waved his arms and vanished.

Ronnie and Penny dove into the portal and escaped before the robots took notice of them. Penny tumbled out of the portal on the other side and blurted hysterically, "Doc, they're coming!"

"Who's coming, Penny?"

"Killer robots from one of Ruger's portals."

"Where's Billy?"

Penny wept and muttered, "He fell through the floor. It's all my fault."

Doc quickly closed the valve on the sphere and shut down the portal.

"What are you doing? Billy's still back there!" cried Penny.

"We have to close it. If these things aren't Ruger's and he can't control them, then we can't handle them either."

Penny knelt in front of the vacant gate and banged her hands in desperation on the cold stone. "We were so close!" she sobbed. "How could this happen?"

Ronnie tried to comfort her. She said compassionately, "Don't worry. We'll get him back."

"You're just saying that."

"No, I'm not. Give me time to come up with a plan. If Billy's alive, we're going to get him back."

Penny placed her head on Ronnie's shoulder and cried. Ronnie felt as though she consoled a little girl. As much as Penny had matured since the cataclysm, she still had that little girl's character - naïve and innocent.

Penny tried to compose herself and said apologetically, "I'm sorry, Ronnie. Every time I think I have Billy back, something takes him away."

"Yes, we're going to have a talk with him about that."

"The more things that happen to us, the more I feel like our bond gets stronger. It's confusing for me but I'm starting to understand."

"God bless you, Penny. Maybe someday I'll understand."

"Haven't you ever been in love, Ronnie?"

"Once, or at least I thought I was."

"What happened?"

"I was only seventeen and he was my prince charming. Unfortunately, I was only a piece of tail to him and part of a bet. He made a public spectacle of my affection and, since then, I've always felt a desire to humiliate men at every opportunity."

"So that's what was going on with you and Randy and Billy."

"Yeah, but he surprised the both of us. He's a good guy. I didn't think there were any left."

"Thanks, Ronnie." Penny put her head down and walked away. She joined the others while Ronnie rousted the dragons for the flight back to the compound. Everyone else had already boarded the trucks and departed.

Ronnie paused, staring at the empty portal and thought about Billy and Randy. It touched her to hear that Penny was so in love with Billy. She didn't think there was any love left in the world, in the old world anyway. Then she fretted, *What if Randy and Billy are both dead?*

John's hand gently gripped her shoulder and startled her. Ronnie jumped and turned around. "John, what are you doing here?"

"I know what you're thinking, but there's nothing you could have done."

"They're like family and they could be dead or dying."

"Let's go check on Randy's condition. Then we'll decide whether or not we can do something about Billy. What about you?"

Ronnie asked curiously, "What about me?"

John looked into Ronnie's eyes and kissed her. They held each other tightly. She paused and sighed contentedly as if a weight had been lifted from her back. John asked, "Are you okay?"

"I needed that." Ronnie placed her arms around him and kissed him again. She remembered the young girl inside her that existed before that horrible day at school. She felt a ray of hope inside and it felt good. Together they flew back to the compound on her dragon.

When they arrived at the post office, the two retreated to her room. Ronnie waited years for a man to earn her respect the way he had. She felt no remorse in giving herself to a warrior and a gentleman like John Murdoch.

When morning came, Ronnie went to the stream alone to wash. She wondered if she had done the right thing. When she saw John's musclebound body descending the trail toward her, she whispered confidently to herself, "Oh, yes!"

John asked, "You okay?"

"Of course. How about I meet you at breakfast?"

"Don't be late." John left her to ponder their relationship.

Later that morning, Ronnie went to the room that they used as a medical facility and met the doctor. "How is Randy?"

"She has a concussion, a broken right hip and a fractured right leg. She has internal bleeding as well. You know, she's lost a lot of blood," explained the doctor.

"But will she make it?"

"I don't know."

The doctor left her alone with Randy. She noticed Penny tending to Jarret. He was unconscious as well. Ronnie felt bad for Jarret. He was starting to come around and she developed a soft spot for him. "What's the word on the kid?" she asked.

"The poison put him in a coma and the doctors don't have a good prognosis for him to recover," said Penny sadly. "How about Randy?"

Ronnie choked up and said tearfully, "She's lost a lot of blood and she's had a head trauma. She's lucky to be alive this long."

"I'm sorry, Ronnie."

"Yeah, we all are." Ronnie stared at Randy's face, broken-hearted. She looked so helpless, lying there with an IV in her arm and a makeshift caste on her leg. *How could this happen?* she thought. *Randy's so strong and fierce?* Ronnie fell to her knees and hugged Randy. Tears flowed down her cheeks. When she regained her composure, she held Randy's hand and pleaded, "Come back to me, Randy, please."

Seneca entered the room and saw Ronnie with Randy. A short distance away from her, Cassius lay on a cot. She knelt by him and placed her head on his chest. She listened to his faint heartbeat and dreamed about their childhood. Tears streamed down her cheek and she wondered if Cassius would ever recover. Ronnie interrupted Seneca's meditation and offered condolences. "I'm sorry about your brother. I guess we're both hurting right now for friends and family."

"Thanks. It's been a rough time," Seneca replied somberly.

"We never really had the opportunity to talk before."

"This nightmare has made friendships difficult."

"Where are you from, Seneca? You don't look like someone from my world."

"I'm a Firenghi, a shape-shifter."

Penny interrupted and hugged Seneca. "What happens next, for us Seneca?"

"Cassius is dying. I must take him back to our people where he can die with dignity."

"Will you be back?

"I don't know. With Billy gone and Cassius in his condition, I don't know what will happen."

"There's always a place in my heart for you. I'm going to have a hard time without you and Billy." Seneca kissed Penny's cheek and promised, "We'll be together again."

Seneca showed amazing strength as she lifted Cassius in her arms. She carried him from the building and disappeared into the forest. Her grief made farewells difficult.

"I wish I had gotten to know her while she was here. She's a rare person," remarked Ronnie.

"Yes, she is. I'm going to miss her," said Penny sadly.

Seamus entered the room and was surprised to find both of the girls there. "I stopped by to check on Randy. How is she?"

"Not good," answered Ronnie.

"Would it be okay to spend a few minutes alone with her?"

"Sure. We're on the way out."

Seamus admired Randy and felt much admiration for her. He ran his hand through her auburn hair and kissed her cheek. After a short prayer, he whispered into her ear, "If you make it through this, I'm going to show you how much I really care about you. There's so much I want to share with you."

Xerxes sat alone on a log behind the post office. He was distraught over how close they came to escaping with the PCU and the sphere. He decided that as soon as he regained his strength, he was going back through the portal. They would power it up, even if for only a few moments, to make the trip back to Ruger's castle. If necessary, he would take the sphere with him. He pondered if the Council of Guardians would send help, unless they were ignorant as to what was happening here. He held his head in his palms and concluded, "There must be a way to get the PCU back from Ruger. I must go back there and find him."

Penny confronted Doc as he studied the sphere. "You're not taking the sphere with you to the observatory, are you?"

"Dr. Miller and I are going to study it and see how it works."

"And what about Billy?"

"He's gone, Penny. You saw it yourself."

"Yes, but we have to be sure."

"If we open that portal, who knows what will come forth from it. If Ruger was frightened of those things you saw, then we should be, too."

"Doc, it's not your sphere. It belongs to Xerxes. It should be his decision."

"Penny, this is a major discovery. This could change everything as we know it."

"Everything has already changed as we know it. If there's ever a chance of going back to our world, Xerxes will know how, not you."

Maggie sauntered over and asked, "What's all the noise about? Is this about Billy's disappearance?"

"It's nothing dear. I was just trying to explain something to Penny and she wasn't buying it."

"It's about the sphere, isn't it?"

"Yes, it is. So what?"

"Doc, you don't have any right to that sphere. It doesn't belong to you."

"But Maggie, you don't understand."

"Robert, you had better think about what you're doing. I'm only going to warn you once."

"But …"
Maggie walked away angrily from Doc.

— ⧗ —

Billy and Brutus floundered in the cold water for hours before they regained their balance. The water was only six feet deep but everything was enveloped in darkness. Billy dove to the stream's bottom and retrieved the silver chest. With only the current to guide him, he waded blindly through the water. He could feel the deadly grip of cold penetrating his bones. If he didn't get out of the water soon, hypothermia would surely finish him off. Billy fretted over Penny. He knew the others escaped, but what about her. What would Ruger do to her? Somehow, his desire for vengeance against Ruger invigorated him.

Billy heard Brutus splashing ahead of him but he couldn't tell what the saber-toothed tiger was doing. When he couldn't think anymore, he stumbled and fell underwater. It didn't matter anymore to him. He was near the bottom and it felt so peaceful that even the cold faded away. His hands released the silver chest and he drifted away with the current. *I'm tired now*, was his last thought.

— ⧗ —

Evening came without incident and the post office was quiet. Penny sat by the fire thinking about Billy's disappearance and whether or not she'd ever see him again. Ronnie joined her and sat quietly. The warm fire crackled and shot sparks up into the starry night sky. Maggie watched from a distance and shared the hurt that the girls experienced. The tragic events that befell Randy, Jarret, and Billy were hard to believe. Maggie never believed that any one of them would ever be hurt or killed. They always had an answer for everything and that gave her the courage to carry on in this new world. But now it was her turn to give them courage.

Doc slept peacefully on the quilt. He wasn't used to so much excitement and he still couldn't accept the supernatural events he witnessed earlier. Maggie saw the sphere on the floor nearby. She knew that Doc wanted to take the sphere to the observatory for analysis, but she also knew that it wasn't his to take. He'd be upset when he found out she took it but he'd have to get over it. Someday he'll understand why she did it.

Maggie carried the dull gray sphere, which was rather light for all the power it was said to have. With the valve closed, depriving the sphere of oxygen, the ball had none of its glowing radiance. When she returned to the campfire, she saw Xerxes and John with the girls. She approached Xerxes and handed him the sphere. "I believe this is yours."

Penny asked, "What are you doing, Maggie? Doc's going to be livid!"

"Doc's wrong. He'll get over it."

Xerxes thanked her for the sphere. "It's necessary for me to have the sphere to continue my mission," he explained.

"Could you tell us about your mission and where you're from?" asked Penny.

"I guess this is as good a time as any."

"We've got lots of that," quipped Ronnie.

"First of all, I am from the Council of Guardians. We're from another part of the universe and our responsibility is to protect the family of human races evolved from the parent race. We took an oath about four thousand years ago to protect each race from the other and from alien races."

"What alien races are we talking about? Are they here today?" asked John.

"No, they are from other star systems and dimensions. Your world has not seen any of them yet, although I fear that Ruger's blunders may change that."

"Is our old world destroyed?" asked Maggie.

"No, it still exists. It's just missing a few pieces."

"Can you undo everything that's done if we retrieve the PCU?" asked Penny anxiously.

"I don't know. It may be possible but it depends how much damage Ruger has done to the network and how much imbalance he has created to the rest of the universe."

"The rest of the universe!" exclaimed John.

"Yes, your race has spawned from a parent race that has scattered clans all over the universe, similar to a group of tribes that departs in different directions."

After a brief pause, he continued, "We, at the Council, set up a network of passages that allows us access to each of the clans of mankind. Our primary assignment is to watch for trouble and intervene when necessary."

"Have you ever intervened on our planet before?" asked Ronnie curiously.

"Yes, on several occasions. Unfortunately, your particular clan is more violent than the other races. Throughout your short history, you have been on the verge of annihilating each other on numerous occasions through war. I don't believe your race is bad, just severely misguided."

"What evidence is there of your intervention?" inquired Maggie.

"We prefer to be discrete about our presence, but at times we have had to bring in sky crafts to carry out our intervention."

Maggie's interest was piqued. "Are these sky craft like flying saucers?"

"Well, we try to imitate your current sky crafts with a variety of lights and we prefer to appear at night to shroud our presence. Our craft can assume a variety of shapes and sizes."

Ronnie wondered how Ruger became involved in the scheme of things. Even more so, she found it harder to believe that such a family tree for man really existed. "So, Xerxes, you're saying that there are other people like us throughout the universe?" she asked.

"Yes. Each of the clans evolved differently, based on their habitats. If you're wondering about me, I am from one of those races, and I am related to you through the parent race."

"But how can that be?" replied John skeptically. "It doesn't fit in with our records of time. We have the Bible and other books of ancient history that mention nothing of this."

"Some of it does. Your interpretations of historical records are based only on what you understand, not on real events."

"Can you prove it?"

"Do you think Noah really built an ark big enough for a menagerie? From time to time, we provided helpful information to guide your race in the right direction."

"Can you give us an example of what kind of information?" asked Maggie.

"Ah, always the skeptic. You must be a woman of science," replied Xerxes with a chuckle.

"Of course, I am," said Maggie proudly.

"A few thousand years ago, my ancestors provided mathematical theorems and formulae to peoples you called Egyptians and Sumerians. We sent some of our people to teach them how to construct objects using this math. We took a simple object like a pyramid to demonstrate mathematical principles that were new to them. To convince them that this new math was a valuable tool, we used the idea of a pyramid having chambers within. They used these chambers as tombs for their leaders."

Penny changed the subject and asked, "Can we go back for the PCU again and find Billy?"

"Yes, we can. The robots you saw in Ruger's castle are going to be a problem, though. They are called Dracor and are a very dangerous species. We have had trouble with them for some time. They are destructive and difficult to kill. It appears that only four of them came through the portal and only because Ruger left it open. We'll have to find a way to dispose of them."

"So, how did Ruger and his demon girlfriend fit into all of this?" inquired Ronnie.

"Diomedes is a witch and was once a powerful Queen from Orion-4, a star in the seventh sector. She had the desire to rule all of the worlds where mankind existed. She knew about the network and how to use it but she didn't have access to it. Later, she traveled to an alien planet and consorted with an Andoran creature. She would bear a child for this creature to evolve a more intelligent bloodline if he would help her obtain certain powers, including the PCU and the sphere. The consequence of her mating with the alien creature is what you saw. Diomedes involuntarily transformed into a mutation of one of the creatures to accommodate the offspring."

"What does this have to do with you?"

"My ancestors discovered the plot and kidnapped the offspring after the birth. Diomedes was lured, using the offspring, into a cell created by energy fields and magic from Firenghian wizards to ensure she never escaped. The offspring were disposed of. As we understand it, she needs the deaths and blood of the entire royal family responsible for her imprisonment to regain her human form and immortality. Then she would exact her revenge in the process."

"Great Mother in heaven. What a diabolical plot," uttered John.

"So where does Ruger enter the story?" asked Penny.

"Ruger was at war with the other wizards in his kingdom. He was obsessed with greed and sought to conquer the wizards. When the tide of the war turned against him, he extracted help from the supernatural. During one of his rituals, Diomedes heard his pleas. She knew she could use him to help her escape her prison. She projected herself into his thoughts in her human form, then provided him with the whereabouts of the PCUs and the spheres that we used to travel through time, dimensions, and space. She also tricked him into transporting her cell to his castle where she could provide further assistance until her release.

Ruger was shocked, however, when he saw her demonic form instead of the lovely woman portrayed in his dreams. She promised him immortality if he could free her. What he didn't realize is that he would have to mate with her to achieve this immortality. At that point, she would probably kill him anyway. I don't believe she wishes to share her gift with any mortal, especially a wizard who might threaten her reign later."

"Something must have transpired between Diomedes and Ruger that he assumed such a grotesque shape," suggested Maggie.

"We believe that he and his followers had second thoughts about helping her and she somehow induced a curse on them to force their loyalty. Diomedes revealed to Ruger the location of an invisible portal near his kingdom. He was able to access the portal and enter the chamber of the Council of Guardians. He killed a friend of mine and escaped with a sphere and a PCU."

"Aren't these things kept secured?" asked Ronnie. "It seems that as important as they are, you would want to protect them."

Xerxes looked down, embarrassed, and then continued, "Each of the guardians wears a PCU on his or her arm. The chamber is host to fifteen spheres; each empowers a device and, when in unison with the other spheres, provides enough power to manipulate large quantities of matter through time and space. Unfortunately, he wasn't familiar with the use of the PCU. As a result, some of your areas were projected into this world. Other masses have been displaced as well but are in areas far away from here. In some cases, whole planets were displaced."

"These 'other masses', are they from different times?" asked John.

"Yes, but some are from other planets and some are from other dimensions. If we were to search other areas of this planet, we would find some strange and unusual life forms. Ruger wasn't able to execute his plan for ridding himself of his enemies, and now he cannot distort any more landmasses. Unfortunately, he's seeking other ways of disposing of his enemies."

"What if we were to go back and find these wizards?" asked Penny.

"Perhaps they could help us and maybe they know where Billy's at, too."

"It would be too risky. They might suspect us as spies for Ruger. If we had no other recourse, it could become a viable option. Would any of you be willing to return with me to finish this?"

"That's why we're meeting here; to discuss going back to the castle and finishing what we started," said Ronnie.

"I can't go and leave Robert but I fear that if he came, he would be a distraction," said Maggie. "He is a science-minded person. If he can't explain things with facts, he can't accept them as reality. I'll stay here and inform him of the purpose of the mission. Perhaps we can be of help from this side of the portal."

"You could take care of the sphere for us. Open it for us to enter and close it after we've had time to cross over. Then, tomorrow night, you'll open the portal at midnight. If we have succeeded, we'll all return. If not, we'll try once more the following night only. Time is critical and we don't want any more foreign creatures crossing over. We have enough to worry about with Ruger's blunders."

"When do you want to leave?" asked Ronnie anxiously.

"I think nightfall would be best. We can use the darkness to provide cover for us."

"I'll talk to Sam. I'm sure we can count on him to make sure nothing comes through the portal other than you."

"Good. Then we'll leave at sunset," Xerxes announced.

The five split up and prepared for another trip to Ruger's castle. They knew this was their last shot at the wizard and, if they failed, it could cost them their lives.

CHAPTER 13

CHEATING DEATH

Billy dreamed he was at his mother's house for Christmas Eve. He sat on the red, velour sofa in front of the fireplace and watched the flames. Each blue and yellow flame licked at the logs stacked neatly on the black iron rack.

It was early and the relatives hadn't arrived yet. The smell of fresh baked apple pie filled the air and the flashing Christmas lights on the beautifully decorated Spruce tree completed the mood. It was a matter of time before either Aunt Madge or Billy's mother would ask the usual question, "Billy, when are you going to find a nice girl and settle down? Christmas is for the children and you are getting older. Soon you'll miss your chance for a family."

Billy wasn't intimidated this year. "I told you, she'll be here soon," he said confidently.

This year was going to be different. He could hear the Volkswagen sputter into the driveway now. "Do I look alright, darling?" his mother asked nervously.

"Relax mom. She's different than the others," Billy said calmly.

Suddenly, he tried to remember what he was talking about. *What others? Who's coming?* His thoughts distorted and he became unsettled as he tried to remember what was happening. As if on cue, he slid back into the dream.

The doorbell rang and his mother rushed to the door. She paused to fix her hair one more time. Billy waited anxiously behind her for Penny to appear. When his mother opened the door, Billy's dream came to a horrible end.

Ruger stood in the doorway, laughing at him. "Well, foolish boy! It looks like Penny isn't going to make it. She's all tied up. Imagine that. And this is mom, I presume." Ruger grabbed Billy's mother by the throat and the tube-like appendages shot from his mouth into her nasal passages.

Billy screamed as loud as his lungs would let him. When he opened his eyes, he was wrapped in a wool blanket and surrounded by strangers. "Where am I?" he cried out.

A tall man wearing a dark robe asked, "Are you well enough to stand. You should eat something."

"How did I get here?" Billy asked.

The man explained, "A tiger dragged you out of the cave. When it saw us, it released you and disappeared into the forest. We pulled you out of the water."

"How long have I been here?"

"Two days. We were worried that you would never come out of your sleep. Sometimes people lose part of their mind when they take the sleep of the dead and then wake up."

Another man in a gray robe asked, "Who are you and how is it that you fell into this particular stream?"

"Who are you people?" Billy asked defensively.

The man wearing the cloak extended his hand to Billy and helped him to his feet. "We are simple folk, fighting for our freedom."

Billy teetered and grabbed onto the man's arm for support. "Who are you fighting against?"

"An evil one named Ruger. He has violated the sanctity of our land and destroyed most of our families. He has called upon evil to vanquish us, but we will not surrender."

"I am Shoran from the region of Redfern," the first man informed him. "This is Tybis, our leader from the region of Sarcasson," explained the man in gray.

Billy froze when he heard 'Sarcasson'. "Is that the same Sarcasson where King Cassius ruled?"

The man's eyes lit up with hope. "Yes! How do you know of him?"

"He and his sister, Seneca, are friends of mine," answered Billy.

The man asked excitedly, "Queen Seneca was with him, too?"

"Yes. Together, we hunted Ruger. Unfortunately, Cassius was captured and tortured. I rescued him and my friends took him back to our camp where our doctors can help him."

"And what of Queen Seneca?"

"She escaped into the portal. My tiger, Brutus, and I fell through a hole in the castle floor, courtesy of Ruger. My friend, Penny, recovered a special device from Ruger but was captured before she could escape," Billy explained. "I have to go back and rescue her."

"What is this device that you speak of?"

"Ruger has stolen a device and a powerful sphere that enables him to travel through time and space. He screwed things up and that's how my friends wound up here in your realm."

Shoran replied, "So that's what he's been up to. We suspected he was trying to summon a demon to slay us."

"Oh, he did that, too. She needed the blood and lives of Cassius and Seneca to recover her powers and escape her prison. Ruger was able to transport her to his castle."

Shoran asked, "What do we do now, Tybis? He's already summoned a demon!"

Billy interjected, "Relax, guys. I think we took care of that problem. The demon's name was Diomedes." The men gasped in horror at the mention of her name.

Billy was surprised that Diomedes was so popular. "So, you know about Diomedes," he remarked.

"Yes. Are you quite sure that you've taken care of her?" inquired Tybis warily.

"When she and Ruger entered one of the portals, I turned off the sphere. The portal collapsed and only Ruger made it out."

"What about Queen Seneca?"

"She continued the search for the control device with a man named Xerxes."

A short balding man in a brown toga stepped forward and said, "I was told in a dream that a man named Xerxes would come to help us. He must be a mighty warrior."

Billy was amused and explained, "Well, not exactly. He's from another world. He knows a little magic, but his strength is in his intelligence. He knows about a lot of things from the future and the past."

The short man, whose name was Grymes, replied excitedly, "He is a seer like me! I knew it."

"Hopefully, you'll meet him and you can decide for yourself."

Tybis announced, "Enough talk! We must eat and prepare a plan for Ruger. Now that we know he's weakened, we can mount another offensive."

"I don't know about that. He seemed pretty strong to me," Billy replied apprehensively. The men dismissed his warning and led him to the campfire to eat.

Billy ate quietly and listened to the conversations of the men around him. Most of them seemed normal like him, but he noticed one particular fellow whose eyes caught his attention. The man wore a sword at his side and a black tunic, similar to the tunics worn by Seneca and Cassius. He was quite tall and his dark facial features reminded Billy of a panther. *Ah, he must be a Firhengi. I'll bet he knows Seneca.*

The man stared at Billy with a cold look in his eyes. Billy became nervous and realized that he hadn't cloaked his thoughts.

The man spoke to Billy telepathically, "So, you know a little about Firenghia, my friend. I'd be careful if I were you. I'm sure there is a side of us you don't know about."

Billy pretended that he didn't know what the man was telling him. He knew he'd have to be careful and cloak his thoughts from now on. *That must be one of Seneca's suitors. I'll probably meet more of the competition before this is over.*

Tybis joined Billy away from the crowd. "Would you care for some grog, Master Billy?"

"I'll try a little. The meat is very good."

"In our land, we take our food seriously." Tybis handed a mug to Billy. He sipped from it and smiled with satisfaction, then handed the mug back to Tybis.

"So how much do you know about us?" asked Tybis.

"Seneca and Cassius gave me a little background. Unfortunately, every time we started to discuss things, we were interrupted."

"How well do you know Seneca?"

"Pretty well, I guess. We've been through a lot."

"Has she told you anything about her throne?"

"What about it?"

"She has until her thirtieth cycle to choose a mate to sit on the throne of Firenghia. If not, the throne is abdicated and the title passed on to the next in line."

"And who might that be?"

Tybis pointed and said somberly, "That dark-skinned man over there. His name is Pantheos. Stay away from him. He's trouble."

"What problems could he have with me? We've never met."

"It's not you. It's Seneca."

"But why?"

"He and Seneca have never liked each other. He feels that he should be the rightful King of Firenghia since the remainder of Seneca's family was murdered by Ruger."

"Ah. He wants Seneca to marry him and make him King?"

"No. He wants Seneca to abdicate the throne to him. He has a mate that no one has seen yet. He has pledged his allegiance to this woman and won't reveal her identity until he's ready."

Billy pondered Tybis' revelation and inquired, "Forgive my suspicions here, but how do you know about Diomedes?"

"Years ago, Pantheos and Ruger researched some scrolls they discovered near Ruger's castle. They came across one in particular that told of Diomedes and her banishment."

"I find it interesting that Pantheos and Ruger both knew of Diomedes. Now Pantheos has this mystery woman whom no one has seen. Doesn't that strike you as funny?"

"Be careful, Master Billy. Those kinds of thoughts will get you killed unless you're cloaking them."

Billy's eyes widened with surprise. "Why would you say that?"

"Several of us suspect that you are Seneca's chosen."

"What makes you think that?"

"You appear to be a mere human but you healed from the sleep of the dead. It seems that you may have inherited some of her qualities."

"Maybe I'm just healthy," Billy kidded.

Tybis grinned and handed Billy the cup of grog. "You don't have to hide your secrets from me. We would welcome you as Seneca's chosen. We respect her and her family, but beware of Pantheos."

"Believe me, I will." Billy assured him. Tybis left him to finish his meal.

Billy thought about what Tybis had implied. If he were to wed Seneca, he would be King of Firenghia. It's not something he ever dreamed of and he knew very little of the people. He looked up at the sky and wondered, *What would mom say if she ever knew I had a shape-shifter with cat's eyes for a wife?*

Billy knew he'd have to give this a lot of thought. Seneca meant a lot to him and he wondered how much he really loved her. Unfortunately, he felt the same way about Penny as he did about Seneca. Seneca mentioned sharing him with Penny. He couldn't bring himself to have a relationship like that. He grew more confused. The fact that Tybis and his friends thought Billy might be their next king didn't make things any easier for him. Then it occurred to him that he might never see either of the girls again anyway if they didn't stop Ruger.

Billy finished the cup of grog and considered how he would get into the castle and find Ruger. The only way he would come back is with the PCU. As he walked toward the campfire, he wondered if his friends would risk looking for him. Penny saw what happened to him and surely would believe he's dead. *Ruger's not known for his charity either, so what about Penny?* he contemplated. *He might have killed her already as well.*

Billy called to Tybis, "I need a few minutes of your time."

"What is it, Master Billy."

"How have you been fighting Ruger? I'm interested in what his defenses are."

"Do you have a plan?"

"Not yet, but I will. I'm going to the castle to rescue my friend Penny. Then I have to get the device from Ruger and, if I'm lucky, I'll get through the portal to see my friends."

"You said earlier that Queen Seneca and King Cassius were with them."

"Yes, they are."

"Ruger's castle has a drawbridge as a main entrance. There are two small entrances on either side of the castle. You can access them by narrow stairs along the outer wall that are difficult to climb. The doors are made of thick oak and are locked."

"Have you ever seen these doors close up?"

"I haven't but one of my men has."

"If the door has a lock, I think I can pick it. Then I'll try to get to the drawbridge. How many men do you have?"

"Our army is at the bottom of the hill. We have about sixty-five warriors left. When we started, there were close to a thousand."

"What happened to them?"

"Ruger turned his creatures loose on us each time we got close to the castle. They kill ten of my men for every one of them that we slay."

"I'll try and assess how many of these creatures he has left. If there are too many, we'll regroup. I don't want to drop the drawbridge and have your men get slaughtered. Where do these creatures come from?"

"To the left of the drawbridge is a tunnel. I don't know where it goes but the creatures always know when we're coming."

"Interesting."

"What if you can't get through the side entrance, Billy?"

"We might need to create a diversion to lure the creatures out. Then I'll sneak in through their tunnel. Do you have any magical skills?"

"Of course, we do. We're wizards. Unfortunately, Ruger has some sort of a protective spell around the castle. Our magic can't penetrate the perimeter of the castle."

"Can you create an illusion of an army of soldiers marching toward the castle?"

"I think we can. Why?"

"If you can use an illusion to draw the creatures out, I'll enter through the tunnel."

Tybis called to one of his men, "Cyrus, you've been to the side entrance of the castle, haven't you?"

"Yes, but only once."

"Is there a key hole in the door?"

"Yes, there is."

"Maybe that's the break we're looking for," suggested Billy.

A voice startled the men from behind. "You won't get in that way."

Tybis exclaimed, "Pantheos! You startled me."

"I'm surprised you wouldn't include me in your plans. Is there a reason for such disrespect?"

"No, Billy was making a plan. I'm explaining what we've tried so far against Ruger and what his defenses were."

"Ah, so now this stranger is our field marshal, leading us into battle."

Billy didn't care for Pantheos' attitude. "So, Pantheos, why wouldn't we be able to open the lock on the door."

"It's barred from the other side."

"And how would you know that?"

"Don't try my patience."

Billy felt a chill come over his body. Pantheos used his telepathy to warn Billy, "I know about you and Seneca. I know you're cloaking your thoughts from me, too. I will deal with you in my own way. Ruger's treatment will seem mild compared to what I do to you."

Billy grew quite concerned about Pantheos' threat. He thought, *Ruger's treatment? How would he know how Ruger treated me? I smell a rat.*

Billy sent a message back to Pantheos to see his reaction. "Pantheos, I don't think you know whom you're dealing with. If you ever want to see Diomedes again, you'd best behave yourself."

Billy watched carefully, to see the reaction on Pantheos face. Pantheos looked shocked at first but then he became irate. He made no reply and cloaked his thoughts from Billy. Obviously, he hit a nerve.

Tybis warned, "He's a maniac, Billy. You'd best stay clear of him."

"That's okay. I know where something of his is locked up and if he wants it, he'll have to behave."

"I don't understand."

"In time, it'll all make sense."

"When do you want us to create this illusion for you?"

"Tonight. I have another idea and we may not have to wait that long to find out. Where did you see the tiger last?"

"Across the stream, near those trees."

"How about my brown sack? Is it still here?"

"Yes, I'll have it brought to you immediately."

"Thank you for all the help. Have someone keep an eye on the window at the top of the left tower. If you get a signal of three lights, prepare your warriors but send your illusion to the drawbridge first. Once Ruger's creatures realize the army isn't real, they'll return to their den. I'll open the drawbridge and you'll bring the real army forward. When you're inside the castle, I'll close the drawbridge to protect your flank from the creatures. I'm not sure how long this will take from the time I get in, so you might have to be patient."

"What are you going to do?"

"I'm waiting for an invitation to enter the castle. If you don't see me back here, you'll know I got in."

"You're an interesting man, Billy. For some reason, I trust you."

"I'll try not to disappoint you. Just be ready."

"If you give the signal, we'll be there."

Billy took the brown leather sack from a man named Cyrus and tied it to his belt. He disappeared into the trees and found a vantage point where he could keep an eye on Pantheos. He worried about what tricks Pantheos could use while shape-shifting and how Pantheos might avoid his detection.

The sun set and the shadows of nightfall crept across the valley. In the daylight, the mountains were beautiful, covered with dense, green forests. The snow-covered mountaintops were a bright contrast to the lush beauty below. But once the shadows moved in, the terrain took on an ominous appearance. Chilled air filtered into the camp, much to the chagrin of the men.

Billy attempted to contact Brutus with his telepathy. If Pantheos took his alter shape, Billy would need Brutus for protection. The saber- toothed tiger emerged from the trees and stood by Billy's side.

Pantheos sat alone, away from the other men. He had an aura of evil about him, with his dark complexion and high cheekbones. His eyes seemed to meet over the bridge of his nose in a narrow point. The strained look on his face indicated something was bothering him. When darkness covered the camp, Pantheos disappeared into the forest.

Billy was pleased that his plan was working. He and Brutus circled around to the area where Pantheos disappeared. Between his senses and Brutus', they easily tracked Pantheos. Confident that Pantheos went to the castle, he ascended a steep trail to the top of the plateau. Billy shivered from the cold air and moved quickly to keep warm. He could see his breath as he exhaled and recalled that the castle was somewhat warmer. Ironically, it would be a welcome feeling.

The castle sat atop the plateau and was surrounded by a moat. The water was covered with algae and had an acrid stench to it. A rotten tree trunk lay across the moat, not quite reaching the ground on the other side near the castle. Billy watched from the trees as a dark shape danced across the trunk and leaped onto the rocky shore. Pantheos was on the move.

The moon broke through the clouds, illuminating the area. The black-stoned castle, however, seemed impervious to the moon's rays and stood like a shadow in the moonlight.

Billy hustled to the edge of the forest and watched Pantheos' alter form shape creep to the rear of the castle. Under the moonlight, Billy saw that Pantheos had clearly taken on the shape of a panther. Brutus wasn't concerned by Pantheos' alter form, much to Billy's satisfaction.

There must be another entrance to the castle. Why else would Pantheos go that way? he thought.

When Billy reached the moat, he surveyed the distance between the end of the log and the shore. Getting wet wasn't a problem until he saw the outline of several large snakes across the slimy surface of the moat. Brutus dashed across the trunk and easily leaped ashore. Billy knew he wouldn't make it so he searched for something he could use as a plank. Frustration set in as he failed to find anything strong enough to support him. He slammed his fist against the bark of the tree and bit his lip to suppress a scream. The pain was excruciating and he was losing his patience.

Billy had no choice but to use a flimsy branch. He was going to make the jump now or never. Carefully, he stepped across the trunk until he could go no further. He laid the big branch across the water to the shore. After backing up, a few steps he rushed across the branch. Just as he reached the solid ground, the branch split and disappeared into the water.

"Shit! I guess I won't be going back that way," he grumbled. His heart raced as he wondered what lay ahead. He plodded across the rocky ground, jumping clear of sinkholes on several occasions. Finally, he found Brutus resting near a cluster of bushes.

"Which way, boy?" he asked. The tiger crouched low and slithered into a small gap behind the bushes at the base of the castle wall. Billy dropped to the ground and followed. The branches scraped at his face and the stones cut into his hands and knees. When he cleared the bushes, he entered the triangular opening in the castle wall.

Billy peered into the darkness and saw nothing. His eyes soon adjusted and, thanks to Seneca's traits, he could see in the dark. He crawled through a section of collapsed tunnel before pulling himself into a wider cave. When he stood up, he was thankful to walk upright. The cave's ceiling was just above his head, which meant an added caution for protruding rocks. Water dripped from several spots, making the stone floor slippery and moss-covered in places.

Billy resumed his pursuit of Pantheos and followed the tracks through the cave. Both Pantheos' and Brutus' tracks were visible on the damp floor. He followed the cave endlessly through the castle's lower levels until he entered a dungeon.

Across the floor, one set of animal tracks stopped and a man's tracks appeared. Pantheos had taken his human form. Billy saw Brutus waiting calmly at the base of a stairwell. He studied the dungeon and found numerous horrible torture mechanisms. The contraptions were covered in moss and cobwebs. Upon closer inspection, Billy saw that the moss was actually rotten human flesh. He was overcome by the rancid odor and felt nauseous. He moved on to a wooden table with arm and leg shackles hanging from the ceiling above it. Stringy, rotten pieces of meat still hung from the limbs.

Billy discovered a pit near the wall. He cautiously approached and peered down at the pit floor. There were bones littered all about the gravel floor. He wondered if this was the access to the drawbridge area. If so, then this was where Ruger's creatures dwelled. Billy reluctantly picked up a mangled arm from one of the torture contraptions and tossed it into the pit.

A dozen ostrich-like creatures sprang from the darkness and swarmed upon the limb. They fought viciously for the scant bit of rotten flesh that remained on the bone. Billy was horrified as Ruger's creatures became more frightening each time.

Brutus sat at the base of the steps with all the patience in the world. Billy wished he could be as relaxed as the big cat. He passed Brutus and ascended the long set of steps. Then he heard indistinguishable voices in the distance due to the echoes in the hallway. He drew closer and peered around the corner. Pantheos and Ruger argued inside another chamber. "How dare you come here and threaten me, Pantheos. I have my hands full with the Dracor and those meddling people. Diomedes is the least of my concerns," shouted Ruger.

"We had a deal and I expect you to keep your part of it. Now, where is Diomedes?"

"I don't know?"

"Open the portal and find her!"

"I can't. I don't have the sphere."

"What will it take to recover the sphere?"

"This Billy character has friends that escaped through one of the portals. I trapped the girl with the device but the Dracor showed up. They attacked me and she escaped. I assume she warned the others and they shut down all the portals."

"What did you do with Billy?"

"I sent him to the bottom of the castle through the floor. Why?"

"He's alive and well, you fool. Now he's a threat to my quest for the throne of Firenghia. Can't you do anything right?"

"Well, Pantheos. You're the mighty warrior. Can't you take care of him?"

"Since you're so incompetent, I'll have to."

Ruger held up a finger and paused. "On second thought, I don't want you to do anything. I think his friends will return to rescue him. They'll have to power the sphere up to do that. Maybe we just need to have a little more patience."

"I'm warning you, Ruger. If Diomedes isn't returned to me soon, I'll gut you like a rat."

"You don't know what Diomedes really is, Pantheos. Look what she did to me."

"That's because you were weak."

"But you've only seen her as a woman in your dreams. She is an evil creature."

"You will not speak of my queen like that! Speak of her with respect."

"You'll be sorry when you find out."

A flash of light followed by a loud blast sent them scurrying. Pieces of rock exploded from the wall. The four Dracor robots entered the room and fired at Ruger. Each blast from the Dracor weapons rocked the castle walls. "Ruger, use your magic!" bellowed Pantheos.

"It won't work on them. I've tried."

"I can't fight them off alone."

"Then start running, Pantheos."

CHAPTER 14

THE SIEGE

Colonel Ray Jackson entered the projection room and greeted Joe Miller. "Good afternoon, Doctor. I got your message. What's up?"

"I suppose you heard about our visitors down where Hatteras used to be."

"Yeah, I was wondering what to do about them."

"I understand that they're primitive and not the most talented at armed conflict," Miller remarked.

"So, you're telling me that guns should solve the problem," Jackson remarked confidently.

"I believe so. I would like to take some prisoners, however, for the sake of research, if you know what I mean."

"You'd like some guinea pigs to analyze."

"Correct. I also understand that our scouts have found the portal through which these things traveled."

"That's also correct. I'm sure you heard that they detected what appeared to be power fluctuations in the portal."

"Yes, Colonel, I did. We're going to take a research team with us and analyze the portal to see what makes it tick. I'd like for you and your men to deal with the neighborhood riff-raff while we perform our research. We're also bringing a valuable piece of equipment, which generates a tractor beam. By reversing the field, we may be able to hold the portal open in the event someone tries to close it on us."

"Have you tested this tractor beam?"

"Yes, and it's been very successful on smaller objects like aircraft. We've never reversed the field to repel an object, though. I'm thinking that the energy in the repulsion may be enough to keep the portal stable while we pass through it."

"We're going through the portal?"

"Yes, we are. It's going to be dangerous but the knowledge we can gain may help us find a way to return to our civilization."

"Then I guess it's worth a shot."

"We'll leave right after dinner. By morning, the portal should be ours."

"Okay, Doc. Let's meet, say 1900."

"That's fine. Thank you, Colonel." Dr. Miller pressed the button on the speakerphone and called his assistant, "Cathy, can you come in here?"

A young woman entered the office. She wore a lab coat, eyeglasses and knee-length dress. "Yes, Dr. Miller. What can I do for you?"

"We're going on a field trip this evening. You're going to handle the data collection."

"May I ask what we're researching?"

"Wormhole technology and time travel."

Cathy's eyes bulged in surprise. "What did you say?"

"You heard me. There's a portal, which leads to another world. I'm going to escort the Marines through it while you gather information on its makeup from this side. I recommend that you bring a spectrograph, Geiger counter, and any other equipment that might help analyze it. From what I see on the satellite images, the field is made up of multiple forms of energy, sound, and light frequencies that we can't identify. I want to know how to control it, create it, and even destroy it, if necessary. If we can do that, then maybe we can return to our old world, assuming it still exists."

"That's amazing! I'll need help but I'll have everything ready."

"Take any personnel that you think will be helpful to you. Tell them I authorized you to organize the team."

"When do want to leave, Dr. Miller?"

"1900 hours. Make sure you're ready."

"Yes, sir!" Cathy left the office excitedly.

— ☓ —

Penny leaned against the back of the flatbed and stared at the stars. Her previous life seemed like something that never was. She changed so much in this new life but everything was so uncertain. Every day that she survived was a blessing for her. When she noticed that one particular star twinkled, she fought to keep back her tears and cried, "Billy, if that's you up there, I miss you."

Ronnie and John approached and heard Penny. They paused a few moments to respect her privacy. John put his arm around Ronnie and squeezed her tightly. He was grateful to have her by his side. Ronnie, in turn, was happy to have someone like John to give her strength.

"Are you alright, Penny?" asked Ronnie.

"I guess I'm just wondering if Billy's alive somewhere."

"We all are. If he's alive, we'll find him and bring him back."

Xerxes and Maggie arrived and interrupted their conversation. Xerxes announced, "We've got a plan. Maggie is going to operate the sphere at designated times. Sam and his boys will protect her while we're on the other side of the portal."

"Do you expect those new creatures to pose a problem?" asked Ronnie.

"Yes, unfortunately. They're part robot and part alien. The only way I know to kill them is to smash the glass helmet that protects them."

"If we get the PCU and close their portal, will we be rid of them?" inquired Penny.

"I'm afraid not. They've surely locked in on the coordinates of the portal and will find a way to return. I think it'll take some time, though. Let's hope they're too busy chasing Ruger to bother with us."

"Where do we look for Billy?"

"If his castle is anything like ours, there should be a stream or a river underneath for drainage and sewage," suggested John. "If it was deep enough, Billy may have survived the fall and is outside the castle already. That also means we could have a hard time finding him."

"If he's alive, I don't think he'll be hard to find," kidded Ronnie.

Sam arrived with Brent and Marty accompanied by their usual cache of weapons.

"Hello, everyone. What time does the party start?" asked Sam enthusiastically.

"Right about now," answered John.

Ronnie took her usual position in the driver seat of the Expedition. Sam put the back seat down and, because of his portly figure, sat in the front passenger seat. Everyone else sat Indian style in the back of the vehicle.

As Ronnie drove them toward the portal, no one spoke at all during the ride. John snored occasionally, prompting a nudge from Penny. Maggie cradled the sphere as if it were her infant. When the Expedition could go no further, Ronnie parked it. "Showtime, people! Let's go," she announced. Ronnie was personally attached to the vehicle and at some point, she knew her gas tank would be empty and she'd have to leave it or find more gas.

John led them up the moonlit trail toward the portal. About half way to the camp, they heard a slow thumping sound. The rhythmic vibration grew louder.

"Oh, no! It's the dinosaur again," complained Ronnie.

"Let's find cover before it gets here," suggested John.

They hurried up the path until they reached the clearing in front of the portal. Xerxes waved everyone into the trees. "Slowly open the valve on the sphere," he instructed Maggie.

At first, there was only a slight flicker within it, but soon a steady blue glow emerged from it.

"You may want to cover the sphere with your sweater," he suggested. "You don't want to attract the dinosaur's attention."

Maggie heeded his warning and immediately covered the sphere with her sweater. She opened the valve a little further and the face of the gate changed shape. At first, it was blurry, but soon took on its swirling effect. The color of the portal changed from dull gray to luminous orange. "That should do it, Maggie. I think we're ready to enter."

Suddenly, two shapes appeared from the portal and stepped down from the gate. They scanned the area. "Oh, no!" exclaimed Xerxes. "It's the Dracor."

"We'll have to drive them back into the portal," John ordered. He stepped from the trees and challenged the two Dracor. "Hey, over here! I believe we have business to settle with you."

The two Dracor accepted the challenge and marched toward John. Ronnie and Penny stepped out to assist him. The three stood shoulder-to-shoulder as the Dracor spread apart. The Crocosaurus lumbered into the clearing and pounced on the closest Dracor. It chewed hungrily until it shredded the metal from the Dracor. The remaining Dracor fled back to the portal.

"Everyone into the portal, now!" shouted John.

"Stick to the plan, Maggie. We'll see you at midnight."

Maggie, Sam, Brent, and Martin stayed hidden while the beast feasted on the Dracor. Sam snickered and said, "Well, if there's anything left of it, we can inspect it."

"Why would you want to do that?" Maggie asked sarcastically.

"Simple. If we know what kind of armor they wear, it may help us find a weak spot."

Maggie waited for five minutes and closed the valve on the sphere. The glow disappeared and the portal closed. When the dinosaur finished its meal, it roared triumphantly as if to remind the world that it was king. It scanned the area one more time and vanished into the darkness. The rhythmic pulsing of the ground grew fainter until it was gone. "Let's go see what's left of that tin can," said Sam eagerly.

Maggie stayed by the portal. In the back of her mind, she worried what Doc would say when he realized that she left with the sphere. He would surely be irate with her but this was the right thing to do.

Sam interrupted her, "Are you okay, Maggie?"

"What? Oh, I'm sorry. Yes, I'm fine."

"What is the first return time?"

"Midnight. If they don't show, we'll try tomorrow night. If they still don't show, then we pack it in. They won't be coming."

"I guess your husband's going to be worried."

"Yeah, I'm sure he will. I hope I did the right thing."

Sam patted her shoulder. "You did fine. Don't worry about it."

They sat around the portal and talked for a while. The discussion centered on everything that happened regarding the portal and Xerxes. Maggie brought the men up to speed on what the portal was about. Sam and his boys didn't quite understand how the portal related to their first battle with the minions in the city. It seemed like such a long time ago.

— ✕ —

Penny emerged from the portal first, followed by Ronnie, John, and Xerxes. She spotted the Dracor fleeing into the green portal on the opposite wall. "John, that robot went into the green portal!"

"No doubt, it's going for reinforcements. I hope Maggie shuts it down as planned." Then, as if on cue, all the portals shut down.

Ronnie was relieved and said, "At least there are two less Dracor to worry about."

"That means there are two left," replied Penny.

"Are you sure?"

"Yes. I saw them come through the portal before I left."

The castle was strangely quiet and the main chamber seemed safe for the time being.

"Where do we start?" asked Ronnie.

"We have to find stairs to access the lower levels," answered John.

"I think I know where they are," said Penny anxiously. "Follow me." She led them up the steps to the landing and proceeded down the hallway. When they reached another large chamber, Penny stopped short and turned into a small vestibule. She stepped through a narrow doorway and carefully descended the cold, dark, spiral stairwell. John removed a torch from the wall and handed it to Penny. The cobwebs and slime that littered the black stone steps disgusted her. When they reached the bottom, they found three tunnels.

"What do you think, John?" asked Ronnie.

"I guess we'll pick one and see where it goes."

"How about we split up and cover all three?" Penny suggested.

"That's the only sensible way to search down here," remarked Xerxes. John was somewhat reluctant but he knew they were right. They didn't have a lot of time to waste.

"I'll go to the left," Penny announced.

"I'll take the right path," added Xerxes.

John looked at Ronnie and replied, "I guess I'll take the center path. Why don't you go with Penny? I'll be fine by myself."

"You'd better be, you big lummox."

John kissed her on the cheek and dispersed down the hall. Xerxes disappeared down the right path. Ronnie sighed and said, "I guess it's me and you, Penny. Let's go find wonder boy." The two girls moved swiftly, with only a torch to guide them. The entire length of the tunnel was covered with cobwebs and the floor thick with dust and dirt.

Ronnie cautioned Penny, "Be careful with the torch. This stuff might burn pretty quickly."

Penny replied disgustedly, "It would be an improvement."

Xerxes came to a split in the tunnel and chose the left side. He proceeded warily until he encountered a webbed wall. He burned away the sticky silk material with a torch and entered another tunnel. On either side of the tunnels were ledges with corpses on them. *These must be the catacombs*, he thought to himself. Xerxes leaned over one of the bodies for a closer inspection. The corpse's hands grabbed his throat. He gasped in horror as the corpse sat upright. Desperately, he shoved the torch at the dead creature's face. The corpse caught fire and an ear-piercing scream shattered the silence. As soon as it released its grip, Xerxes rushed back toward the split. As he raced down the tunnel, several of the corpses reached greedily for him. He swatted at them with his torch.

— X —

Penny slowed down, prompting a bump from Ronnie. "What's the matter, Penny?"

"I thought I heard something." They paused to listen for a moment.

"What did it sound like?" asked Ronnie.

"I'm not sure. It was either the wind blowing through the tunnel or something howling from far away."

"That's absurd. Let's keep going."

The second time Penny heard the sound, Ronnie heard it too. "What the hell was that?"

"I don't think that was the wind," replied Penny.

"Maybe, we're getting close."

"To what?"

"I don't know."

— ⚹ —

John followed a series of tight crevices and hazy caves. Something about the area gave him the chills. When the haze cleared, he saw a primitive table made from rocks and a slab of stone. An old pot sat on top of the slab. John wondered who in their right mind might live down there. Across from the table was a hole in the wall about four feet in diameter. He had an eerie feeling that he would meet the inhabitant soon enough. He decided that Billy couldn't be there so he retreated.

As he backed away from the hole, a woman's voice called to him, "Where are you going, stranger? It isn't polite to leave without at least greeting an old woman."

John kept backing toward the tunnel, content to ignore the voice and exit the area. He nearly reached the tunnel when a bony hand gripped his shoulder and frightened him. He turned and was mortified at the ghoulish sight before him. An old, hunch-backed woman with leaches and maggots on her body glared at him. The stringy gray hair swayed as if it were alive. The eyes were cold and blank, yet alive.

John tried to draw his sword and strike at her, but something stopped him. He wasn't sure if it was fear or magic, but he froze. "Who who are you?" he stuttered.

"I am Rena. Whom might you be?"

"I am John Murdoch. What do you want with me?"

"Why have you come here, John Murdoch?"

"I'm looking for a friend. He was dropped into the depths of the castle."

"Ah, another of Ruger's playthings."

"You haven't answered my question. What do you want with me?"

"Why do you think I want anything from you? I am just an old woman waiting to die. I am cursed to walk these tunnels until my body decomposes into dust."

"Who did this to you?" John asked sympathetically.

She tightened her grip on his shoulder and said, "Come now. You and I both know the answer to that. I could stand to eat something and slightly nourish this frail body of mine."

John knew that she was referring to him. "Is there something I can do for you?"

"So, you offer. Is it out of fear or is it pity for an old hag?"

"I will not lie to you. Yes, I fear you and pity you. It seems unjust to punish someone in a fashion such as yours. That being the case, I feel some desire to right the wrong."

"You speak from the heart. Perhaps I will spare you."

"That act of kindness would be appreciated."

"As for what you can do for me, I want Ruger. I crave his heart. That's all I want before I die."

"But what good would that do? You can't get back what he's taken away from you. It's a part of your life that you can never regain."

"How old do you think I am, stranger?"

John was clueless. "I have no idea, but I sense that you may not be as old as you appear."

"I am younger than you. I am Ruger's daughter. I tried to stop him from delving into the black arts and hurting our family and this was my punishment."

"Then I have one more reason for wanting to slay him," replied John.

"I know the one you seek. He is the wolverine."

John didn't understand what she meant. "I am looking for a man called Billy."

"Yes, he is the wolverine that I see."

John wondered if the woman was senile. "Do you know where I can find him?"

"He is closer than you think."

"But where? Can't you tell me?"

"He is closer than you think. I want Ruger or else …" The woman faded mysteriously into the haze.

John checked his shoulder to see if he was dreaming. The marks were still present from the woman's icy grip. He didn't understand what she meant about a wolverine. A cold chill caused him to shudder. He rushed through the tunnel until he reached the intersection. Only then did he stop to catch his breath and regain his composure. Without warning, Xerxes rushed from the other tunnel and collided with him. "Holy Mother above, Xerxes!" cried John. "You scared the life from my body."

"We need to keep moving!" shouted Xerxes.

"Man, you act as if you've been chased by the dead."

"Funny you should say that. Look!" John held the torch in the direction of the other tunnel and saw the corpses staggering toward them. "Quickly, this way!" he ordered.

They rushed into the third tunnel, desperate to stay ahead of the zombies. Fortunately for them, decayed bodies don't move very fast.

"Xerxes, it looks as if no one has been through these tunnels in ages. I hope Penny and Ronnie were able to find their way through this mess."

"I hope so too because we have nowhere else to go."

"I couldn't help notice that whomever Ruger captures, he either kills them or damns them."

"That, my friend, could be a gross understatement. You still don't know what he's capable of."

— X —

Penny and Ronnie reached a split in the tunnel where one path spiraled upward and the other continued straight.

"What do you think, Penny?"

"If Billy's alive, he'd be down here somewhere. If we go up, we're going to confront Ruger."

A distant howling echoed through the tunnel. "It could be a man howling like that. Maybe Billy's hurt and he's trying to attract our attention."

"But what if it's a trap?"

"This whole place is a trap. I think we should go up."

"Oh, I hope you're right, Ronnie."

"Believe me, so do I."

— X —

Billy entered the chamber and looked about. It was a dining chamber, large enough for a feast. In the middle was great oak table surrounded by twenty-four chairs, each one also carved from thick oak. Billy wondered how such heavy objects were brought up to that part of the castle. To the right, he saw the doorway where the Dracor entered the chamber. He decided his odds were better if he went that way. At least his path would be unimpeded for a short while.

When he passed through the doorway, he found another long hallway. He chose to go left and search for an entrance to the tower. At the end of the hall, he found a spiral stairway located to the rear of a vestibule. He ascended the stairs until he reached a landing at the top of the stairs. There was a small window on the right and another spiral stairway on the left. Behind the stairs was a small wooden door.

Billy peered out the window and looked across the top of the wall at the other tower. He realized that he needed to climb the next set of stairs. A small door, which led onto the ramparts, was located nearby. It was used for defending the castle in battle. The next set of stairs extended indefinitely and Billy's legs tired. When he finally reached a window at the top, he waved the torch three times. He peered out and gazed across the forest. Somewhere out there, Tybis' army waited for this signal.

Billy hustled down the stairs to the hallway. He grew anxious as he rushed through the halls to another landing. A short distance from where he stood, was the corridor to the drawbridge? Below him were large gates latched shut by pieces of timber. *What kinds of horses use a gate that big?* he pondered nervously.

Billy found a small set of stairs that led to a ledge. Mounted on the ledge was a wooden wheel with iron spokes protruding from it. He traced a cable from the wheel up to a pulley on the ceiling and out to the drawbridge itself. He climbed up on the ledge and grabbed a hold of the spokes. At first, it was difficult to rotate the wheel, but once he moved it, he discovered that it had a ratcheting device, which prevented the drawbridge from dropping to the ground on the other side of the moat. He pushed with all his strength on the wheel, until the ratchet released. Each time he moved the wheel, the drawbridge opened about a foot.

When the drawbridge was finally lowered, Billy returned to the tower and watched for Tybis' army to approach. He worried about Ruger and Pantheos. It was strange that he hadn't crossed paths with them.

Shoran pointed excitedly toward the tower and exclaimed, "The signal, Tybis. The signal!"

"Yes, I see. We must create the illusion and prepare the men." The two men returned to camp and summoned the other wizards. They assembled around the fire and chanted incantations. After the fourth repetition, a dark cloud formed and covered the valley between the wizards' camp and the castle. When it settled to the ground and cleared, an army of warriors holding torches stood in its wake. They promptly marched to the castle as a unit.

Tybis left the group and watched from a vantage point high above the valley. He studied the area intently as Ruger's watchdog creatures emerged from the tunnel near the moat. They rushed through the illusion, thrashing about fruitlessly. Eventually, the ignorant creatures realized that they were fooled and returned to the tunnel.

— X —

Dr. Miller and Colonel Jackson stepped out of the portal into Ruger's castle and surveyed the area around them. "This is phenomenal!" Colonel Jackson uttered in amazement.

"We've traveled through a wormhole into another time or another dimension. I'm not sure which," replied Dr. Miller.

One by one, the Marines exited the portal with a deer-in-the-headlights stare. They were as astonished as the Colonel was. When the last soldier arrived, Colonel Jackson ordered them to form up. He divided them into two groups and briefed them on what their mission was. His rollout was interrupted when a shuffling sound attracted his attention.

Emerging from a tunnel was a large contingent of zombies. Colonel Jackson gasped, "What the hell? Men, take up firing position! Aim for the heads, on my order." The men were horrified at the sight of dead creatures stalking them.

"This isn't right. This is evil. What are we doing here?" shouted one Marine.

Colonel Jackson ordered, "Shut up, soldier! Ready. Aim. Fire!"

The Marines fired repeatedly but the wall of zombies kept coming. Several of the rotting creatures fell as their heads exploded from the force of the gunshots. When the creatures got close, the Marines broke rank. They used their rifles like baseball bats and swung at the creatures' heads.

Dr. Miller and Colonel Jackson stood to the rear of the melee and watched in horror as the zombies overwhelmed the soldiers. The chamber was filled with horrible screams. The Marines retreated down the steps into Diomedes' former chamber.

Colonel Jackson looked concerned as he monitored the battle closely. "Stay here, Doc." Jackson drew his saber and joined in the melee. He was fearless in combating the creatures, while venting his anger for the loss of so many of his men. His fierce fighting inspired the men and they pushed the creatures back into the main chamber. Eventually, they terminated the last zombie.

He counted the remaining number of his soldiers still standing. "Thirteen out of fifty. Those sons of bitches killed thirty-seven of my men," he bellowed.

"Are you okay, Colonel?" asked Dr. Miller.

"Yes, but this was steep. We're not splitting up for the search. It's too dangerous."

"I agree, Colonel."

"Men, we're searching the upstairs. Secure the hallway and take up defensive positions."

— ⚥ —

Tybis ordered his men forward to the drawbridge. Shoran escorted him and inquired, "Do you think Billy's plan will work? I know he means well but how do we know that the creatures won't return?"

"It's the best and only shot we've got," answered Tybis. "We have to try."

When they reached the halfway point of the valley, Tybis saw that the drawbridge was down. "Let's go. We've got to get into the castle before those creatures change their mind."

The warriors lined up behind Tybis and Shoran. They followed them across the valley and into the castle. Tybis ordered two of his men to close the drawbridge behind them. They cautiously proceeded down the corridor toward a darkened courtyard. Four small torches spaced evenly apart barely gave off enough light to make a difference. On the left were gates secured with thick beams of wood.

"Wow, Tybis! What kind of animals live in a stable that big?"

"I don't want to know. Keep walking, Shoran."

One of Tybis' men stopped abruptly. "Tybis, I've stepped on something."

"What is it?"

"The block under my foot - I think it triggered something when I stepped on it."

"Don't move."

Tybis lifted a large rock and carried it to the man. "Set this onto the stone as you slide your foot off. It should hold the stone in place until you move away." Tybis ordered the others to clear the area until they figured out what the stone triggered.

"Okay, Cletus. Slowly move your foot and place the rock there."

Cletus removed his foot and placed the rock on the stone block. He breathed a sigh of relief.

"It worked, Ty …" The stone block unexpectedly popped back to its original level and the floor dropped twenty feet down leaving a pit about twelve feet square.

Tybis rushed to the edge and looked down. Cletus lay in agony with a broken leg. The bone stuck out in a gory configuration and blood spurted onto the stone floor. Two ostrich-like creatures leaped out of the darkness and tore Cletus to shreds. Tybis grew nauseous and vomited. He regained his composure and ordered his men forward.

Shoran put a hand on his shoulder and asked, "Are you alright, Tybis?"

"No, but it doesn't matter, does it?"

"I guess not."

— ☓ —

Penny and Ronnie ascended the stairs, guided only by the meager light from the torch. "Something isn't right," said Ronnie uneasily. "I have this strange feeling ..."

A deep, husky voice surprised her and said, "Like someone was behind you."

Ronnie turned around and shrieked, "Who the hell are you?"

"Keep moving or I'll gut you right here."

Ronnie drew her sword and replied boldly, "I don't think so."

The two dueled briefly but Pantheos clearly overmatched her. The stairwell was too narrow for Penny to be of any help to her. Pantheos locked swords with Ronnie and slammed her nose with the hilt. She fell unconscious to the ground, her nose broken and blood streaming onto the steps. Penny trembled with her sword in hand. Pantheos laughed at her and said, "Don't play with me, woman."

"What do you want from me?" asked Penny, trembling.

"I suggest you stow your sword before I remove both it and your hand."

Penny quickly put the sword into the scabbard. She wondered who this stranger was. Certainly, he was going to be trouble. "Get going!" he ordered. "I'll tell you what you need to do."

Pantheos shoved Penny into the upper section of the tower. She entered and saw Ruger, peering out the open window. Pantheos followed her and announced, "It's time to settle some scores, Ruger. Get out of the way."

Pantheos saw Billy at the window of the other tower. "Ruger, give me your torch."

Ruger handed the torch to him. He was curious to see what Pantheos had in mind. Pantheos laid the torch on the window ledge and used his telepathy to communicate with Billy. "I believe I have something of yours. Perhaps we can make a trade."

Billy was surprised to hear from Pantheos. He tried to ignore him and cloak his telepathic abilities, but once again, Pantheos was in his head. "Come now, Billy. You can't keep playing these games with me. Look over at the other tower and see what I have of yours."

Pantheos grabbed Penny by her ankle and belt. He dangled her from the window. She screamed hysterically as she looked down at the rocks far below. Billy was mortified when he saw her hanging perilously. "Alright, Pantheos! No more games. What do you want from me?"

"I want Diomedes back. You will open the portal and find her."

"But I can't open the portal. I don't have the sphere."

Pantheos pulled Penny inside and held her in front of him. He ran one of his pointed nails across her neck. Blood trickled from the cut he inflicted. "My, how red she bleeds. Would you like me to continue?"

Billy was frantic. "Don't hurt her Pantheos!" he pleaded telepathically. "I'm coming over. I'll think of something."

"Oh, I'm sure you will. I'll be waiting."

Pantheos shoved Penny against the wall. "Don't move, you little whore, or I'll rip your throat out." Penny lay across the cold stone floor in near hysteria. She fought to regain her composure and the fact that Billy was alive made her heart flutter briefly with joy. The possibility of Ruger or

Pantheos slaying him before her very eyes terrified her. Billy would need her help and she had to be ready.

"Make sure you open the right portal, Ruger, or else," Pantheos warned.

"You don't understand how difficult it is to operate this device."

"When Billy provides you with the power, you'd better find it. My patience is wearing thin with all of you."

Billy and Brutus reached the bottom of the stairs and paused. "I'm coming up, Pantheos. Let her go."

"Lose the tiger, now!" Pantheos ordered.

Billy patted the tiger's head and said, "Sorry Brutus, I'm on my own this time." When he ascended the stairs, he found Ronnie lying on the steps, unconscious with blood streaming from her nose. He couldn't do anything for her right now so he continued up the stairs.

"That's right, leave the woman. She'll be fine," chided Pantheos.

When Billy reached the top of the stairs, Pantheos backed off, allowing him to enter the room.

"Billy, it's really you!" Penny yelled excitedly.

Billy saw the stream of blood from Penny's neck wound and the stains on her blouse. "Your neck - are you alright?"

"It's not bad."

Billy helped her to her feet and hugged her. "I was afraid you were dead but I never gave up hope," said Penny tearfully.

Pantheos was amused by the lovers' reunion. "Does she know what you really are?" he taunted. Billy didn't know what Pantheos referred to.

Pantheos laughed cynically and taunted Billy again, "Does she know you can shape-shift or haven't you told her?"

"I don't change shape like you do, Pantheos. What do you want from me?"

"You'll help Ruger open the portal and rescue Diomedes or I will dismember your whore, piece by piece."

"If you call her that again, I'll ..." Billy drew his sword.

"You'll what? Humor me."

Billy dueled briefly with Pantheos but as he did to Ronnie earlier, Pantheos quickly separated Billy's sword from his hand. Billy retreated away from him. "Change your shape. Show her what you really are," goaded Pantheos.

"I told you; I don't change shape! I never did and I never will."

"Enough bravado!" Ruger interrupted impatiently. "Open the portal now!"

"I can't! Don't you understand that?"

With a quick stroke of his sword, Pantheos cut Billy's cheek and punched him in the face. Billy fell to the ground, stunned and bloody.

"Leave him alone," cried Penny. "I know how to open the portal."

"Tell me how!" Ruger commanded.

Penny looked at her watch. It was quarter to twelve. "Fifteen minutes. The portal will open in fifteen minutes."

"What is that to me, woman!"

"It means very soon. I'll tell you when."

"You had better be telling the truth."

Penny huddled in the corner with Billy and waited for midnight. She nuzzled against him and dreamed of a faraway place. She hoped, *Maybe someday, we'll have a chance to start over again, just like before.*

Billy's mind cleared and he felt Penny's caresses. "Penny, what did you tell them?"

"At midnight, Maggie will open the portal, but only for a few minutes. Maybe they won't find Diomedes in time."

"For our sake, they had better."

Penny checked her watch and announced, "Get ready, Ruger. It'll open anytime now."

Pantheos ordered, "Ruger, you'll go in and find her. You make sure you bring her back to me."

"Why do I have to do this?"

"Just do it, Ruger!"

Ruger pointed the control device at the wall and punched in five digits. At first, nothing happened. He grew uneasy and fidgeted. Then the portal formed. At first, it was slow to take shape, but then its swirling appearance grew and the mist became orange. Ruger reluctantly entered the portal. He stepped cautiously through the orange sands and mists.

"Diomedes, can you hear me? Where are you?"

Diomedes raspy voice screeched from somewhere in the mist. "Ruger, get me out of here!"

"Where are you?"

"Over here, you fool!"

Ruger cowered. He hoped that she was gone forever. To his left, he saw her drifting a short distance from the sands of the orange path. There was no way that he was going to risk his life for her.

Perhaps I'll tell Pantheos that she isn't here, he thought.

"Ruger! Hurry, you bumbling idiot."

"Yes, that's what I'll do. To hell with her."

Penny suggested to Pantheos, "The portal will only be open for a short while. You may want to help Ruger."

"Why, so you can escape?"

"Come on! How far do you think we'd get? We aren't stupid."

"You're right. But if you do run, I'll make sure you die slowly and painfully."

"I told you, we aren't going anywhere!" Penny said defiantly.

Pantheos glared suspiciously at them and then proceeded into the portal. He found Ruger backing toward him at the entrance. "Where are you going, Ruger? Leaving so soon?"

"No, I just don't know how we're going to reach her."

"We'll make a chain. I'll hold your ankles and you'll reach out to her."

Ruger didn't like the idea but he was caught. He had to play this out and hope for the best. Diomedes recognized Pantheos and immediately created the illusion of her former self. Pantheos only knew Diomedes' appearance before she was transformed into the horrible creature she became. He had no idea what evil he was consorting with.

"Pantheos, help me!" Diomedes pleaded.

"I'm coming, Diomedes. We'll save you." He pushed Ruger down on his stomach and grabbed his ankles. He swung him out from the path. Ruger floated effortlessly with little gravitational effect in the portal. Moored only by Pantheos' hold on his legs, he reluctantly reached for Diomedes and grabbed her clawed hands. Pantheos pulled them both back on the path.

Diomedes fell to one knee and lowered her head. Pantheos consoled her. "It's okay, my love. I'll never leave your side."

Ruger rushed out of the portal. Diomedes raised her head and pulled Pantheos' face to hers. It was then that his dream erupted into a nightmare. Her illusion faded and Pantheos was face to face with the most horrible creature he ever imagined. Tentacles emerged from Diomedes' chest and snared him. With little resistance, he was pulled into the horrible mouth that made up her chest cavity. He screamed in agony as the tentacles dragged him into the gaping mouth.

Diomedes laughed sadistically. "You're right, Pantheos, you fool. You'll always be a part of me, an inside part." She let out a blood-curdling scream as she ingested his quivering body. When the tentacles retracted into her cavity and the chest plates closed, Diomedes transformed herself into Pantheos' figure.

Billy and Penny stood by the stairs, cradled in each other's arms. Ruger paced across the floor, nervously waiting for Pantheos to return with Diomedes. Billy suspected that something wasn't right. They should have come out right behind Ruger. Pantheos form finally emerged from the portal just as it closed. He glared at the two of them with an evil leer.

"Something's happened to him. He doesn't look right," whispered Penny.

Pantheos pulled Billy from Penny and slapped him to the ground. Billy tried to get up but Pantheos kicked him down again. Ruger wondered what happened to Diomedes but he was happy that she didn't make it out of the portal. Billy became enraged and his body tensed up.

"What do we have here - a shifter!" remarked Pantheos, who then transformed into a black panther. Penny was astonished as she watched the transformation take place. She was nauseated by the sound of cracking bone and the tearing of muscle and tendon.

Billy hunched over in pain, holding his abdomen. Sweat poured over his brows and he bit into his lip so hard that blood ran down his chin. He gasped for air and convulsed as he transformed. His muscles and tendons stretched and tore more dramatically than Pantheos' did. Thick, matted hair sprouted from his skin and his body transformed.

Penny watched in awe as Billy took his alter shape – a wolverine. At first, she was frightened, but then she realized that this is what Seneca was and perhaps what she, herself, was to become. Strangely enough, Penny felt a certain pride for what Billy became.

Billy felt much anger toward Pantheos, but he didn't feel right. He felt mobile and dangerous. Then, he realized he had taken his alter shape. At first, he was afraid but he quickly adapted to the new form. He stalked the panther with a lust for killing that he never experienced before.

As Penny watched the panther's actions closely, she noticed something terrible. It had Diomedes' eyes. "Billy! The panther's eyes – they're red!"

Billy heard Penny but he was focused on his opponent. He and Pantheos stalked each other in a circle, each waiting for the first opportunity to strike at the other.

Penny yelled again, "It's not Pantheos! It's Diomedes in his form."

This time Billy heard Penny and felt a renewed confidence. He could defeat Diomedes in the form of an animal. Diomedes couldn't fight with Pantheos' skills, despite using his shape. Billy lunged at the panther and took the first swipe. His claws ripped a piece of flesh from the panther's flank. The panther spun and lunged clumsily at Billy. He sidestepped the panther's assault and poised to strike again.

Suddenly, the panther leaped at Penny. She wasn't surprised by the move and stood with her sword drawn. The panther knocked her down but she pierced its side with her sword. Her shoulders bled from the wound inflicted by the panther's claws and her chest hurt from the force of its weight.

Billy pounced quickly on top of the panther, gouging and ripping at the back of its neck. The panther rolled away from Penny and staggered to its feet. Penny was incensed by its attack on her. She transformed as Billy did. She was overcome by the excruciating pain and stumbled across the floor. Knowing what was happening made her transformation much easier to tolerate. She writhed in pain, though, for what seemed to be eternity.

Billy relentlessly attacked the panther. Unfortunately, Diomedes adapted to the new skills of the panther. She sidestepped a lunge from Billy and turned the momentum against him. Suddenly, Billy was pinned to the ground and the panther prepared to deliver a deadly blow to his throat with its fangs.

Penny completed her transformation and took the form of a snow leopard. Her new shape was long and slim with thin, but muscular limbs. Her coat was thick and white with dark spots. Penny felt the same lust for blood that Billy did. Immediately, she targeted the panther's throat and tore into the tender flesh of its neck with her teeth. She felt a strange satisfaction as she continued her attack on the panther. She wasn't sure if it was vengeance or bloodlust. Either way, it was an overpowering desire.

The panther squealed and rolled across the ground, writhing in pain. Blood gushed from the gaping hole in its neck. It staggered to the stairs, took a last look at Penny, and tumbled down the steps. It fell over Ronnie's unconscious body and came to rest at the base of the stairwell. Brutus was startled and leaped away from the dead animal in disgust.

Billy and Penny each transformed back to their human shapes. Neither one could remember much of the transformation, except for the severe spasms. When they became cognizant of their surroundings again, they both sat naked on the cold floor, gazing at each other in disbelief.

"Holy cow! That was scary." stammered Billy.

"I thought it felt kind of gratifying, don't you think?" Penny remarked coyly.

"At first, it was different, but now, I don't know. It bothers me a little bit."

"You looked kind of cute with all that hair."

"That's it? I was cute! Didn't I look vicious or mean?"

"Well, yeah, but you were cute, too."

"Well, Miss Spotted Leopard. You looked kind of cuddly yourself. Just remind me not to aggravate you. You really tore up Pantheos or Diomedes or whoever the heck that panther was."

Billy stood up and helped Penny to her feet. "Thanks, Penny. I owe you for saving my life."

"No, I owe you for saving mine, time and time again." Penny then inspected Billy's naked body and commented, "Not bad."

"While you're thinking dirty thoughts, I'm cold. Where are my clothes?" kidded Billy as he blushed. Penny laughed at him and stepped aside so he could dress. "You're looking quite perky yourself," he joked.

Now it was Penny's turn to blush. "I think we'll resume this conversation at the earliest convenient moment."

"Ooh, I like when you talk like that," Billy remarked.

Just as they put on their stretched and torn clothing, Ronnie entered the room, holding her hand across her nose. "What the hell are you two babbling about? My nose is busted."

"Where did Ruger go?" asked Penny.

"I don't know but he's running out of allies. Pantheos and Diomedes are gone and I hope it's for good this time," replied Billy.

"We've got to find him."

"What about me?" complained Ronnie.

"Hang in there," Billy urged. "We're almost through with this."

Brutus waited faithfully at the bottom of the stairs, eying the panther's carcass suspiciously. Billy descended the stairs and stroked the tiger's head. "Come on, boy. We still have some work to do." The tiger followed obediently.

John and Xerxes heard voices echo through the hallway. "Xerxes, it sounds like the girls have found Billy."

"Yes, it does. I hope they found Ruger, too."

The trio appeared from the stairwell and entered the hallway.

John immediately noticed Ronnie's swollen nose. "Ronnie, what in the world …?"

"I should have killed the bastard," Ronnie grumbled.

"I can't believe Ruger did that to you," replied John, surprised. "We'll get him yet."

"It wasn't Ruger. It was Pantheos."

"Who's Pantheos?"

"He's gone or Diomedes is gone. They are both gone. Hell, nothing is simple around here. That was the panther's carcass lying at the bottom of the steps," explained Billy.

Ronnie muttered, "That makes no sense at all. Never mind, I'm getting used to things not making sense around here."

John put an arm on Billy's shoulder. "It's good to see you again. You look like you've lost some weight or else you need some new clothes."

"Yeah, it's the clothes. They're stretched out of shape a bit."

"I see Penny has the same problem. I won't ask what happened."

"Yeah, it's better that way."

"Did you find Ruger?" asked Xerxes anxiously.

"Yes, but he escaped. He couldn't have gone far, though," replied Penny.

"Why don't we head to the main chamber," suggested Billy. "I believe we have some friends coming to join us."

Billy took Penny by the hand. She walked on his left. Brutus walked on his right. The others followed him, keeping a safe distance from Brutus.

— X —

When Tybis and his men reached the other side of the courtyard, they heard a squeal from inside a nearby doorway. Tybis sent two men to check it out. After several minutes, Tybis called out to them but there was no answer. He sent two more men to investigate the noise. They entered the doorway and disappeared as well. Once again, Tybis called out to them and again, there was no answer. This time he sent six men to investigate and again achieved the same result. His patience wore thin and he sent twelve men through the doorway. Again, there was no sign of them.

Tybis had enough. He had just lost twenty-two men without a sound. It was time to get out before any more of his men disappeared. Whatever evil lurked there had silenced a large portion of his army without a sound. "Let's get out of here! Follow me, men."

Tybis led his men through another tunnel. He waited behind them to see if they were followed. His men marched until one of them stumbled. A loud clinking sound filled the air and four pendulums, two from each wall swung across their path, slicing the first warrior into sections.

Tybis heard the screams and wondered what misfortune befell his men this time. He rushed to the front of the group and watched as the giant pendulums swung back and forth before him. Tybis estimated the gap between the giant blades by the separation between the slots in the wall. "Listen up, men. There's enough room to step between the blades, one at a time."

"How are we going to do that?" complained one man.

"I'll show you." Tybis stood in front of the path of the first blade and patiently timed its pass. He could feel his heart racing as he prepared for the first move. When he was ready, he took the first step. He almost lost his balance as he quickly planted both feet before the path of the second blade. The breeze from the blade behind him blew past the back of his neck and sent chills down his spine. When he regained his composure, he timed the pass of the second blade and took the next step. Again, he made it into a safe position. He could feel the sweat beading on his brow as he timed the third blade's pass. Again, he stepped successfully past the arc of the blade.

Tybis took a deep breath as he realized he only had one more blade to pass. He timed the pass of the blade and stepped safely across. He sighed with relief as he wiped the sweat from his forehead. "Okay, who's next?"

"I am," said Shoran confidently. He carefully stepped through the blades, just as Tybis had done. He, too, took a sigh of relief when he successfully cleared the last blade.

The next man stepped successfully past the first and second blade but froze before the path of the third. Two other men had passed behind him and were stalled between the first and second blades. Tybis tried to encourage him to make the next step, but the man lost his nerve. He ordered him to focus his attention. When the man finally took the next step, it was a horrible scene. The blade split his body, sending it in two halves into the path of the other blades. Blood splattered from each blade during the next few passes.

The other men were frantic and refused to cross. Three of Tybis' men attempted to pass the blades at once. Two of the warriors frantically made it past the first two blades but the third warrior was struck immediately. The remnants of his body against the other two, forced them into the path of the third blade. There was a moment of silence as Tybis contemplated the next move.

The silence was broken by a scream. Then, another scream pierced the air. The two Dracor caught up with Tybis' men and sliced them to pieces. Tybis was appalled as he watched the remainder of his army slaughtered by the two machine-like creatures. The warriors tried to defend themselves but their swords could not penetrate the Dracor armor. The only consolation Tybis had was that he and Shoran were safely past the blades.

"We must continue to hunt Ruger on our own," Tybis said somberly. The two men entered a long stretch of hallway and reluctantly continued their search.

— X —

Doc Smith arrived at the portal and called out for Maggie. He was startled when Sam and Brent leaped out of the bushes.

"Who's there?" shouted Sam.

"It's Doc. Where's Maggie?"

"I'm over here," Maggie answered from the side of the portal.

"Maggie, I was worried about you. Why didn't you tell me what you were doing?"

"I didn't think you'd understand."

"The others went through to look for Billy, didn't they?" he queried.

"Yes, they did. They just missed the first escape time. There is one more chance to open the portal for them. If they don't make it, then we quit and go back."

"Any problems so far?"

"Only one. That's what's left of it over there."

Doc Smith walked over to the crumpled pile of armor and analyzed the remains.

"These things are part android. Someone must have made them this way."

"They must be a very intelligent species of barbarians to construct themselves into killing machines," commented Sam.

"I wonder how far their intellect goes."

Maggie mentioned, "Thank God for the dinosaur. It handled the situation pretty easily."

"Sam, I need one of your men to escort me through the portal," requested Doc.

"Right now?"

"Yes. We're going in for some quick reconnaissance."

"Take Brent with you."

"Are you sure you know what you're doing?" asked Maggie.

"Yes, Honey. Stay here and work the sphere. Give us two hours and then open the portal."

Maggie turned the sphere's valve and watched as it began to glow. The portal formed and took on its orange shape. Doc and Brent hurried into the swirling mists. The two men reached the main chamber and were horrified at the carnage that surrounded them.

Bodies of soldiers and rotted corpses littered the ground. "What in the hell were the Marines doing in here?" exclaimed Doc.

"Don't ask me. I thought you had all the answers."

Doc saw the light from a torch at the end of the long tunnel underneath the landing and heard footsteps. "Quick, get inside the doorway, Brent."

The two men hid and waited to see who was coming. Colonel Jackson waved his men to one side of the hallway. He heard the voices coming toward them and doused the torchlight.

When Billy stepped into the hallway, Colonel Smith attempted to grab him. Brutus quickly stepped between them and glared at the Colonel. "Oh, Geez! Call him off!" Colonel Jackson screamed.

"It's okay, Brutus," said Billy calmly

"Sorry man, we didn't know who was coming. Who are you?"

"Billy Brock. These are my friends; Penny Nichols, Ronnie Vander Slice, John Murdoch and Xerxes, one name."

"Billy Brock. You wouldn't happen to be Doc Smith's Billy Brock?"

"Yes I am."

Dr. Miller came forward and asked, "Is Doc here, too?"

"No, he's not."

"How did you and your men get in here, doctor?" inquired Ronnie.

"We found a way to keep the portal from our location open."

"That was foolish," replied John. "You don't know what could pass through that portal at any time. That's why we shut them down except to pass through."

"We need to get back to the main chamber," ordered Billy.

"You know your way around here?" asked Colonel Jackson.

"Yes, I do."

"We'll follow you then."

They followed the labyrinth of hallways to the landing above the main chamber. "Wait here. I'm going after Ruger," said Billy determinedly.

"I'm going with you," insisted Penny.

"Then get a torch and come on." They descended the stairs in the middle of the hall.

Doc Smith entered the chamber and saw the Marines and Dr. Miller. "Joe Miller! What are you doing here?"

"Doc! I reversed the polarity on the tractor beam and used it to keep the portal open at Hatteras."

"It's not open now, is it?"

"Yes. Why?"

"You've got to close it! There are dangerous aliens around here in robotic armor. They accessed the castle through one of the portals and locked onto the coordinates of that portal. If they get the coordinates to Hatteras, they could invade us too. These things are dangerous and guns aren't going to stop them."

"Shit! Now what do we do?"

"Get your men out now! Shut down your tractor beam. I'll be in touch when we get out."

"You heard him, Colonel. Get the men into the portal ASAP," ordered Dr. Miller. The Marines anxiously left and the portal closed.

Billy and Penny entered another hallway at the bottom of the stairs. There were numerous doors along the left side. Penny asked, "Are you sure you know what you're doing, Billy?"

"Be serious, Penny. Does anybody?"

The right side was lined with unlit torches. "Light the torches," instructed Billy.

Penny obeyed and lit each of them. He approached one of the doors and peered inside through a barred window. He couldn't see anything.

"Why are you looking in there? I doubt he's hiding from us."

"Just take care of the torches, Penny."

Billy opened the door slowly and peered in. A tall woman with tattered clothes lunged from the corner at Billy's arm. He retreated but the woman grabbed his arm. She snarled rabidly and fought to hold on. "Get over here, Penny!" he screamed.

Penny rushed to his aid. "What is that thing, Billy?"

Billy struggled to pull his arm out and close the door. "Stick the torch inside, fast!"

Penny reached in with the torch and scorched the woman's face. The woman shrieked and retreated into the corner. Billy pulled his arm out and locked the door. "Phew! That was close."

Billy leaned against the side of the door and breathed a sigh of relief. The woman's face appeared in the window. She reached through the bars and grabbed Billy by the throat. Penny shoved the torch against her arm. Billy spun away and escaped her clutches.

The woman had ashen skin and white eyes with no pupils. Her mouth was full of sharp, pointed teeth. Drool splashed from her mouth onto the floor near Billy's feet. Her high cheekbones indicated that she wasn't human. The woman gnawed madly at the wood around the bars. "What the hell is that thing?" asked Billy as he trembled.

"Maybe it's one of Ruger's lab experiments."

The woman disappeared from the door and the hall became quiet again. Penny looked petrified and cowered against the wall.

"Thanks, Honey," Billy said and hugged her.

Penny sobbed and then hollered, "Billy, you're a big jerk!"

"Look, if you can't handle this, go back now."

Penny became irate and cried, "Maybe I will." She stormed away from him.

Billy entered the next room with the torch in front of him. There was a variety of torture gadgets hanging from the walls. A corpse sat in a wooden chair in the middle of the room. It wore a cage over its head. The cage had numerous guide holes with long metal, pins pushed through into the corpse's skull. "Ugh. How horrible?" he muttered.

Billy scanned the remainder of the room and muttered, "What a sick bastard he is."

Penny rushed into the room. "Billy! The door's locked. We can't go back."

"Ruger's nearby," Billy announced anxiously. "I can feel him."

"Yeah, and we're locked up with his guinea pig creatures!"

"Penny, stop it! We'll be fine."

"We're never going to escape this place."

"Keep thinking that way and we won't." Billy left the room and proceeded to the next door. He felt the door with his hand and paused. Penny stood by the last door. "I'm not going in any more rooms," she said adamantly.

"Fine, stay out here."

Billy sensed someone was in the room. He quietly lifted the latch and pushed the door open. Cobwebs dangled from the ceiling in front of him. Billy waved the torch across them and burned them away. He entered the room and saw nothing. "That's strange."

Penny peered inside and noticed an opening in the lower wall. Two wooden poles stuck out near the floor. "Billy, what's that?"

Billy approached the opening and knelt down. He held the torch in front of it.

"Somebody's in there." Billy attempted to reach inside with the torch but an invisible barrier blocked him. He tapped on the barrier with his knuckles.

"Ruger sealed him in there."

Penny entered the room and looked closer. "Can you pull the poles out? They extend through the seal."

"It's worth a try."

Billy grabbed both poles and pulled on them. They slid noisily across the stone floor. "It's working!"

The poles were part of a wooden stretcher. Billy pulled the stretcher out of the hole and saw an old, decrepit man strapped to it. Several tubes were connected to his arms, legs and chest. The tubes were small and filled with blood. Billy unstrapped the man.

"Are you sure you know what you're doing, Billy?"

"Of course, I do. The poor guy's a prisoner here." Billy removed the tubes from the man's body. He noticed that they ran through a small hole in the rear of the man's tiny prison. "That's really freaky. Ruger's using his blood for something."

"Billy, we really need to talk about this. We're gonna get killed here."

Billy turned his back to the man and hugged Penny. "Look, all we have to do is find Ruger and kill him. We're this close."

Meanwhile, the man transformed into a huge beast with a protruding jaw and sharp teeth. Penny noticed the creature and pushed away from Billy. She looked horrified.

"What is it, Penny?" When he turned around, the creature stood in front of him. It was much taller than he was.

"Oh, shit!" muttered Billy. The creature grabbed Billy by the throat and pushed him against the wall. Penny screamed and retreated out the door. Billy's eyes bulged from the pressure on his throat. He used his telepathy to communicate with the creature. "You're a shape-shifter, too. What region are you from?"

"Sarcasson, why?" replied the creature telepathically.

"I'm a friend of Cassius and Seneca."

The creature set Billy down and released its hold on him. It transformed back into the old man. "Why have you come here?" the man asked.

"We're hunting Ruger."

"You can't touch Ruger. He's too powerful and is protected by evil forces."

"We've taken care of some of his forces."

"Diomedes will protect him."

"Diomedes is dead. So is Pantheos."

"What?"

"We've rescued Cassius as well. The device Ruger uses to power his evil has been recovered. He doesn't have much left."

"Then perhaps we can defeat him."

"Would you join us?" asked Billy.

"I must go now." The man rushed from the room and hurried down the hallway.

"Not bad for an old man on his death bed," joked Billy as he massaged his throat.

"How can you joke about this?" chided Penny.

"What else can I do?" Billy paused in front of another door.

"Please, Billy. No more rooms."

Billy opened the door and entered. In the middle of the room was a stone slab. Something large lay underneath a sheet. He approached the slab and noticed the blood-filled tubing. He traced it from the wall to whatever lay under the sheet. Penny looked in and saw the slab and its subject. "Billy, leave it alone. It can only be trouble."

"Penny, wait outside," ordered Billy, irritated by her nagging. Penny stepped back and watched from the hall.

Billy examined a small table with numerous instruments. He recognized various cutting knives, scalpels and probes. He took one of the scalpels and cut the tubing. Blood flowed from the tubing onto the floor. Billy paused over the sheet. He needed to know what was under it. He reached for the sheet and pulled it back slowly. The face was that of Pirocles.

"Well, I'll be." Billy pulled the sheet completely off. Pirocles head was attached to a body assembled with parts of different creatures. The arms were leathery tentacles about four feet long with stingers protruding from the last four inches of the appendage. The torso looked to be of a baby dinosaur, similar to the Crocosaurus they encountered earlier but without the tail. Under the tentacles were two powerful arms from a large gorilla.

"And they thought Frankenstein was screwed up," Billy remarked edgily. Then Pirocles' eyes opened, startling him. Billy gasped, "What the ...?" The tentacles wrapped tightly around Billy before he could escape. Penny screamed hysterically. Billy struggled to get loose but Pirocles squeezed him tighter.

"Penny, help me," Billy pleaded faintly.

Pirocles raised the second tentacle over Billy's head. The stingers protruded a little bit further. A clear liquid dripped off the ends of each stinger. "Please, Pirocles, don't do this."

Pirocles laughed sadistically. "You thought Ruger was your only worry. Now you have me to deal with."

Penny drew her short sword and rushed at Pirocles. Pirocles turned and saw her coming, but too late. Penny shoved her sword into his throat and pulled the sword sideways. Pirocles knocked her across the room with one of his powerful arms. She lay stunned on the floor while he stared at Billy in a sick sort of way. Billy felt the tentacle loosen slightly. Pirocles' head fell from his shoulders and struck the floor with a thud. His body crumpled to the ground. Billy struggled to rid himself of the tentacle.

Penny stared at him from the ground and said nothing. When he finally freed himself, he picked up Penny's sword and handed it to her. She took it and sheathed it without saying a word.

"Thanks, Penny. You saved my life."

Penny stared sadly at Billy. He didn't understand why she looked that way. "What's wrong?" he asked, baffled by her reaction.

"My heart breaks every time you nearly get killed. All you can say is 'what's wrong?'"

Billy put his arms around Penny but she pushed him away. "For once, Billy, you ought to stop thinking about yourself and consider what you put me and your friends through."

"When we get out of here, we'll talk about it."

"Will we?"

"Let's go. We have work to do," he said angrily. Billy stormed down the hall and descended another stairwell into the bowels of the castle.

Penny bristled at him until a chilly breeze blew into the room. Sensing that someone or something else was near her, she rushed from the room and followed the hallway to the next stairwell.

Billy slipped on the damp stone steps and tumbled halfway down. The torch fell thirty-feet to the floor below. He groaned and pulled himself into a sitting position. Blood trickled down his forehead from a laceration. He felt lightheaded and rested. "I'm getting too old for this crap," he complained.

Penny descended the stairs and looked down at him pitifully. "Can you help me up?" he asked.

"You're a big boy. You don't need anyone's help. Remember?" Penny left him and continued down the stairs.

Billy slammed his fist on the step. "Damn it, Penny!" He stood up and leaned against the wall for support. "Penny, wait for me!" There was no response. "Come on. This is ridiculous," he complained.

Penny entered Ruger's laboratory. Torches lined the wall, casting eerie shadows around the lab. A long table was positioned in the middle with numerous test tubes and various colored solutions. Small, blue flames heated several of the glass containers. Skulls were placed at regular intervals with holes bored in them. Candles burned in the holes for light at the table.

Billy caught up with Penny. He placed his hand on her shoulder and startled her. She trembled and glared at him. "Please, Penny. I'm sorry."

"Don't ever scare me like that again or, so help me, I will punch you in the face!"

"I'm sorry. When I get scared, I become quiet and focused. I'm not trying to shut you out."

"I'm telling you; I've about had it with your 'Billy the Hero' act." She reluctantly stayed.

"This is Ruger's laboratory," Billy remarked as he looked at the lab equipment. "I have a feeling he's not far away."

"Yeah, I sense him, too." They heard the faint sound of running water. Billy held his torch up high to see the source of the sound. "Looks like there's a break in the wall in the back corner."

"Maybe it's a way out," Penny answered hopefully. They crept cautiously across the lab toward the broken wall.

Billy held the torch through the gap and saw a large underground cavern with a wide river flowing through it. A chilly breeze flowed through the wall into the lab and rippled Billy's hair. "That's where your breeze came from, Penny."

"No way! It came from the other direction. I'm telling you; it was Ruger."

"Maybe it was." Billy stopped in front of another wooden door and stared at it.

"Do you have to open it?" asked Penny nervously. "We haven't had much luck with doors."

"We could be missing something important."

Penny grew frustrated and bellowed sarcastically, "Go ahead, Billy, open the door! I wouldn't want you to miss anything."

Billy ignored her and pulled the door open without another thought. Inside, he saw a row of iron-barred cells. He entered the corridor and scanned the cells. Each cell had a glowing portal against the rear wall. "I think Ruger practiced with the PCU down here," suggested Billy.

Penny entered and stood in front of one of the cells. "I guess he learned his lesson after the Dracor came through."

A large lizard crept up to the bars behind Penny. Its long tongue reached toward her waist. "Penny! Look out!" shouted Billy. The lizard's tongue hungrily wrapped itself around Penny's waist. Billy drew his sword and struck at the tongue, easily severing it. The lizard howled and retreated into the portal.

"I hate this place! Take me out of here, please, Billy."

Billy comforted her. "Soon, Penny. Soon."

"Damn you, Billy!"

Billy followed her into the lab. "What do you want me to do, Penny?"

"Get me the hell out of here for a start."

"And how do I do that?"

"We can go that way," she said as she pointed at the broken wall.

"Alright, we'll do it your way." Penny looked suspiciously at him. "Go on," he urged her. "I'll follow you and we'll see how much better you fare."

Penny approached the wall and stepped through the gap. Billy warily followed her through the darkness to the bank of the river. She surveyed the area, wondering which way to go.

Billy drank from the water and suddenly saw the reflection of hundreds of red eyes. "Penny, douse the torch," he ordered her sternly.

"Why? What's wrong?"

"Douse the friggin' torch, now!"

Penny stuck the torch in the water. She was hurt by Billy's shortness with her. "Are you happy now?"

"Back up toward the laboratory, slowly."

"Billy, stop it. You're scaring me."

"Look up then, and see for yourself, damn it!"

Penny looked up and saw the eyes. "Oh my gosh! Look at them all!"

"Still want to argue about it."

Penny moved purposely toward the opening in the wall as hundreds of shadows descended to the ground from the cavern ceiling.

"They look like people but they sure aren't," remarked Billy somberly.

Penny looked back at the laboratory and saw several of the creatures standing in front of the wall.

"Billy, they cut us off."

"Oh, shit! I'll bet that's where Vampyra upstairs came from." Billy quickly removes his clothes. "What are you doing, Billy?"

"I'm shape-shifting. I'll get them away from the lab. As soon as they leave, get out of here."

"But what about you?"

"Damn it, Penny! Listen to me for once in your life. Get the hell out of here!"

Billy shifted into his wolverine shape. He dashed toward the creatures near the lab. They spread their winged arms and waited. Billy lunged at one of the creature's legs and tore a chunk of flesh from it. He raced away toward the river. The creature fell to the ground, wailing in pain. The other creatures hunted Billy.

Penny raced through the wall and left the cavern. Billy leaped onto a rock above the creatures. He noticed one that stood out among the others. His telepathic ability sensed some communication from that particular creature to the others. He jumped off of the rock and raced after the creature. It rose from the ground, but Billy lunged at it and tore into its neck with his teeth. The creature wailed and tumbled into the river with Billy hanging from its neck.

The other creatures flapped their wings and wailed in horror as their leader disappeared into the depths of the river. Billy held the creature at the bottom until he was sure it was dead. When he came ashore, the creatures were in a panic.

Billy raced toward the lab as fast as he could, as four of the creatures flew toward him. He stopped quickly, allowing them to collide with each other. Instinctively, he jumped on the back of one creature and sprung toward the wall.

Another creature lunged at him and caught a piece of his flank. Billy howled in pain but made it into the lab. The creatures remained in the cavern away from the torchlight. Billy slid onto his side and transformed into his human self. He trembled as he lay on his side.

Penny cradled him and hugged him. "It's alright, Billy. You made it." When she helped him sit up, she saw blood on the floor from Billy's side. "Oh, Billy! You're hurt bad."

"No kidding." He staggered to his feet and tried to dress himself.

Penny offered, "Let me help."

"Are you sure you want to. After all, I don't need anyone, do I?"

"Stop it! Stop it right now!" Penny noticed for the first time that Billy had tears in his eyes. "You're crying. I never saw that before in you." Billy looked away from her, embarrassed. "Billy, that wound is bad. Let me look at it."

"Don't bother. Any more ideas for getting out of here?"

Penny became upset with him. "You can be such an ass, Billy!"

Billy staggered to another stairwell in the lab. The steps were wooden and rotted. "You can't go up there. Those steps won't hold you," warned Penny.

"So what? Maybe I'll fall to my death." Billy took one of the torches and struggled up the stairs, using the wall to brace himself. Penny heatedly watched. She refused to give in this time to him. The steps creaked under Billy's weight but they held him. When Billy reached two broken steps, he carefully stepped over them and continued upward. He thought he heard something under the stairs and paused. There was no further noise so he climbed further.

Penny felt the chilly breeze from the other direction and became frightened. She looked around the lab but saw no one. Reluctantly, she climbed the wooden stairs. Billy reached the top of the stairs and pushed the door open. He pulled himself through and recognized the hallway. He knew he was a short distance from the landing.

Penny nervously ascended the wooden stairs. She reached the broken steps and held her torch over the dark opening. Suddenly, a hand reached from under the step and grabbed her ankle. Penny screamed as loud as she could. She dropped her torch on the steps behind her. The step she stood on broke. She fell through but clung to another step. "Billy! Help me!"

The step creaked as the weight of Penny and her unknown assailant strained the rotted wood. Billy rolled on his back and moaned, "Now what?" He struggled to his feet and descended the stairs as fast as he could without falling. He saw Penny's head and arms above the stairs. "Hold on, Penny!"

Billy stretched over the opening and saw someone hanging from her legs. He instructed the assailant, "I'm reaching down for you. Take my hand or you'll both fall." He reached down into the darkness and ordered, "Take it before you both fall!" He was startled when a hand reached out of the darkness and grabbed his.

Billy instructed Penny, "Hold on. I'll pull you up next." He pulled the other person up and was surprised to see the old man. "Take hold of the steps."

The old man wrapped both his arms around the step and clung tightly. Billy pulled Penny safely up on the stairs.

"I'll pull him up by one arm. I need you to pull his other arm."

"But Billy, he nearly killed me!"

"Penny, listen to me!" Billy pulled the old man up to his waist. Penny grabbed his other arm and pulled him up. When they lifted him high enough, he braced his legs against the sides of the broken stairs.

"Thank you both for saving me," the old man said feebly.

"We'll see how thankful you are. Let's get out of here," Billy remarked cynically.

Penny rushed up the stairs ahead of them. Billy waited for the old man to walk ahead of him. He labored behind the man while clutching his side. When they reached the hall, Billy pointed toward the landing. They walked in a single file, close to the wall; Penny first, followed by Billy; and the old man.

"Why did you help him first?" asked Penny hurtfully.

"Because there's no way I could pull both of you up and I don't think he was going to let go voluntarily."

"What if I fell? Would you look for me?" Billy purposely hesitated. "You wouldn't look for me, you ass!" she shouted at him.

"Of course, I would," Billy replied and chuckled briefly.

"So, who are you? You never told me," Billy asked the old man.

"I'm Germain, Pantheos' father."

Billy was stunned. "I'm sorry for your loss," he said respectfully.

"Pantheos was a good son once. He was a brave warrior and was a key leader of the Firenghian tribes. Ruger met with him one day and twisted his goals and ambitions. When they became involved with Diomedes, I knew I had to stop him."

"So, Ruger imprisoned you?"

"No, my son did. Ruger used me as one of his experiments."

"What did he do to you?" asked Penny.

"You saw my alter-shape. It's an aberration. How can I be proud of a beast like that?"

"It's what's in the heart, Germain. No one can blame you for what they've done to you," replied Billy.

"My people will never accept me like this."

"Give them a chance. They might surprise you." The three of them entered the main chamber.

"I was never so happy to see this room," said Penny cheerfully.

John, Ronnie, Xerxes and Brent waited near the portal. "Hey, you're back in one piece!" shouted John.

"So far. Any problems?" asked Billy.

"No. It's been unusually quiet."

John saw Billy's side and was concerned. "What happened to you?"

"Oh, some vampire people tried to eat me. I guess I didn't taste very good or they would have finished."

"Billy, I don't know how you do it," said John with a chuckle. Penny bit her finger and looked away in anger.

They descended the stairs and joined the others. Billy put his hand up, motioning for silence. Ruger entered the chamber and crept toward the stairwell. He muttered to himself in anger as he stormed across the floor. "Hey, Ruger, going somewhere?" shouted Billy.

"Ah, you're still around," Ruger replied in mock surprise. "Where's Pantheos?"

"Gone."

"And Diomedes?"

"Gone."

"That makes my job that much easier. I guess I can thank you for your efforts. With that said, it's your turn to die. I'll make sure this time."

"I don't think so, Ruger," challenged Germain. "You poisoned my son. You must pay."

"Ah, so Billy's bringing out the trash to defend himself from me."

Germain chanted an incantation and clapped his hands together. The room echoed with a loud bang and Ruger was thrust against the wall. After recovering from the initial shock, Ruger laughed at him.

"Is that all you have, Germain. My you've fallen a long way from the old days."

"Germain, you don't have to do this. I can handle him," said Billy.

"It's a matter of family honor."

John took Billy's arm and advised, "He's right, Billy. I would want the same."

Germain shouted another incantation and approached Ruger with his hands extended forward. Ruger clutched at his heart and swore. Germain stood face to face with Ruger and said, "Meet your maker."

"No, meet yours," Ruger replied angrily. He grabbed the man by the throat and spun him against the wall. He shouted his own incantation and Germain shook violently. Ruger repeated the incantation and Germain exploded in a cloud of dust. He turned to Billy and glared at him. "Now, it's your turn to die."

Billy reached into the sack and pulled out the skull from Ruger's silver chest. Ruger smiled and bowed to Billy. "I see you and I are at a draw – for now."

Rena quietly emerged from the stairwell behind Ruger with a curled knife.

Billy laughed at Ruger and taunted, "You never were a very smart wizard, were you?"

Ruger smirked and said wryly, "You'll pay for your disrespect soon enough."

"I don't think so, Ruger. Look behind you."

Ruger turned around and saw only the flash of the blade that cut his arm off. Rena smiled sadistically as she placed the next incision in his chest.

Ruger fell to his knees and gasped, "Why, Rena?"

"How about 'Why, father?' Do you have an answer for that?" She carved his heart out mercilessly and bit into it. Ruger stared wide-eyed at her in shock. His last bit of life seeped from his body and he dropped to the stone floor.

Rena shuddered, convulsed and fell to the ground as well. Red smoke billowed from her body until she was obscured. Ruger lay lifeless on the ground nearby. His severed arm quivered for a few moments before it, too, lay still.

Billy saw the PCU strapped to the arm. He grabbed the arm and tossed it to Xerxes. "I believe you wanted this, Xerxes."

Xerxes reluctantly caught the arm and removed the PCU. "Thank you, Billy, I think." Xerxes tossed the arm on the floor. Brutus obligingly took the arm to a corner and gnawed on it.

"What's left to do?" asked Billy. "We have the sphere and the PCU. Ruger, Diomedes and Pantheos are gone. Is the nightmare over yet or do we have a new cast of characters to push us to the brink of insanity?"

"To my knowledge ..." started Xerxes.

The red smoke from Rena's body cleared, catching everyone's attention. Her body twitched erratically and she rolled over. She sat up and ran both of her hands across her face. She became the woman she once was. The spell was broken. Everyone was stunned by her appearance.

"Look at her; she's beautiful!" exclaimed Brent.

"The curse is broken! I'm cured!" Rena cried out excitedly.

Tybis and Shoran rushed into the chamber from the other tunnel.

"What's going on here?" asked Shoran. They saw Ruger's lifeless body on the ground and the hole in his chest.

"It's over, isn't it?" said Tybis somberly.

"Yes, it is," replied Billy. "Where are the other warriors?"

"We're all that's left."

Billy was mortified. "What happened?"

"Creatures with heavy armor shredded them."

"The Dracor. There are only two left."

"What do we do about them?" asked John.

"I'm not sure. When is the portal going to open again?"

"In about twenty minutes," replied Doc.

Rena approached John and held his hand. "Thank you for your help. I never thought I'd be free of Ruger's curse."

"You're welcome, ma'am, but I really didn't do anything."

"I wouldn't be here if you hadn't given me hope."

"When the portal opens, everyone goes through. I'll stay here and deal with the Dracor," ordered Billy.

Penny grabbed Billy by his shirt and chastised him, "You've done enough! Why do you keep doing this to me?"

"Penny, I've got the skull. The Dracor will destroy itself."

"So what? No one will be here to fear them?"

"Because it will continue to hunt. That's all it knows how to do. These men, Tybis and Shoran, are from Seneca's land. The Dracor will hunt their people until no one is left."

Suddenly, the Dracor appeared in the tunnel. They flashed their mechanized arms with sharp blades. "I guess it doesn't matter now, does it?" grumbled Billy. "Everyone get back."

Brutus growled viciously and stalked the mechanized monsters but Billy quickly called him off. The tiger reluctantly backtracked away from the creatures.

The Dracor stalked Billy and crouched before him. Billy pulled the skull from the sack and held it out toward the creatures. The eyes of the skull glowed bright red as the Dracor charged at Billy. Both Dracor became engulfed in a bright flash of light and vaporized into metal dust.

Billy breathed a sigh of relief. "Wow, I was afraid that the skull wasn't going to work in time."

Penny came to Billy's side and hugged him. "Now, I think the nightmare is officially over," he declared.

"I'm sorry for being angry with you," Penny said humbly.

"Well, we're going to work on that."

"But I was so worried that you might be killed again."

"Did you think Ruger killed me before?"

Penny looked down at the ground shamefully. "Yes, I did. I was devastated, but I had to know for sure."

"What about the others?" he asked.

"We all needed to know," she answered.

"That's really nice."

"Thank you, Billy, for all your help," said Tybis. "It looks like our work here is done. When can we see Seneca and Cassius?"

"Cassius was dying and our doctors couldn't help him," answered Penny. "Seneca took him home to die among his people."

Billy was surprised and responded disappointedly, "Seneca left without saying anything to me?"

"She didn't look well, but she said she'll see us soon."

"Then we'll travel back to Firenghia and find her."

"For once, I'll agree with you," Penny said.

"Would you mind if we go back with you, Tybis? I'd like to say goodbye to Seneca."

"Is it goodbye, Billy?"

"I guess we won't know until I see her."

"Would you give her my thanks for all her help?" asked Xerxes.

"She'd appreciate it, I'm sure."

"I'd like to offer my condolences for her brother Cassius as well. I must take the sphere and PCU back to the Council immediately and place it where it belongs."

"You're leaving us, Xerxes?" Billy asked in surprise.

"Yes, but I will join you in a few days. We have some important issues to discuss."

"Brent and I will go back to the camp," said Doc. "I assume Ronnie and John will be joining us."

"I've had enough castles for one lifetime. Let's get out of here," added John anxiously.

"Then we'll see you soon." Doc and Brent hurried into the portal first, followed by John and Ronnie.

Billy offered his arm to Penny. "Shall we?"

"Of course," Penny said and smiled at him.

Tybis related to Billy how he and his men encountered the traps in the castle. He was heart-broken that his warriors were slain and now hoped they saw the last of the formidable Dracor.

Billy led them across the courtyard and contemplated how to safely exit the castle. He found an alternate path back to the drawbridge to avoid the pendulums and the trap floors. He and Tybis climbed onto the ledge and lowered the drawbridge, hopefully for the last time. Outside the castle, they looked back and held a moment of silence for their lost comrades.

CHAPTER 15

RESTORATION

When they reached the valley later that morning, everyone felt confident that the danger was over. "What happened to the creatures in the tunnel, Billy?" asked Tybis.

"They were all part of Ruger's magic. They disappeared when Ruger died."

Billy noticed that Tybis and Shoran were still a little nervous. "Don't worry, we have Brutus for protection."

"I'll feel much better when we reach Firenghia," replied Tybis.

Penny followed and said nothing. Billy looked at her curiously. She just smiled and held his arm affectionately.

When they arrived in Firenghia, a man in a white robe greeted them. "My name is Talomar. Seneca is expecting you."

"Where is she now?" asked Tybis.

"On the hill. They pray for Cassius and for your triumphant return."

Billy surveyed the village as they walked through. It was a simple place with thatched huts and ox-drawn carts. Tybis motioned for them to follow him across the village to a small hill with a large shady tree on top.

"Is it always this quiet, Tybis?" asked Penny.

"There aren't many of us left. But if Cassius is dying, they are no doubt praying for him." Tybis placed a finger to his lips, indicating silence as they approached the hill.

The citizens of Firenghia and Sarcasson stood at the base of the hill. Under a large tree at the top of the hill was a wooden altar upon which Cassius lay. Seneca stood in front of the altar, facing Cassius. She wore a long white robe with gold trim. Upon her head was a gold tiara, decorated with lovely flowers. Incense burned in small urns positioned around the hilltop. Seneca's back was to them but she knew they were there. She chanted a prayer for Cassius and paused in silence. She used her telepathy to communicate with Billy. "I knew you could do it. I knew you were the one."

Seneca turned and faced the congregation. "My people, today is a day of great sadness and wondrous joy. Today is a new beginning for Firenghia, Sarcasson and the rest of our world. I welcome our friends who have just returned with this great victory: Tybis, mage of Sarcasson; Shoran, mage of Red Fern; Billy Brock and Penny, warriors from another land. Please, come forward so all may show their appreciation for your great victory."

Tybis and Shoran walked proudly up to the altar and stepped to either side. Billy and Penny stopped in front of the altar and gazed at the still figure of Cassius.

"When we focused our powers in close proximity in the castle, we shattered the transparent ball that imprisoned me. Let's hold hands and try to help Cassius heal," suggested Billy.

"Perhaps you're right," replied Seneca. "Maybe our collective powers are strong enough to heal him."

Seneca and Penny extended their hands to Billy and to each other. Tybis and Shoran joined, too. They concentrated together for Cassius to heal. The congregation watched anxiously and wondered what great power the group possessed. Tybis and Shoran glanced at each other, wondering what new surprise Billy had for them with this rite.

Cassius opened his eyes and smiled weakly. "What took you so long, Billy? I thought you'd figure out how to use your powers much sooner than this."

"If I didn't have to look for your sorry butt, I might have had time to learn about them first."

Slowly, the color came back to Cassius' face. His breathing became stronger. "Thank you so much, all of you."

"Cassius, we have so much to tell you," Seneca blurted excitedly.

"Please tell me that we've defeated Ruger."

"Yes, my brother, he's gone."

Tybis and Shoran jumped and danced in jubilation. "Cassius lives! Cassius lives!" they chanted. Everyone cheered and chanted for Cassius.

Seneca put her hands up for silence and the congregation promptly obeyed. "Tybis, would you speak first? Tell the people of our victory."

"Yes, my queen." Tybis nervously stepped forward to address the group and said, "It's been a long time since I could bear good news and it's been longer since I've heard good news. I'll be brief and direct. We've waited too long. Ruger has been defeated!" Everyone cheered.

Tybis allowed them a moment of applause before proceeding; "Pantheos has also been slain. He conspired with Ruger for the throne of Firenghia." The crowd stirred in surprise.

"Both men summoned the witch Diomedes but ..." Whispers of fear circulated among the crowd. "But Diomedes has been slain as well." Another round of cheering ensued.

"Many have wondered what our Queen, Seneca, would do before her thirtieth cycle, which falls on the new moon in three days. I'll allow her to reveal her intentions to you." Once again, the congregation roared in approval as Seneca stood by Tybis' side.

"As you all know, our laws dictate that I must choose someone to share the throne with me by my thirtieth cycle. Well, I have met one person of extraordinary character, strength and wisdom. I have met another who is pure, caring and strong in fortitude. These two individuals behind me have all of the qualities of a wise ruler."

Seneca stood back and pointed to Billy and Penny. She could see by Billy's expression that he was confused and concerned. Seneca projected telepathically, "Don't worry, Billy. I know you'll be happy with my decision."

Billy tried to read her thoughts but she was careful to conceal them from him after her initial message. "I now bear a child, Billy's child," Seneca announced proudly. She paused as the crowd filled with whispers. Tybis smiled in satisfaction.

Penny knew what Seneca wanted and she was supportive even though it meant sharing Billy with her. Together they had a special bond. Billy was as surprised as anyone. He suspected that Seneca had placed him in a position he couldn't say no to. He wasn't ready to leave his world for hers but instead of growing angry, he was patient.

Penny watched his expression intently and projected to him, "Just relax, Billy. Seneca would never hurt you."

Billy projected back to her, "I don't know what to say. I didn't know."

Penny emphasized, "This is a great moment for her. Don't ruin it." Billy wiped a bead of sweat from his forehead and swallowed hard.

Seneca continued, "There is also a law that states if the Queen does not share the throne with a mate, she may retain her title and throne should she bear a child who would inherit the title at maturity. With your approval, I invoke that law. If you do not accept me as your queen, I will graciously step down."

Tybis spoke to the audience, "Seneca has proven herself worthy of the title of Queen of Firenghia. Is there anyone here who would not have her retain that title? Let him or her speak now." Everyone looked around suspiciously for objectors, but no one spoke up.

"Does everyone agree that Seneca should remain the Queen of Firenghia?" The air was filled with a deafening roar of approval. People chanted Seneca's name and clapped. Musicians played a Firenghian victory tune.

"Why didn't you tell me?" Billy asked.

"Would it have made a difference how you felt about me?" replied Seneca.

"Yes! Yes, it would!"

"I was afraid of that."

"No, not like that. It would have erased my earlier doubts that you might have used me to get to Ruger."

"What do you think now?"

"I love you, Seneca, but I love Penny too."

"So do I, Billy. What's the problem?"

"Um, I … I don't know. Let me think about this for a while."

Seneca faced Penny and they exchanged smiles. They had a special bond that in some ways was sisterly and in other ways was magical. When the musicians finished their song, Seneca held her arms up for silence.

"I want everyone to know that Billy won't be staying in Firenghia. He and Penny share a life together in their land. However, we will see him from time to time, as I'm sure he'll want to ensure his son grows to be of fine royal character. I hope I haven't disappointed any of you by not selecting a mate to rule as king, but my child will more than make up for that absence as will Billy's good will to the people of Firenghia."

Once again, the crowd cheered. This time they chanted, "Billy, Billy!"

Tybis stood up and the crowd silenced. "We have fought battles with Ruger and his evil creatures for many cycles. A few days ago, we pulled Billy from the river by Ruger's castle. I knew right away that he would be the one to set us free. I also knew he had the traits of a Firenghi and that he would have an impact on our future. I pledge my loyalty to Billy, Seneca, their child and all of Billy's friends for what they have done for us."

After more cheers, Tybis raised his hands again for the crowd's attention. "In addition, we found Rena, cursed by Ruger's own hand many moons ago and imprisoned in the bowels of his castle. She personally ended his life and ended the evil that imprisoned all of us. Without all of these heroes, we would not have this victory today."

Seneca welcomed her cousin with open arms. Rena tearfully approached the altar and hugged Seneca. "Would you like to speak, dear cousin?" asked Seneca.

"No, not yet," she whispered.

"Would you like to speak, dear brother, or would you like me to say something for you?"

"Tell them that I too pledge my loyalty to Billy and his friends," replied Cassius. "Billy saved my life." Seneca repeated Cassius' words to the people and Cassius waved.

The crowd again erupted in cheers, chants and songs. The men set up tables in the middle of the village. The people brought forth great quantities of food and drink. Their festival erupted in a matter of minutes.

Billy helped Cassius from the altar and down to the tables. "What will you do next, Billy?" asked Cassius.

"I guess we'll see if Xerxes can undo what Ruger has done to our worlds. If so, I hope to return to my own world. I've learned a lot from you and Seneca. I can never thank you enough."

"Nor can I."

"Penny and I have a lot of catching up to do as well."

"It's time for my victory celebration with Billy," said Penny elatedly, clutching his arm.

Seneca gleefully hugged them. "Gee, Sis. You can stop already," kidded Cassius.

"But everything is so perfect today. I will have a child in four moons and our kingdoms are free again."

Billy overheard and couldn't help wondering about the timing of Seneca's pregnancy. "Seneca, can I ask you something?"

"What is it?"

"You said that you would have the baby in four moons. It wasn't that long ago that we met. It was actually just a few weeks ago, only a half-moon ago."

Seneca laughed at Billy. "You still have so much to learn about Firenghi. A Firenghi woman bears a child in five moons or less."

Billy rubbed his chin and thought about this dilemma. He looked at Penny and was about to speak, but she cut him off. "Don't even say it, Billy. If we ever got married, you'd have to wait four or five months for appearance's sake."

"Just great!" he moaned. The two girls laughed at him and then Penny and Seneca each kissed him on the cheek. "Cloak your thoughts, dummy," he reminded himself.

"Billy, you're a lucky man," remarked Cassius.

"But Cassius, it isn't like it seems. You don't know what they put me through. It's always two against one."

"That's why I prefer to stay alone. Sarcasson law doesn't require me to choose a mate."

A tall, blonde woman approached Cassius from behind and placed her arms around him. "Cassius, I was so worried. Don't you to ever leave without telling me again. I thought we talked about that last time."

Cassius placed his hand on his forehead as the others laughed at him. "Billy, take me with you!" he pleaded. "I'm sure there are things we need to deal with yet."

"No, Cassius. He's mine for now," declared Penny. "Besides, your woman needs you."

"We'll leave you alone, Cassius, so you can rest with Xanther. I'm sure the two of you have a lot to catch up on as well," said Seneca playfully.

Before Cassius could say another word, Xanther embraced him and kissed him.

Billy felt bad, bailing out on his friend like that. Penny read his thoughts and frowned at him. "Forget it, Billy. It's our turn."

Why are women always so bossy? Billy pondered.

"Because men are so darn hard-headed," answered Penny aloud.

"You are welcome to stay in that hut over there," offered Seneca.

"It belonged to my sister before Ruger killed her. I'm sure the two of you could use some rest."

"Thanks, Seneca. In fact, I think we're going to retire right now," said Penny anxiously.

Penny pulled Billy into the hut and laid him down on the crude bed. He still felt severe pain from the wound on his hip and cringed. "I think I know what you need, Billy." Penny removed her sneakers and looked up. Billy was asleep on the bed already.

Penny sighed disappointedly. "Men. What good are they?" She undressed and lay beside Billy. After watching him sleep for a few minutes, she placed her head on his chest and put her arm around him. Soon, she slept as well.

Brutus entered the hut and lay next to the bed. He watched over them until the middle of the night when he discretely disappeared into the trees.

— X —

Maggie waited anxiously at the portal. "Another five minutes and they'll be out. You'll see," said Sam confidently.

"It's difficult to sit here and wait without having a clue as to what's going on. They could either be dead or having the time of their lives."

Sam looked at his watch. "It's close enough, Maggie. Turn on the portal." She turned the valve on the sphere. It glowed steadily and the portal formed. Sam warned Martin to be ready with his weapon, just in case. John and Ronnie emerged first.

Maggie asked frantically, "Where's Doc?"

"He's okay. Leave the sphere on while Xerxes closes the other portals."

"Does that mean it's over?"

"Yes, it is. Xerxes has the PCU."

"That's great!"

— ⧖ —

Xerxes pointed the PCU at each of the portals that illuminated. One by one, he closed them with a series of codes.

"It's done, isn't it?" asked Doc.

"Yes, it is. We can go now."

"There was so much to be learned from this. It's knowledge I'll never know."

"It's not all knowledge, Dr. Smith. There are some magical and supernatural elements too."

"I still don't get it."

"Some day you will. Let's go." The two men entered the portal, leaving the castle for the last time.

When they emerged from the portal, Maggie scolded Doc, "I thought you changed your mind about coming back. What took you so long?"

"I was just taking a last look at something I'll never see or know again."

"You need some rest, Honey," she suggested.

"Heck, we all need some rest. Perhaps Nigel and Krill have some more of that scotch back at the camp."

"All of you can rest in the back of the truck. I'll drive," offered Sam as he looked around. "What about Billy? Where'd he go?"

"He'll be back later. He has some business to tend to," replied John.

"You know, this has to be the strangest damn experience that's ever happened to me and I still don't understand what's going on," complained Martin.

"Just think of it as a bad dream," replied Sam.

"What happened to your nose, Ronnie?" asked Maggie.

"She had an accident. It's broken," explained John. Maggie realized that Ronnie wasn't happy about it and said nothing further on the subject.

When they reached the post office, everyone quickly dispersed. It appeared that a quiet night was in order. John escorted Ronnie into her room and helped remove her boots. She fell asleep before he could say good night. John undressed and lay beside her. He kissed her cheek and said 'goodnight'. She sighed with a smile.

— X —

Xerxes carried the sphere into the forest and found a secluded location. He energized the sphere and pointed the PCU at a large rock. After punching in several digits, a transparent portal formed. He stepped through and returned to the Council of Guardians. The portal led him directly into the center of the Orb Chamber.

The Orb Chamber was a large round room with white marble walls. The walls were adorned with sheer, white curtains made from lace. Fifteen pedestals of shiny black stone were placed equidistant around the room. There was a sphere on top of each pedestal with the exception of one. Xerxes carried the sphere to the vacant pedestal and placed it on top. Nine men in white robes entered the chamber and watched anxiously.

"Well, Xerxes, it appears that you have done well. I see you've recovered the orb and the controller," said one of them.

"Yes, Goliathan. We were successful. However, I would not have succeeded on my own without the help of several individuals."

"They were instrumental in your success?"

"Yes, they were."

"And what of the people of Earth? How do feel about their progress?"

"I think they've come a long way. They formed a group to defend and feed the weaker of the species. There was no cannibalism or power struggles. They exhibited intelligent survival instincts and never lost sight of who they were."

"They obviously have learned some things about our technology. How do you feel about that?"

"I think these particular people are responsible and can be trusted with our technology."

"Very well. We have other important issues to discuss."

"I expected so."

"First, we have debated for quite some time, how to recover from Ruger's intrusion. We also contemplated, during your absence, who will replace Golmar. As you know, Ruger killed him to steal his PCU. After much deliberation, we have decided that you would be worthy to take his place as a member of the Council of Guardians."

"I I'm flattered, Goliathan. I would be honored. Thank you."

"With this title comes the right to have the controller as your own. Come forward."

Xerxes approached the men and knelt down on one knee. Goliathan opened a scroll and performed the Rite of Induction into the Council. Once the rite was completed, Goliathan posed a question to Xerxes, "As your first official responsibility, you will attempt to undo the damage that Ruger has done. How do you propose to do this?"

"Obviously, I would like to return all the individuals back to the time before Ruger's interference. In what capacity, I would like to discuss with them first."

"Do you feel that any of them are worthy to join our allegiance and fight for the Council?"

"I believe so, Goliathan."

"This Council gives you permission to recruit those whom you think are worthy to join us. Ruger's actions had a devastating effect on everyone and we realize that we, too, are vulnerable. We can use people with strength and wisdom. We have isolated the tribe of Earthlings long enough. You may share the technology with appropriate individuals along with the responsibilities and consequences that come with it. In addition, I believe we'll need their help with our other issues."

"Other issues?"

"Yes. We'll discuss them when you've completed this restoration."

"I understand. Thank you." Xerxes departed the Orb Chamber through an opening in the curtains. He was excited over his promotion and never expected to replace his friend Golmar.

When he arrived in his quarters, he tossed his raggedy clothes on the floor and took a hot bath. It felt so good to be relieved of the weight of Ruger's debacle. After relaxing for a while, he thought about his friends and what he should do for them. Since the Council never had this problem before, there were many unanswered questions. Could he send everyone back to the moment before Ruger changed each one's fates? Would they remember everything that happened? What about those who were injured or killed? What would he tell his friends? Perhaps, he considered, just the truth or some portion of it. After a good night's rest, he would return to meet with them at the post office.

— ☓ —

Everyone at the post office rested well until noontime when they met for lunch. The conversations revolved around Xerxes and whether or not he could send them back to their own world. Billy and Penny returned from Firenghia and joined them.

"Has anyone seen Xerxes since last night?" asked Doc.

Everyone shrugged their shoulders and shook their heads indicating a 'no'.

"I'm sure he was anxious to return the sphere and the device to the Council he spoke of. He'll be back," assured Billy.

"What if he doesn't?"

"Then we'll stay here," said Maggie calmly. "Don't worry so much."

Ronnie was concerned about Randy's condition. She inquired, "Doc, did anyone go with Randy to Dr. Miller's observatory?"

"Jerry, Seamus and the pilot took them. They're in good hands, I'm sure. I'll be in touch with Joe by radio after lunch and I'll ask about all of them." Ronnie was relieved to know that Randy was taken where she could receive decent medical attention.

Penny noticed how each of their friends seemed to be pairing with a mate. She felt good about that. Perhaps, with Ronnie and Randy occupied, she wouldn't have to worry so much about Billy running off on secret adventures every day.

When they finished lunch, Billy asked the group, "If Xerxes can reset time and send us back, what do all of you want to do?"

"John and I would like to stay together," replied Ronnie. "It doesn't matter where. I imagine Seamus and Randy feel the same way."

"I didn't realize the two of them had become that close," remarked Penny.

"Well, since Billy's off the market, we both decided to grab a man while there were still some good ones available," kidded Ronnie.

"So, I was second choice?" John asked hurtfully.

"That was before I met you, Sweetie." Ronnie rested her head on his shoulder and squeezed his arm.

"What about you, Billy?" she asked.

"I don't know. I'd like to go back and see my mom. Except for her, I find this life a heck of a lot more interesting than my old life."

"And you, Penny?"

"I think I'd like to stay with Billy, at least for a little while."

"What do you mean 'a little while'? I thought you said you loved me?"

"I'm teasing, silly," Penny said and kissed his cheek.

Billy blushed as everyone laughed at him. "Outnumbered again. Damn it!"

Xerxes entered the building and approached the table. "Good morning, friends. How is everyone, today?"

"Marvelous, Xerxes. How about you?" asked Billy.

"Very well, thank you. I have a lot of things to discuss with you, but before we begin, I need to tell you a few things."

"Time is all we have," quipped John.

"First of all, the Council is greatly in your debt. They send their thanks. In regards to sending you back to the time before Ruger's disaster befell you, the Council has never had to deal with a situation like this. What we are going to do has never been done. Therefore, many of your questions will not have answers."

"Why not tell us what you can do?" suggested Billy.

"Each of you risked your life to help me resolve this issue."

"It was a little more than an issue, Xerxes," kidded Billy.

"Yes, well, you all performed valiantly and because of that, I would like to make some recommendations. Because of our success, I have been given a seat on the Council of Guardians. Therefore, I now have certain powers that I didn't have before. First, Dr. Smith, you and Maggie are the science minds here. The Council feels that it is time we share our technology with the people of your world. However, there are responsibilities that you must bear. Should you or any of your race abuse this technology, we would be required to interfere and revoke it from you. That is not a pleasant experience since your minds would be purged of the knowledge. You and I will discuss those responsibilities later."

"I thank you, Xerxes. We won't disappoint you," said Doc gratefully.

"As far as those who were injured and killed, I don't believe that they will be cured or brought back to life by resetting time. I could be wrong, but I doubt it."

"At least, we can get Randy and Jarret the proper medical attention," remarked Ronnie.

Billy looked at Ronnie's nose and joked, "Yeah and a good nose doctor, too."

Ronnie covered her face in shame. "You're such an ass, Billy!"

"Some things never change, Ronnie," added Penny.

"Yes, I see that."

"It's only fair that I repay you for all the abuse I took from you and Randy," replied Billy.

Xerxes continued, "Somehow, you must find a way to explain the disappearances of those who were killed and your return to different places than where this started."

"I've been thinking about that," answered Doc. "My colleague, Joe Miller and I will persuade the government to set up a department for the understanding and application of your technology. I can also persuade the government to cover up the disappearances of those who died here. They have the ability to do that."

"I understand that Ronnie and Randy would like to stay with John and Seamus. That creates several complications. However, I have a suggestion. When Randy is well enough to travel, I would like the girls, John and Seamus to join our alliance as warriors. You seem to be quite adept at that role and we could use your help."

John smiled at Ronnie. "I believe that would be an excellent idea."

"Count us in, Xerxes," said Ronnie.

"I will return you together with Dr. Smith and Maggie to the observatory. When you are ready to join us, I will know. I'll find you."

"That's fine with us," she responded, pleased.

"I extend my offer to you, Billy and Penny, but I don't believe either of you is ready to leave your world behind."

"Thank you, Xerxes. I think that's pretty accurate. Penny and I still have some family to tend to. But, should you need our help, I'm sure we could get away for a little while."

"Thank you. I'll bear that in mind. Are there any other questions before we begin?"

"Xerxes, will we really ever see you again?" asked Billy.

"Why do you ask?"

"Well, after all we've been through, I feel like all of you are my family. Can we get together somehow, from time to time?"

Xerxes reached into his pocket and pulled out two silver chains, each with a small transparent ball. He handed one to Billy and one to John.

"If you want to reach me, place the orb in the palm of your hand and call for me. I'll answer you."

"Thanks, Xerxes. I will," said Billy.

"Before we do this, I'd like to exchange phone numbers with Billy, so we can stay in touch," requested Doc.

"Very well. I'll wait."

Sam hustled up wearing a black backpack. "Hey, where's everybody going? Don't forget me."

"How can we forget you, Sam?" said Billy giddily.

"Is it true that we're going back to our old world, Xerxes?"

"Yes, do you have a problem with that?"

"Well, yeah, I do. I had so much fun with you folks that I'd like to stick around for more. I don't have any family and my only obligation is alimony. I'd certainly like to skip that any way I can." Everyone laughed.

"Can you use one more warrior, Xerxes?" Billy asked. "He's great with battle strategies and fighting with a club."

"I'm sure I can. Welcome, Sam. You'll go with the others until I'm prepared for you. Are you all ready?"

Everyone anxiously chanted, "Yes!"

"The others of your race will remember only a dream and a sketchy one at that. Close your eyes and relax."

CHAPTER 16

NEW BEGINNINGS

Billy sat at the kitchen table pondering over all that happened. "Was it all real? It seems like a dream already." When he stood up, he clutched at his ribs and hip. "Ouch! Oh, yeah. It was real."

Billy went upstairs to shower. His next thoughts turned to Penny. I wonder what she's doing right now. *It would be nice if there was a fire burning in the fireplace, candles on the table and some nice romantic music on the stereo. Perhaps Penny would be waiting for me in a negligee on the couch.* He laughed and dismissed it as a dream. "Well, it was worth the thought anyway," he said giddily and then climbed into the steamy, hot shower.

Penny sat at home and wondered what Billy was up to. Then Billy's thoughts popped into her head and she realized that they still had Seneca's traits and mental capabilities. *So, Billy is feeling romantic tonight,* she thought deviously. She grabbed the phone book and looked up Billy's address. *Hmm, 562 Cobbler Street. I think I know where that is.* She grabbed her purse and rushed out to her car. Hurriedly, she sped down the freeway enroute to Billy's house.

When she arrived at Billy's house, she allowed the VW to coast to a stop in front. She nearly ran to the front door; she was so excited. Penny turned the doorknob and the door opened. She entered the house quietly with Billy in his bedroom.

On top of Billy's refrigerator were four candles in gold bases. She placed them strategically around the living room: one on each end table and one at each end of the mantle over the fireplace. Next, she started a fire in the fireplace. It took a little patience, but she soon had the fire burning nicely. *June is a funny time to have a fire going but after what we went through, who cares?* she thought.

Next, she raced through Billy's CD collection. "Ah. Mr. Brock is a bit of a romantic. What an interesting variety he has. Engelbert - that will work." Penny turned the TV off and placed the disk into the CD carriage on the stereo. She lit the candles and changed into the a sexy night gown.

Billy heard the music coming from downstairs. "Engelbert. That's strange. Must be a concert on TV."

When he walked into the hallway, he suspected something wasn't right and paused at the top of the steps. He immediately noticed that the lights were dimmed. Billy rushed down the steps and was stunned to see Penny laying across his couch.

"What's the matter, Billy? I've never seen you at a loss for words before."

"How did you know?"

"I can still read your thoughts, you dirty man."

"Penny, you look ..."

"Billy Brock, shut your mouth and come over here right now." Billy seated himself beside Penny. "Now it's our time," Penny said as she placed her arms around him. They shared the night wrapped in each other's arms.

When dawn came, they finally separated from each other. "So, are we going to take the plane to Philadelphia and finally do this presentation?" Billy asked.

"Uh-huh. Now that we can read each other's minds, it should be a piece of cake." They laughed and nestled together again.